# The Gods at Number23

## Also by author Lisa Keeble – From His Perspective

You might think you know human history, but you've never viewed it From His Perspective.....you like a good laugh, right? In the beginning, there was darkness and The Boss liked the darkness. He'd spent years creating the darkness. He was proud of the darkness. Unfortunately, his assistant Norbert liked to snack while working and had a very sensitive nose. Had he not been in charge of monitoring the black holes this may not have been a problem but, as it was, a violent sneeze launched a single biscuit crumb into the darkness, and it was no more. A huge explosion rocked the Factory (better known to us as Planet Earth) and, for The Boss and Norbert, the real work began - they had to deal with life. Life, as they found out, had an awful habit of not staying true to their designs, however carefully they drew up the blueprints. Suddenly, there were fish who wanted to live on the land, a dinosaur who went around killing everything it met, and then, of course, there was man — the Boss' most distinguished and regrettable invention.

## Praise for From His Perspective

"Author Lisa Keeble writes with smooth confidence and a sense of timing which is rare in written comedy fiction. Even when you see her jokes coming, there's always an additional sting in the tail or a wry aside to offset your expectations, which keeps the reading experience fresh throughout."

Readers' Favorite Review


"This wonderful book is delightfully different. Although it is really comical, it also screams about poignant lessons for us all. So many lessons which we could all benefit from to make the world a greater place in which to live. From His Perspective is wonderfully intriguing and thought provoking."

Goodreads Review

"Hilarious and imaginative take on the origins of life in the universe. Well written and highly enjoyable to read. Lisa has wit and a way with words that will have you romping through this book with ease."

Goodreads Review

"I laughed till I cried. The earth and its history as seen by the creator. It's laugh out loud funny but true history it's just told with a comic turn. I wish I could have learned history this way it would have been a lot more fun."

Amazon Review

"I have woken my husband up when I've been reading it in the middle of the night because I was laughing out loud or shaking the bed if I tried to suppress the chuckle. Caution for those with weak bladders!"

Amazon Review

"This book had me giggling from start to finish. the author has a great sense of humour, I'll be keeping an eye out for anything else that they produce !"

NetGalley Review

For Adrian. Always


The Gods at Number 23 was written during the Covid-19 pandemic of 2020 and probably stopped me from losing my marbles completely. Thanks to Will and my parents, Jim & Barbara who were only ever a phone call away during that impossibly lonely time.

*There is in general good reason to suppose that in several respects the gods could all benefit from instruction by us human beings. We humans are - more humane.*

Friedrich Nietzsche

*The Gods are too fond of a joke*

Aristotle

## The Gods at Number 23

Zeus looked down on the Parthenon, a scowl on his face. The view hadn't changed in hundreds of years, plenty of tourists but not a single bloody worshipper. Something had to be done. He had been resting on his laurels, enjoying a life of luxury and debauchery for so long that he hadn't realised people had stopped believing in him. He'd sent a survey round to all his fellow gods and goddesses, and it was clear that their customers, the human race, were not at all satisfied.

The gods were arrogant and didn't normally give a stuff what anyone thought of them but, without thought there was no belief and without belief, the gods were nothing. Not only that, with a lack of believers, came a depletion of their vast wealth, and that just could not be tolerated. As their fortunes dwindled, they'd all had to economise which had been very stressful as none of them knew how to prepare a budget. They had even had to downsize, meaning that the gods of ancient Rome and ancient Greece had all taken up residence on Mount Olympus, mainly because it had the best views. However, gods were never meant to live in close proximity and relationships were strained to put it mildly.

Before a full scale war broke out on Olympus, they had to try to revive their fortunes, so they were forced to come up with a plan. After many heated arguments, they decided that the only way they could prevent their own demise was to, once again, engage with human beings. Lots were drawn and the five losers ended up in a small, semi-detached house in Brighton....

## Chapter 1

Hebe, goddess of youth and beauty, was brushing her long, burnished hair and contemplating the day that lay ahead. She would definitely have to go to the market to get some avocados. She was going to make a face mask for each of her housemates – god knows they needed one – before heading off to her job on the make-up counter in Boots. As she continued brushing, she felt a tiny bead of sweat break out on her porcelain forehead, and she glared at the fireplace impatiently. A fire, which burned fiercely, the single flame reminiscent of a large penis, roared in the hearth.

"Vesta, do you have to? It's about 90 degrees in here." She fanned her face with her hand and moved further down the sofa. Moments later, there was a whoomph, a small pop and then a second, older woman was standing in the living room. She looked harassed and also slightly grubby; despite her best efforts, it was impossible to keep a working fireplace really clean.

"You know it's where I feel most comfortable Hebe; why must you complain so? I don't see why I can't have a few minutes to myself with everything I do around here." Vesta used the reproachful voice of the willing martyr. Hebe rolled her eyes as she watched Vesta straighten cushions and pick up plates that had been left on the table by the side of the sofa, tutting all the while. She was the goddess of the hearth and home, so tidying up came naturally to her. Hebe rose elegantly from the sofa and moved over to the mantelpiece, so she could look in the mirror that hung on the wall above it. "You don't have to do all the housework you know; we're all perfectly capable of cleaning up after ourselves."

She turned this way and that, admiring her flawless beauty. She had alabaster skin; dark, almond-shaped eyes; and a perfect rosebud mouth that was currently pursed as she wondered why Vesta didn't follow any of the diet plans that she'd so carefully prepared for her. She also couldn't understand why she hadn't abandoned her traditional toga in favour of more stylish and exciting human clothes. She had offered to take Vesta shopping, but she seemed more interested in housework or sitting in her damn fireplace.

"Oh yes, I can just see Hades or Pan running the Hoover around or unloading the dishwasher. Don't be ridiculous Hebe, if I don't do it, we'll end up living in a filthy hovel and you know it." She looked disdainfully at Hebe, who was still admiring herself, and took the dirty plates out to the kitchen where she wrapped a pinafore around her ample waist and set about cleaning up. A lock of her long, light brown hair fell forward, and she brushed it back impatiently as she reminded herself that quarrelling with her housemates would serve no purpose. Her mouth turned down and her startling blue, but very tired, eyes focused on the mountain of washing-up in the sink "Gits!" she thought to herself "I miss the days when I had my virgins to do all this for me." She sighed deeply and turned on the hot tap before reaching for the washing-up liquid. "Dad would cry if he could see me now. I'm sure this isn't what he meant when he made me goddess of the hearth and home."

Vesta had lived a sheltered life, surrounded by her priestesses, who were prized for their chastity; they were universally known as the Vestal Virgins. In her more reflective moments, Vesta couldn't help but wonder if her life would have been more interesting if she'd been surrounded by goddesses like Hebe, but she would never admit it.

Hebe called out that she was going to work, and Vesta responded with a curt "Bye." As she shrugged on her perfectly fitting coat, Hebe wondered about Vesta's demeanour; on the one hand, she was naïve and seemed dedicated to taking care of their home; on the other, whenever she took refuge in the fireplace, a giant phallus could always be found burning there. "Oh well," she thought "each to their own." As a goddess, she was used to strange peccadilloes, but she rarely wasted much time thinking about others. "I wonder if the new Dior Spring eye make-up palettes have arrived."

With that, she was out the door and on her way to the North Street branch of Boots, ready to start another day of beautifying humans. She liked a challenge. Goddesses don't wear make-up as a rule, so when Hebe had discovered the world of cosmetics, she was immediately captivated. Before they'd come to Brighton, she'd always assumed that human females were pretty much like goddesses, and she'd been sadly disappointed. So much so, that she'd applied for the job in Boots. Her current mission in life was to beautify and keep the humans looking as young as possible for as long as possible. The other gods and goddesses had neglected to tell her that humans are not immortal, so she was certainly destined for further disappointment.

## Chapter 2

Saturn was the god of time, wealth and agriculture, and he certainly hadn't intended that his daughter, Vesta, end up as a drudge for a houseful of lesser gods in a small, semi-detached house in Brighton but, then again, he hadn't foreseen that people would stop believing in the concept of all-powerful, random deities either. As it was, he was struggling to hold on to his house on Capitoline Hill, especially as he had a wife and two mistresses to support. His boss, Zeus, had made it clear in their last annual general meeting that, unless Vesta, Hebe and the others didn't gather up some believers while they were in Brighton, they'd all be out on their ear.

"Oh well," he thought "At least her Uncle Janus is there to look out for her." This offered some small comfort as he ploughed his way through a stack of invoices for new gowns, given to him that morning by his wife,

Ops. "Goddess of riches and prosperity my arse," he muttered to himself as he rummaged around in his desk drawer hoping to find some loose change.

Saturn was a powerful god and very popular with the ladies, given his impressive musculature and penchant for wearing little more than a carefully draped sheet and some fig leaves, but as belief in the old gods dropped off, his powers were waning.

"In the good old days, I'd have just conjured up a coffer full of gold, but now..." he clicked his fingers experimentally and a copper penny popped into existence. "Oh bugger." He added the penny to the small pile of copper coins on his desk and wondered if there were any nymphs roaming around the palace that he could sell on e-Bay. The god's study of modern-day humans had proven useful, but even the express delivery of a fully functioning nymph to their front door seemed to do nothing to strengthen their belief. From his buyer's feedback, it seemed as though the humans just figured that the wood nymphs had come from a Chinese robotics company and were disappointed that their inclinations extended to little more than wanting to do the gardening. If human thoughts immediately turned to robotics when they saw a wood nymph rather than a gift from the gods, what hope did they have to reignite belief? He had thought about trying to lay his hands on a shipment of succubae, but from what he could gather, anyone who had a succubus wouldn't let it go unless it was prised from their cold, dead hands. That in itself wasn't a problem for him, but Zeus had insisted that they try to curb their more extreme urges in an effort to ingratiate themselves with the humans.

Just then there was an enormous clap of thunder, and the great double doors of his office flew off their hinges and across the room.

"Was that really necessary?" Saturn glared at the angry-looking god with the white beard who had just, literally, stormed into his office. "We don't need the thunderclaps and lightning bolts every time you want to have a meeting you know." Saturn knew that he should be more respectful to his boss, Zeus, but he really wasn't having a good day, and he was fed up with having to keep replacing his office doors; they were heavy.

"That's the problem with gods these days," boomed Zeus "no sense of the dramatic. No wonder the humans aren't interested in us anymore. With their guns and their bombs, they don't even bat an eyelid at an ominous clap of thunder or a well-placed lightning bolt. It's depressing."

Zeus threw himself into a leather armchair and sat there pouting until Saturn offered him a drink. "Well, it's a bit early for me," said Zeus, obviously delighted "but if you're having one..."

Saturn sighed and poured out two glasses of red wine; the bottle was almost empty, and he had only another case or two left in the cellar. "I must have a word with Dionysus," he thought to himself. "If I can catch him when he's sober. Alternatively, I could just get one of the kids to break into his lock-up; he's always so pissed, I'm sure he'd never notice if a case or two went missing." He was trying to remember which of his kids was still around (in his wilder days he had eaten a few and could never recall how many he had left) when Zeus' thundering voice broke into his thoughts.

"I've seen the reports that you put together on the progress of Vesta, Hebe and the others, and I've got to be honest with you Saturn, I am not impressed. They're supposed to be persuading the humans to worship us again, but they've achieved nothing. Vesta does no more than she does at home; Hebe has got a *job*, whatever that is, and the gods seem to spend most of their time drinking which they did quite enough of here."

Saturn sighed. The problem with Zeus was that he had no patience and no understanding of the time it took to reignite the flames of religious fervour. It didn't help that he really didn't like humans; on one occasion when he was feeling particularly pissed off, he had flooded the entire world with the help of his brother Poseidon. It was only when his wife pointed out that wiping out the human race would make gods rather redundant that he relented and saved two of them so that the species could continue.

"I told you this would take time Zeus; they are integrating with the humans; it's all part of the plan. We need the humans to start thinking about us again, about what we can offer them, but even then, it's a long way from thought to belief. When they are fully accepted, they will be able to influence human thought and bring them back to the old ways."

"Influence? How?  Vesta never leaves the house; Hebe works in a place called Boots showing human females how to hide their physical flaws, and Janus just can't seem to make up his mind what he's going to do. As for the other two....." he trailed off and rolled his eyes before drawing his bushy white brows into their habitual frown.

"Zeus, you know why we sent Pan. He's very *persuasive*. The human females love him. He's already formed numerous attachments."

"Yes, yes, yes, I'm sure he has, randy little sod, but is he doing anything to promote belief in us or is it like he was when he visited us here – 'wham, bam, and thank you Vestal Virgin?'"

Saturn glanced away trying to hide the guilt in his eyes; it had been his idea to send Pan. He vaguely recalled a particularly drunken evening when Pan had popped over with a case of rather good wine. The next thing he knew, Pan's name had been added to the sacred list of gods and goddesses who'd be travelling to Earth. As soon as he realised, he tried to get Pan's name removed, but the list had already been laminated, and everyone said it was too much bother to create another one. "Who said 'beware of Greeks bearing gifts'?" he thought. "Whoever it was, I should have listened."

"He's definitely talking to all of the human females before he beds them, and I think, if we give it time…"

"Oh, it's always the same with you Saturn, 'Give it more time.' You don't seem to realise that we don't have much more time." Zeus was angrier than usual, and Saturn could see small sparks flying from the end of his fingertips. He decided to change the subject as he didn't want to risk his second-best armchair being reduced to a pile of ash.

"Hades seems to be getting on all right; he's certainly keeping the others in check. Well, apart from Pan, but you know what he's like."

"Keeping the others in check? How will that help us get more believers?" growled Zeus, irritably.

"It was your bloody idea to send him!" Saturn yelled.

"Oh I know." Zeus waved his hand dismissively, "I just wanted rid of the miserable bastard, never could stand him and his bloody moaning."

Saturn was incredulous. "He's your brother!"

"Don't remind me. I thought I'd seen the back of him when Poseidon and I packed him off to the Underworld, but he still wasn't bloody happy, and as for that wife of his..."

Saturn had heard enough. This was the problem with Zeus; he always blamed others for his own mistakes and, because he was the boss, no-one ever picked him up on it. "You can't blame Persephone for being a bit down every now and again. She didn't want to marry him, but *you* insisted."

Zeus' eyes turned dark as the memory resurfaced. He was great at compartmentalising his own errors and shutting the door on them, and he didn't like it when someone opened it. Saturn was too annoyed to notice the warning signs and ploughed on.

"Even your own wife told you it was a bad idea, but would you have it? No! As bloody usual you just carried on in your own sweet way, trampling over everyone else's feelings." He stopped speaking abruptly as a large vase, full of roses exploded, raining petals down on both their heads. He turned to Zeus, glaring at him.

"Well, that was just childish."

The argument between Zeus and Saturn raged on for several months, during which time they failed to monitor the goings on down on Earth, which was probably just as well.

## Chapter 3

Vesta heard the front door slam as Hebe left for work and heaved a sigh of relief. She longed to change back to her flame self and take up residence in the fireplace, but she knew that, if she didn't keep up with her chores, the house would become uninhabitable. As far as Vesta was concerned, uninhabitable meant a single unwashed plate in the sink or a cushion that wasn't perfectly aligned, a mind-set that ensured housework was a full-time job. As goddess of the hearth and home it wasn't really a challenge for her, but she'd much preferred it when she had an army of virgins at her beck and call. As she pulled a floor rug two inches to the left, she heard a loud bang upstairs and sighed deeply. "Oh great," she thought "they're up."

She wandered into the kitchen and took a wine glass, and two mugs from one of the cupboards and put two slices of wholemeal bread in the toaster. She then rummaged around in the fridge until she found some sausages and a packet of bacon. Filling the kettle and putting it on to boil, she wondered why she went through this ritual every morning knowing full well that her efforts would be thoroughly unappreciated. Once the sausages and bacon were in the pan, she made a coffee and a chamomile tea and then pulled out the Tupperware container housing muesli that looked exactly like the sweepings from the bottom of a hamster's cage.

There was a clattering on the stairs and the sound of male voices that grew increasingly louder as their owners made their way to the kitchen.

"Morning guys," said Vesta politely. She tried her best to be kind and thoughtful, but she still found herself saying it through gritted teeth. There was a loud scraping noise as heavy chairs were pulled along oak floorboards as Hades, Pan and Janus sat down. They were still deep in discussion and ignored Vesta as she prepared their breakfast.

"We need to consider past behaviours so that we can accurately predict future actions, I've been saying that all along," Janus argued as he pulled his coffee mug towards him and took a sip.

"Yes, but that's you all over isn't it? You look back or forward but never see what's right in front of your nose. Humans don't have any use for gods anymore; most of them don't even know who we are and, even if they do, they don't revere us. Do you know, I found a statue of me on bloody Amazon the other day? They even had one of Cerberus, my bloody dog! I used to instil bowel-curdling fear into people; Cerberus, single-pawed, kept the legions of the dead in line in the Underworld, and now we're just a cheap pottery ornament for the mantlepiece. Bastards!" Hades took a long draught of his chamomile tea and poked at his muesli viciously with a spoon.

Pan had his mouth full of sausage, but he waved his fork irritably at Hades before swallowing hard and then taking a long slug of red wine. "Will you stop sodding moaning Hades? We all remember the good old days you know. My life used to be nothing but sexual excess and binge drinking, and now look at me." He rolled his eyes and dipped a forkful of toast into his egg yolk. Hades and Janus just stared at him for a long moment until he raised his eyes from his breakfast and said "What?"

"Well, nothing's bloody changed for you has it? You're still out there getting plastered every day and rodgering some poor unsuspecting human female senseless every night." Janus' voice was incredulous.

"Oh yes, that's true I suppose," Pan conceded "But I can't chase nymphs anymore, can I? Honestly, these human females just don't seem to have any stamina *and* I can't seduce them in my goat form. I tried it once with this human female called Tracey, and she just petted me under the chin and then slapped me on the head when I tried to eat her dress. No imagination, that's the problem with humans." Known as the god of the wild, shepherds and flocks, Pan could change, at will, into a goat or, for nymphs and goddesses with somewhat specialised tastes, half-male and half-goat. Millennia of switching between forms had left him with rather base tastes and terrible table manners. In the human realm, Pan had to blend in, but with his striking face, dark flashing eyes, muscular upper body and long, well-toned, extremely hairy legs, he no more blended in than Lady Gaga in a convent. He usually rendered human males mute with jealousy, but he was certainly popular with human females who swarmed around him in droves. Although it annoyed Janus and Hades in the extreme, they had to admit that it served their purpose.

Vesta was whipping plates away from the three of them as soon as they'd take their last mouthful of food, so she could get started on the washing up. Once everything was clean and tidy again, she could get back to her fireplace.

"Any chance of a refill?" Pan was holding up his wine glass and looking hopeful.

"No!" Vesta's voice was curt and brooked no argument. "Go out and do something useful. Try to remember why we're all here, will you!" She was trying to keep her patience, but she hadn't had so much as a "good morning" from any of them and no thanks for the breakfast that she'd prepared.

"Wooah, stroppy! That time of the lunar cycle is it Vesta?" Pan was laughing uproariously and nudging the other two who were trying to pretend they didn't exist. Vesta didn't lose her temper often, but when she did, it was something to behold. She had been known to bury her virgins alive in the Field of Wickedness for doing nothing more than falling for the amorous charms of a satyr if she were having a really bad day. Hades and Janus stood up slowly and carefully and then backed away from the kitchen table. Pan was oblivious to the tension in the room as he was slightly drunk and still chuckling at his own joke. There was a sudden whoosh and where Vesta had been standing, there now hung a great column of fire that was seething and spewing out hundreds of tiny, dancing flames, one of which leapt onto Pan's beard.

"Oh shit!" Pan leapt from his chair and thrust his chin under the tap, frantically grasping for the faucet; the smell of burning hair and singed flesh filled the kitchen. "Bloody hell Vesta, it was only a joke, you didn't have to go all fire demon on me."

Vesta was, once again, her calm, serene self. She clasped her hands in front of her and lowered her eyes to the floor in a parody of supplication. "Get out, Pan, before I start looking for other hairy bits of you to burn," she said quietly, rigid with self-control.

The three gods sidled out of the kitchen before turning and running upstairs. Vesta returned to her cleaning, trying to ignore Pan's voice as he complained to the other two, "Honestly, I don't know why she's so touchy, I really don't. I was only having a laugh."

Once upstairs, Janus berated Pan for his lack of sensitivity towards Vesta.

"You know that she has only ever kept the company of virgins, Pan. She's never been exposed to your sort of bawdy behaviour, so she's bound to react badly." Janus was known as the god of two faces and was adept at seeing both sides of any argument, a trait that the gods and goddesses, as well as his human acquaintances, found extremely irritating.

"React badly? I wouldn't mind if she'd cried or was embarrassed, but she set fire to my bloody beard. That's not the action of an innocent, whichever way you look at it." Pan was examining the small bald patch in his beard in the dressing table mirror.

"Oh, don't keep on Pan," Hades interjected irritably. "Sometimes you just have to be the bigger god and let things go."

"You're a one to talk." Pan turned on Hades "What about you and Sisyphus? Don't you remember the time that he locked you in your own handcuffs? I thought that you'd you never let it go."

"He cheated death!" Hades spluttered indignantly.

"Only the first time. You got him the second time," said Pan reasonably. "And what did you do? You made him push a boulder up a hill for all eternity; all the way to the top, it rolls back down, and you make him push it all the way back up again. Talk about over-reacting!"

"That wasn't me; that was Zeus." Hades voice was indignant; he didn't like being lumped in with Zeus who was pretty unhinged at the best of times.

"Right, that's enough," Janus leapt up and stood between the pair of them. "We're going out. Vesta was right, we were brought to Brighton for a reason and we need to get on with things. Come on, get your coats."

Hades had a dark, stubborn look on his face. He folded his arms across his chest and glared at Janus. "You do not command me, and I will not follow you. I have my own plans."

No amount of cajoling could persuade him to move so they left him in the bedroom, alone.

There was much grumbling and moaning from Pan, but he followed Janus downstairs, grabbed his jacket from the coat stand in the hall and marched outside as Janus held the door open for him.

Hearing the front door slam, Vesta flicked her tea-towel across the last breakfast plate and retreated, gratefully, to her fire.

"Finally!"

## Chapter 4

Hebe had just arrived at work and was putting her bag and coat in her locker whilst, simultaneously, ignoring her co-workers. In the three months she'd worked at Boots, she'd discovered that all attempts at friendship were doomed to failure. She'd tried to explain to Bethany, very kindly, that if she lost 20 pounds, she'd be much more attractive to the opposite sex. Brian still refused to speak to her after she'd advised him on skincare. Apparently pointing out that his boyfriend would be much happier if Brian had fewer blackheads wasn't considered constructive advice. Chelsea had been reduced to tears after a lecture from Hebe on the importance of regular facial features, and rumour had it, that she was booked in for a nose job later that week.

All of Hebe's colleagues had been on the receiving end of her "helpful" suggestions at one time or another, and she was universally disliked. Unfortunately, her physical perfection made it impossible for them to fire criticism back at her, so they just settled on ignoring her.

The situation wasn't helped by the fact that she was the best saleswoman the company had ever had, and Mr. Jenkins, the department manager, had hinted that she was destined for great things in the world of cosmetic sales. Of course, what neither her colleagues nor Mr. Jenkins knew was that, although her powers were diminished in the human world, she had still retained enough that she could make anyone who visited her counter look younger and more beautiful. After two days on the job, she'd realised that she'd also need to sell them some sort of product if she were going to keep it, but after that epiphany, it had all been smooth sailing, and word had spread amongst the women of Brighton.

Hebe gave herself a final once over in the mirror attached to the back of her locker door. She was dressed in an immaculately tailored red suit and had paired it with a simple navy-blue blouse, and she looked stunning. She then closed her locker, ignored the stage whispered, "Stuck up bitch!" and wandered out onto the shop floor, her high stiletto heels clacking softly as she walked. She was not surprised to see that a small queue had formed in front of her counter despite the fact that the shop had only just opened. She put a smile on her angelic face and addressed the woman at the front of the queue.

"Good morning Madame, how lovely to have you with us today. How may I be of assistance?"

Hebe had undergone a week of training in customer service before starting the job and had found it utterly tedious but had also discovered that a polite enquiry as to the customer's requirements caused less trouble than, "So I'm guessing you want to be less ugly then." The woman before her was about 50 and had obviously not taken care of herself; she was overweight and the skin on her face was heavily lined. Added to that, her mouth was a thin unsmiling line and her eyes were hooded and bloodshot.

"I need something to help with my skin…..now I'm getting a little older……maybe you can help…?" The woman looked distinctly uncomfortable and had relayed her request in a conspiratorial whisper. "A little older," Hebe thought to herself, mentally rolling her eyes. She smiled at her client and reached behind her to pluck a product from the many that graced the shelves; it didn't really matter which one.

"If you'd like to sit in the chair Madame, I'll apply some of this….um…." she glanced at the bottle in her hands "night-time hand softening cream and you'll see remarkable results, I promise you."

"Hand cream? You're going to put *hand cream* on my face?" The woman was clearly unsettled, so Hebe forced her gently back into the chair and slathered the cream all over her face whilst, at the same time, performing certain enchantments designed to promote youth and beauty. The woman presented a bit of a challenge even for the goddess' talents, so Hebe added a tiny drop of ambrosia from a stash that she'd taken from Zeus before they were sent down to live with the humans.

"Madame, you can trust me." Hebe smiled and looked pointedly at her watch. "We now have to wait exactly 2 minutes and 42 seconds for the cream to do its work; no more and no less if we want the best results."

This was utter rubbish, but Hebe had found that a little theatrical flourish worked wonders with her aging clientele. Not only that, but the woman had glued her eyes to her own watch and completely forgotten that her face was liberally smeared with hand cream. The queue of women in front of her counter had grown and there was now a small crowd standing in front of her; all the women were leaning forward with bated breath. After exactly 2 minutes and 42 seconds, Hebe took a small silk cloth from a pile under the counter and began removing the cream, when she had finished, there was an audible gasp and Hebe permitted herself a small self-satisfied smile. "Voila!" she exclaimed as she handed her customer a small mirror.

"I.....I.....oh my god...," the woman stuttered before promptly bursting into tears. Her skin was smooth, without a blemish; her lips were fuller, and her eyes wide and sparkling. She took Hebe's hand. "I don't know how to thank you, my dear." Hebe gently removed her hand. She had an aversion to physical contact with humans unless they were perfect specimens of manhood, and they, she'd found out to her disappointment, were few and far between. She, once again, reached out behind her, taking another small bottle of the hand cream from the shelf and a small silk cloth from under the counter.

"That will be £500 madame, thank you. I am happy you are pleased with the results." The woman looked a little shocked but took the bottle and the cloth before rummaging around in her handbag in search of her purse. She handed over her credit card with one hand and examined the little bottle with the other; she wondered if pure gold was one of the ingredients. It was then that she saw the small white label taped to the side. She tapped Hebe on the arm cautiously "But my dear, the price on the bottle is £24.99." Hebe pushed the credit card machine towards her so that she could enter her pin number "Yes, but you also purchased this and it's essential to the process; it's called a goddess cloth and it is made of extremely fine silk. I could take off the price of the cloth if you'd like, but I do find that the results I get from using it are quite miraculous."

Her customer looked uncertain for a moment as she worried what her husband would say when he saw the credit card bill, but then she caught sight of her reflection. "No, no, I must have the cloth as well if, as you say, it's essential."

"Another satisfied customer," Hebe thought to herself. She was pleased that she'd managed to put the name "goddess" in her sales pitch and link it with the concept of a miracle. She was quite sure that the woman would have made the mental connection; it wasn't much, but it was a start. "Now who's next?" She took a slight step backwards as a surge of women, credit cards in hand, rushed towards her.

Her colleague, Mercedes (real name Daphne) who worked on the adjacent Chanel counter, shook her head in disbelief. She'd worked in cosmetics for years and knew damn well that there was no product that could achieve such outstanding results in less than three minutes. She knew a couple of plastic surgeons who couldn't achieve results like that in three hours, so what was Hebe's secret? And what kind of name was Hebe? "I bet she's really called Jane and doesn't even spell it with a Y," Mercedes thought. She'd love to be able to complain to management, but what could she say? That Hebe was probably called Jane and could perform miracles? They'd probably give the bloody woman a promotion and a pay-rise. "I hate that bitch." Mercedes' lip curled in disdain as she began to organise her display of nail polishes. "There's just something not right about her."

By 11 o'clock, Hebe had sold more products in a few hours than all of her colleagues, put together, managed to sell in a week. Deciding that she'd had enough for one day, she called out to Mr. Jenkins as he walked past her counter.

"I'll be off now Mr. Jenkins, see you tomorrow." With that, she marched off the floor and went to the staff room to retrieve her coat and bag.

"Aren't you going to say anything?" Mercedes was glaring at the manager with her arms folded. "If that was one of us, we'd be sacked on the spot."

Mr. Jenkins knew that he should chastise Hebe, but she was contributing a great deal to his monthly bonus, and Mrs. Jenkins was demanding that they go to Malaga in the summer.

"When your sales are as high as hers, you can take a half-day occasionally as well, Mercedes. As it is, I think you have a delivery to unpack, don't you?" He nodded towards the two large boxes that were stacked, one on top of the other, beside her counter.

Mercedes gritted her teeth, seething at the injustice of it all. "Yes Mr. Jenkins."

She was determined to discover Hebe's secret, or, at the very least, trip her over the first time the opportunity presented itself. She calmed herself with images of Hebe falling flat on her face as she viciously ripped open the boxes and resolved to call her boyfriend and demand that he take her out for a drink that evening. Preferably several, large drinks.

## Chapter 5

Janus and Pan had left Hades at home to sulk and had spent most of the morning wandering in and out of the shops that lined Brighton High Street. They made a striking pair. Pan had thick dark hair and a small goatee beard; his eyes were so dark brown that they were almost black and his cheekbones so high and sharp, they could cut cheese. Women often said that he had the look of Johnny Depp and the body of Chris

Hemsworth. Had they seen him in his natural form they'd be comparing him to a randy old goat; they would not be wrong with either comparison.

Janus, on the other hand, had a full beard, dark curly hair and a straight nose. In his god form he was also clean shaven, had straight dark hair and a Roman nose. Janus had two faces and he liked them both, but Zeus had pointed out that, if he were to walk among humans, he could only take the one face. Pan was much taken with modern street wear and was sporting low slung jeans with rips at the knees, an oversize sweatshirt and a leather jacket; whereas, Janus was dressed in a beautifully cut dark suit, with a soft pink shirt and navy blue tie.

"What are we going to do? I'm bored." Pan kicked ~~out at~~ an empty Coke can that had been dropped on the pavement. It hit an old man, who was some two hundred feet away, on the back of the head, so he and Janus quickly retraced their steps. Pan was inclined to forget that he was physically many times more powerful than the average human.

"You know very well what we have to do; we have to manipulate, persuade or bully the humans into believing in us again and that means, firstly, getting them thinking about us. Zeus' instructions were perfectly clear."

Pan huffed impatiently "Yes, I know that, but how are we supposed to get their attention for long enough? I've seen wood nymphs with longer attention spans, and you know how flaky they are."

Janus thought for a moment "I suppose they've got a lot to worry about. They don't have any special powers; they're not immortal and, for the most part, they're not a particularly attractive bunch. We just need more time to study their behaviour, that's all." He glanced across the road "The Camelford Arms, that looks like as good a place as any to study; fancy a drink?"

"Do you have to ask?" Pan called over his shoulder as he set off towards the pub at a brisk trot, leaving Janus to follow, sedately, in his wake.

Five minutes later they were seated in a booth, a pint of bitter and a glass of red wine before them. Janus was studying the ketchup-smeared menu wondering what to have for lunch, and Pan was flicking through a local paper.

"I think I've figured out what the humans are worried about, the males at least." Pan was skimming through the ads on the back page.

"What do you mean?" Janus had extracted a paper serviette from the glass mug on their table that served as a receptacle for cutlery and, apparently, old chewing gum wrappers. He wiped his sticky fingers and looked at Pan expectantly.

"Well, look at this." Pan angled the paper so that they could both read it at the same time. "Erectile disfunction? 'Woodit' is for you. Trouble maintaining an erection? Try new 'Ardon Ultra.' There's loads of them; no wonder human men look so bloody stressed all the time. I almost feel sorry for the poor bastards."

Janus had to agree that this could be a major problem. "If you are right, how does that help us? They've obviously found a solution. What do you want for lunch, eggs, chips and beans?"

"Yes, that will do, and can you ask them to throw on a couple of sausages, I'm starving." Pan pulled out his smartphone and started typing furiously.

"How can you be starving? You had breakfast only a couple of hours ago." Janus had opted for a bacon sandwich. It never ceased to amaze him how much food Pan could put away.

"Hhhm? What?" Pan looked up from his phone. "Oh. Well let's just say I burned off a fair few calories last night. I had a date with nineteen-year-old twins and then their flatmate came home early, and one thing led to another." He grinned lasciviously before turning his attention back to Google.

"Incorrigible!" Janus muttered as he strode over to the bar to place their order. After the barman had persuaded him to add a fried egg to his bacon sandwich and assured him that no meal was complete without a basket of crispy wedges, Janus re-joined Pan at the table.

"Are you still on that phone? What are you looking at?" He waited for a moment and busied himself extracting the cutlery from the pint mug. "Pan!"

"What? Oh sorry. I've just been doing some research on the human solution to their wilting phallus problem, and I think I've had an idea." He passed his phone over to Janus "Look. The pills work, but they take away one problem and give them a load more – headaches, nausea, muscle pain, the squits…the list just goes on and on."

Janus scrolled down. "Bloody hell! You'd think they'd just put up with a wilting phallus, wouldn't you?"

Pan looked at him incredulously "Are you joking? Who in their right mind would put up with that? I've never wilted a day in my life, and, if I ever did, I'd do whatever it took to un-wilt it, even if that involved two lolly sticks and a ball of string!" Pan was shouting by the time he got to the end of the sentence.

"Alright, calm down. Anyway, as I said, how does this startling revelation help us?" Janus leaned back slightly as a young lad, wearing a badge that said, "My name is Kevin. I'm your waiter," on his grubby white polo shirt put down a plate in front of him. Pan took his own plate and a basket of fries and put them on the table. "Thanks." He waved the waiter away dismissively before tucking into his lunch; it was greasy and there were suspicious looking black flecks in his beans, but he was hungry, ~~and~~ so he tried not to think about it.

"It's simple Janus. Human men have a problem we can solve without giving them other problems, that will reduce their stress and make them more amenable to a spot of ancient god worship, right?" Pan emphasised his point by waving a sausage around.

"Careful, you're flicking bean juice all over the place." Janus mopped a speck from his tie with a paper napkin. "Well yes, I suppose so but, if we do put something together to solve the problem, how do we sell it to them? I guess we could take a stall in the Marshalls Row market." He pondered as he took a bite from his sandwich. "Oh bollocks!" Egg yolk dripped onto his tie. "That's going to stain." He wiped at it furiously with a fresh napkin that he pulled from the container on the table. The egg stain blended perfectly with Pan's baked bean juice and the rubbing seemed to only make things worse. He sighed, took off the tie and put it in his pocket before turning back to his sandwich. He was disappointed to see that the egg yolk he'd rather been looking forward to eating was congealing all over the plate.

"Just you let me worry about that," said Pan polishing off the last of his sausage. "I've got a plan; I just need to have a quick chat with Saturn."


## Chapter 6

Saturn was, in fact, in no mood to have a chat with Pan or anyone else for that matter; all he wanted to do was have a nice lie-down with a damp water sprite. As it was, he was stuck in his office listening to Hades moan about life amongst the humans. He'd been chugging back wine in an effort to dull his senses enough so that Hade's monotonous whingeing would lull him to sleep, but he'd developed a tolerance over the millennia and it just wasn't working.

"Hades! Enough! What do you want me to do about it? Would you prefer to go back to the Underworld? If so, you need to be speaking to Zeus and not me; his office is only upstairs. If you leave now, you can catch him before he goes out for lunch."

Saturn was losing patience rapidly. As he looked at Hades, he felt a sense of distaste; the unkempt beard, the perpetually downturned mouth and the narrowed, suspicious eyes irritated him. Hades was not unattractive, far from it, but his constant griping and complaining made him very unappealing. "And he wonders why we packed him off to the Underworld! Even with that we had to dress it up as a promotion before he'd move his sorry arse." Distracted by these thoughts Saturn had stopped listening to Hades for a brief blissful moment but then he was dragged back into the present by his monotone, whining voice.

"You don't understand, Saturn, the humans are not like us. They are weak, without power and they have no respect. The other day I was standing at the bus stop, minding my own business, when a young male human called me a 'stingy cockwomble' just because I refused to buy alcohol for him. If I had him down in the Underworld, Cerberus would be having him for lunch, let me tell you."

"Yes, yes, yes." Saturn was trying to tune out the moaning, but then, suddenly, he sat up. Something had been bothering him since Hades had walked into his office. "Hang on a minute; what are you even doing here? How did you get back from the human world?"

"I sent an email to Zeus, and he said that I could come back for a visit as long as I promised not to disturb him. That's another thing about humans; they are so obsessed with their ridiculous technology they don't even interact on any real level..." He stopped speaking abruptly as Saturn grabbed his arm.

"Since when has Zeus had an email address, and why haven't I got it? If I had his email address, he wouldn't be coming down to my office every five minutes demanding progress reports." Saturn flung himself back in his chair and reached for a third bottle of wine; his stocks were low, but if ever there were a day for drinking himself into oblivion this was it.

"I don't know why he hasn't given it to you. Have you asked? That's your problem, you know; you're just like the humans, never thinking about anyone but yourself. Do you know, the other day I was speaking to a human, explaining the perils that awaited him in the Underworld if he didn't mend his sorry ways, and he just walked off! I was mid-sentence and he just ignored me. Let me tell you..." He lowered his wagging finger as he saw the dark look on Saturn's face. Hades was not known for his empathetic nature, but even he could see that the god was on the point of losing his temper. He folded his arms defensively and said, "Anyway, you wanted my report?"

Saturn replied through clenched teeth. "No, I didn't want your report; you just showed up here and started bloody moaning. If you've got something to report, why didn't you just tell me as soon as you walked in, and you could have saved us both a lot of time? I hope you've got something good after all this." He took a long draught of his wine before picking up a quill and some parchment to take some notes. Emails and spreadsheets were all very well, but he still preferred the old ways; there was something comforting about writing with a fine quill. He looked at Hades expectantly.

"Well?"

"We're going to fail," Hades announced bluntly. "Humans are stupid and too arrogant to understand that there are beings who are superior to them and far more powerful."

"So, you've got nothing?" Saturn rose from behind his desk and opened the doors to a long metal storage box that was attached to the wall. "You haven't discovered anything new and, basically, you just came up here to bust my balls." He reached into the box and pulled out a long, finely bladed scythe. Hades looked nervously from Saturn to the scythe and considered his best course of action. The scythe's blade was a blur as it came towards him and, before he could react, it sliced through his beard, depositing the bottom three inches in his lap. Saturn's eyes were blazing with fury and it was obvious ~~that~~ he was winding himself up for a second swing.

Hades rose slowly from his chair, beard hair falling to the plush carpet beneath him and backed towards the door. "Right, I'll be off then. Good to see you Saturn; no need to show me out." With that he turned and ran as fast as he could, not even bothering to open the door in his hurry to escape Saturn's wrath. He could hear a roar behind him as he dived back into the human realm. He arrived back with Saturn's parting words still ringing in his ears.

"And you'll pay me for that bloody door as well, you bastard!"

Hades walked into the kitchen of Number 23 still sweating, his heart thumping. "Vesta, where are you?" he called out. "You'll never believe what Saturn's just done."

Vesta was in the living room, straightening a lace doily that was half a centimetre out of place but, on hearing Hades' voice, she immediately took her flaming form and sought refuge in the fireplace.

Hades sighed and went to the kitchen to make himself some lunch. "I can't believe Saturn didn't even offer me a sandwich." he thought to himself "Tight git."

## Chapter 7

In her hearth, Vesta could allow herself to dwell on the past and take pleasure from it. Hers had been a life of complete tranquillity. Served, as she was, by her many worshippers, she had little to do but burn gently and ensure that her sacred flame took a pleasing form. She kept only the company of women and was therefore not subject to the will of her male counterparts. She spent no time with Zeus, Hades, Janus or any of the other gods, so she didn't have to put up with their lechery or misogyny as her sister goddesses had. She'd had celebrations in her name, sacrifices had been made to honour her and her virgins kept their chastity, in her name, for a period of thirty years.

She heard Hades' footsteps retreat from the room, as he took his ham sandwich and a glass of milk up to his bedroom, and she allowed waves of pleasure to wash over her. Unfortunately, she hadn't heard Hebe come home.

"What the bloody hell is that?!"

The screech cut through Vesta's reverie, and for a moment she was disorientated; however, habitual fire was to her, coming suddenly into anthropomorphic form was no joke. Her usually pristine white robes were covered in soot smudges, and as she tried to exit the fireplace, she tripped over the grate and fell, head-first, into the living room. Her natural serenity was lost, as was the greater part of her dignity but that was nothing compared to the humiliation of Hebe's discovery.

"I...I can explain." Vesta stumbled to her feet and took Hebe by the shoulders.

"Get your hands off me! I can't believe you Vesta; all this time you've been giving us all your holier than thou act, and you're no better than the rest of us. I thought you were meditating whilst you were in the fireplace not getting your jollies." Hebe shrugged off Vesta's hands and flung herself on the sofa.

"It's not what you think....well actually, yes it is exactly what you think, but what would you have done in my place? Thousands of years surrounded by bloody women, nothing to do all day but gossip about hairstyles and fashion, I was going out of my mind." Vesta brushed the worst of the soot from her robes and tried to regain her dignity. "I have needs you know. I thought my luck was in with Silenus. I'd seen him admiring me as he passed my temple and I thought he seemed quite nice, not that I had an awful lot to compare him with. I sneaked into one of the great feasts and pretended to be asleep hoping he would find me and...well you know, but the stupid git brought his donkey with him and the damn thing made such a fearful racket everyone came over to see what was going on. Someone told Dad, and he screamed at me and then chased Silenus off and that was that. The gods couldn't bear to see their precious virgin violated. I wouldn't have minded so much if I had been violated, but I didn't get so much as a snog." Her mouth turned down, her face a picture of bitter misery as she collapsed on the sofa next to Hebe.

"But why Silenus? He was old and fat and, more often than not, off his face with drink. Why set your sights so low?" Hebe was not usually a sensitive soul, but she could see that Vesta was distraught. They hadn't spent much time together as Hebe had little time for simpering virgins, but she'd always thought of Vesta as being cold and unfeeling.

"Who else would want me? Saturn, my dad, is ridiculously over-protective; who do you think shut me away with the virgins in the first place? Silenus was the only god I might have a chance with because he was always so drunk, he wouldn't care about incurring Dad's wrath."

"Oh Vesta, you poor thing!" said Hebe as she pulled her sister goddess into a hug. "I don't blame you at all for what you've been doing, but damn woman, the size of that thing!" Hebe burst out laughing and Vesta even managed to raise a small smile.

"Well, if you're going to create a flaming phallus, there's no point in half measures." Hebe was shocked to see Vesta throw her a wink and a sly grin.

"Do you know what Vesta? You have really gone up in my estimation this afternoon. I think you and I could grow to be good friends. Come on let's go and have a drink and let our hair down."

"Do you really think we should? What if the gods come home and want something to eat? And I've just remembered, I really need to do some washing after lunch." Vesta was desperately thinking of excuses to avoid going into the outside world.

"Bugger the gods, they can shift for themselves, and the washing can wait. Come on." Hebe grabbed Vesta by the arm and dragged her towards the stairs. We're going to get changed; I'll do your hair and make-up, and we're going to go out and enjoy ourselves. It will do you good."

Vesta had dug in her heels, but Hebe was a lot stronger than she looked, and Vesta found herself being lifted off her feet and hoisted, bodily, up the stairs.

"You're not going to take no for an answer, are you?" Vesta resigned herself to her fate.

Once upstairs, Hebe plunked Vesta down in front of a mirror while she rummaged through her supply of beauty products. She was a great favourite with the suppliers and had a huge array of free samples to choose from. It was partly because she was such a great saleswoman and they all profited from her success and partly because she had the face of an angel and the body of, well, a goddess.

An hour later, Vesta's hair had been arranged into an elegant up-do; her eyes had been widened, and her skin brightened with make-up. She was dressed in some of Hebe's clothes which were, admittedly a little tight, and a pair of high heels.

"Come and take a look at the full effect." Hebe guided Vesta over to the wardrobe which had a full-length mirror on the door. Vesta stood and then promptly stumbled; high heeled shoes take some getting used to when you've spent your whole life wearing flat, gilded sandals. However, she was pleased with what she saw, and she and Hebe were soon headed into Brighton.

## Chapter 8

Pan and Janus were still sitting in the pub, fleshing out Pan's idea for ridding male humans of their most pressing concern. The preparation of the formula was easy enough; they were waiting for a return email from

Saturn about packaging and distribution and now were trying to come up with a name.

"We need something a bit elegant, Pan. 'Admiral Winky's Wake-up' really lacks a certain gravitas, don't you think?" Janus was not impressed with Pan's suggestions.

"All right, what about the Bald Bishop Rising? That's got a nice clerical tone to it." Pan was on his sixth glass of wine and enjoying himself mightily.

"No, no, no, we need something more clinical sounding, like the human remedies." Janus thought for a moment and then said, innocently. "What about Janusite?"

"Oh yes, very modest! Look we're trying to get away from the clinical stuff. We want the humans to know that our product is all natural and will resolve their problem without them having to suffer a whole load of side effects." He took another slug of wine and grabbed a handful of peanuts that the barman had left on their table in an effort to ensure that they didn't decamp to another drinking establishment. "I've got it! 'Randy Goat'! It's the perfect name."

Janus was underwhelmed. "So, basically, you're just naming it after yourself?"

"Well, why shouldn't I? It was my idea after all. Oh don't look like that, Janus. Tell you what, how about we call it Panacea? We can say that it will remedy all their *short-comings*." Pan giggled to himself as Janus rolled his eyes. "And…and..the humans need to start thinking about us again, so what if we create three different doses – mild, medium and strong? We could name them Apollo for the males who just need a bit of a pick-me-up, Dionysus for those who want to get back their inner bull and…" Pan thought for a moment as he took another slug of wine "…Zeus! We'll make that the strongest version, for the human males who need a jump start." Pan roared out laughing and slapped the table, causing the bowl of peanuts to go flying.

Janus tutted and scooped up most of the peanuts. "You may well laugh Pan, but I think you could be on to something that will definitely get the human males thinking about us again. Daft as you are sometimes, I think you could have a knack for this sort of thing."

Pan stopped laughing. "Seriously?" His phone beeped. "Oh, hang on, I've just had a reply from Saturn. He says that we'll need to organise bottles and some labels, and he'll get hold of the packaging. Apparently, he's got an account with e-bay so we can use that to sell the stuff….I wonder what he's been selling? Oh, well never mind, let's have another drink to celebrate."

Just then, by unhappy coincidence, Hebe and Vesta walked into the dimly lit pub.

Pan was walking unsteadily towards the bar when he spotted them. "Girls! What are you doing here? What do you fancy to drink? It's on me. Come and join me and Janus, we can all snuggle up in the snug." He winked lasciviously.

Hebe turned to look at Vesta and, using the skill peculiar to all females, they telepathically agreed that, considering all the pubs that there are in Brighton, they'd had the peculiar misfortune to walk into this one. They moved as one, turning on their heels and leaving the way that they'd come in.

Pan raised his arms in a gesture of disbelief. "What? What did I say?"

Once they were safely outside, Vesta rolled her eyes and sighed in exasperation. "*Now* do you understand why I prefer to stay in the hearth?"

"Sister, from what I saw in that fire today, I'm surprised you ever leave; all of the pleasure and none of the aggravation! Honestly, what is it with males? They all seem to think that we'll just run after them like eager little puppies, desperate for a bit of attention!" Hebe linked arms with Vesta, and they marched down the road in search of a drinking establishment that wasn't playing host to dissolute and drunken gods. They were both blissfully unaware of the growing line of human males following them, all eyes fixed on Hebe's long, dark hair and luscious, leather clad behind. The undulations were almost hypnotic, and several of the men were drooling uncontrollably despite being 100% certain that this woman was way out of their league and would be unlikely to piss on them if they were on fire.

The two goddesses turned abruptly as they reached the open door of the Pull and Pump, leaving the men outside wondering how they'd got there and why they had dribble on their chins. The pub was still crowded, although the lunchtime rush was over, but as Hebe entered the bar area, a young and attractive barman beckoned to her and asked her what she'd like to drink, much to the annoyance of all the other people waiting to be served.

Hebe flashed a looked at him which caused the barman to shudder involuntarily. He coughed and surreptitiously tried to rearrange the front of his trousers. "I'll have a nice cold glass of Chardonnay, I think. What about you Vesta?"

"Just a glass of orange juice please." Vesta was unused to bars and was feeling distinctly out of place. She felt sure that the other gods and goddesses would disapprove of their perpetual virgin (she'd never been inclined to disillusion them) frequenting such an establishment.

"Two glasses of Chardonnay please." Hebe gave their order to the barman with a wide smile and a flick of her hair. With astonishing speed two glasses of white wine arrived in front of her. "These are on the house love." The barman's eyes were slightly glazed.

"I said I wanted an orange juice." Although Vesta was mildly miffed that Hebe hadn't seen fit to comply with her request, she took the proffered glass.

"You are not coming out for a drink with me and sitting there with an orange juice. We're going to enjoy ourselves." Hebe picked up the drinks. "Could you arrange for some food to be sent to our table as well please?" She gave the barman another stunning smile, and he rushed off in the direction of the kitchen, ignoring the cries of "Oi" from the people still waiting to be served.

Sometime later, Hebe and Vesta had eaten a delicious late lunch of warm lobster salad. The barman had pointed out Hebe to the chef who was then thrown into a culinary frenzy as he tried to prepare something fit for such a beautiful creature. They also were steadily working their way through a chilled bottle of Chardonnay. After her initial reservations, Vesta found that she rather enjoyed alcohol and was beginning to see the appeal of the world outside her fireplace. She was also surprised that she was enjoying Hebe's company so much; they had found much common ground.

"My life was much like yours growing up you know." Hebe took a delicate sip of her drink and leaned back in her chair. "Dad was never around very much and when he was, he invariably decided to show up as an eagle – I never did figure out why. You know Zeus, right? Course you do. Anyway, he made me cupbearer, so I had to follow the gods-in-chief around, making sure they never ran out of ambrosia; they couldn't even be bothered to say thank you half the time. Mum had me running around after Ares, my brother, in what free time I had, and he was a right little bastard, I can tell you." She picked up the bottle and realising it was empty, signalled to the ever-alert barman to bring them another. "You know what he was known as don't you? Ares?"

Vesta shook her head.

"The personification of sheer brutality. On his fourth birthday, Mum arranged a party for him, with a jester and everything. I won't tell you what he did, but that poor Jester was jingling when he walked for days afterwards. Well, I say walked but it was more liked hobbled." Hebe shuddered at the memory

"I know what you mean." Vesta was slurring her words slightly but, nonetheless, took another gulp of wine. "I was forced to go to every bloody human wedding. Can you believe that? Every single one. And was I allowed to have a bit of fun, enjoy myself? Have some wedding cake? Was I? Bollocks!" Vesta never usually swore but that wasn't to say that she hadn't learned a few expletives from Pan since they'd been living at Number 23. "Janus came with me every single time and made sure that I just stood in the doorway and looked serene. Serene, I ask you? Do you know how difficult it is to look serene when you've attended 25,000 weddings, and you need a pee because bloody Janus was in a hurry and said there wasn't time to go before we went?" Vesta was swaying very slightly in her seat.

Hebe wondered if ordering the second bottle of wine had been a good idea. "Oh yes, we always have to do what the gods want don't we? I wouldn't mind if they even treated us with a bit of respect, but they don't. I remember this one time, I was wandering around at some party on Mount Olympus, serving ambrosia, and one of the gods stepped on the back of my robe." Hebe narrowed her eyes as she recalled the event. "You know how flimsy those brooches are that secure them?"

Vesta nodded happily as she tried to bring Hebe's face into focus.

"Well, the clasp broke, and my robe just fell to the floor, leaving me naked in the middle of a bloody party. Honestly, I was mortified. Can you imagine?"

The young barman had just returned to their table with another bottle of Chardonnay. He overheard the tail end of Hebe's story and stopped dead in his tracks. He hadn't been gifted with much of an imagination, but he had enough to be able to picture the scene. His lower body jerked, and he quickly plunked the bottle of wine down before running as fast as he could to the toilet.

"What a strange one he is; have you ever seen anyone run like that?"

Vesta shook her head and then rather regretted it as the room started to spin slowly.

"Anyway, I was sure that god had stepped on the back of my gown on purpose, and I never did get an apology, just a load of lecherous comments about my 'assets' for years afterwards. Bastard." Hebe stared morosely into her empty glass and reached for the bottle.

Vesta thought carefully for a moment as she mentally tried to form a coherent sentence. She took a deep breath and then announced. "Do you know, I think we might actually be better off down here with the humans. I don't have to put up with boring virgins all day and you? Well, the way these human males behave, they'd happily be your slaves." Vesta reached for her wine as Hebe topped up her glass once more.

"It's only because I'm beautiful. I mean, you've seen, they don't even look at you." Hebe was reaching that state of drunkenness where her innate lack of tact was coming to the forefront. Vesta was even more drunk but not so much that she couldn't recognise an insult when she heard one.

"I'm sure they would look at me if you weren't there thrusting your breasts at them and flicking your hair all over the place, distracting them. I've got my own charms, you know; they're just not so obvious as yours. I had loads of admirers back home, thank you so very much." Vesta didn't mention that they were mainly virgins. After a few years of complete separation from males, they began to appreciate the attractions of their goddess and she often found herself the subject of a crush.

Hebe waved her arm impatiently at Vesta, sloshing a fair quantity of wine over the carpet.

"Oh, don't take it so bloody personally, I'm just stating a fact – I am beautiful, so gods and human men want me. It's a simple as that. They don't care if I'm intelligent or witty or well-read. If you think about it, it's pretty insulting in a way."

Vesta looked over at the barman who was still flushed after his visit to the bathroom; he was gazing lovingly at Hebe. He'd been joined by the chef, the pot washer and the nine men left in the bar, all of whom should have gone back to work ages ago.

"Yes, I can see; it must be a real chore being you." She was too drunk to worry about keeping the bitterness from her voice. "However do you cope? Aren't we ordinary looking females lucky we don't have your problems? Putting up with men adoring you wherever you go and hanging on your every word. My heart bleeds for you." Vesta poured the last of the wine into her glass.

"You're hardly ordinary looking. You're quite beautiful compared to the human women." Hebe's eyes flew wide open. "Vesta, I've just had an idea. I think I know how we can get the humans believing in us again. Hey, what happened to the rest of my wine?"

Vesta didn't hear her; she was lying face down on the floor of the bar, gently snoring. Hebe reached down to pick her up.

"Damn, we'll need to find a taxi." She said loudly, looking coyly at the bar's remaining customers. Twelve men frantically Googled "Brighton Taxi Firms" before rushing over to Hebe and Vesta, ostensibly to help Vesta back into her chair but, mainly, to gawp at Hebe. She tried to pay her bill, but the men wouldn't hear of it, each thrusting their wallets at her, apart from the barman who was screaming, "It's on the house"' at the top of his voice.

"Oh, good grief," thought Hebe as she flashed them all a luminous smile of thanks and dragged Vesta out to the waiting taxi.

## Chapter 9

"Are you going to put the kettle on?" Janus and Pan were back at Number 23 and, despite his considerable alcohol consumption, Pan was still lucid and eager to pursue his plan and bring "Panacea" to market.

"I suppose so; what do you want, coffee?" Janus was in the kitchen trying to figure out how to work the kettle.

"Yep that would be great. I need to sober up a bit; I've got to ring Zeus." Pan thought for a moment. "Actually, since I've got to ring Zeus, can you put a shot of brandy in it?" Pan was scrolling through his phone whilst fervently hoping his boss was in a good mood; it was unlikely, but Pan was, by nature, optimistic.

"Where the bloody hell is Vesta when you need her?" Janus was muttering to himself as he tried to find the coffee. After searching in numerous pots and jars, he tracked it down and then it was just a case of finding a spoon and re-boiling the kettle. Twenty minutes later he carried two cups back into the living room and set them down on the table, careful to ensure that he used coasters; the last twenty minutes had taught him new respect for Vesta.

"There you go." He indicated Pan's coffee. "How did you get on with Zeus?"

Pan took a sip of the hot liquid, grateful for the burn of brandy.

"Oh, not too bad, you know what he's like. He tongue-lashed me for a few minutes, but then he got a little tickle in his throat and had to stop yelling, so I managed to get a word in edgeways."

"So, what did you want to talk to him about?" Janus called out from the kitchen. He'd found some biscuits during his search for the coffee and was feeling a bit peckish.

"I need to see Aphrodite. 'Panacea' needs to be as effective as possible, and I could do with her help to refine the ingredients." Pan relaxed back on the sofa and put his feet up on the coffee table.

"Aphrodite? Wow, she's a feisty one; are you sure about this? Chocolate digestive?" Janus offered the packet.

"Oh, lovely thanks." Pan helped himself to two. "She's feisty all right. I had a run in with her a few centuries ago, and I've still got the scar, look." He pulled back his thick black hair from his forehead and indicated a faint scar.

"What did you do?" Janus had had enough experience with Pan's lecherous ways to know that he probably deserved the scar.

"Don't look at me like that Janus, you know what Aphrodite was like – always up for a good time. I just pressed my advantage when she was a bit tipsy and flirty." Pan helped himself to another biscuit and tried to feign innocence.

"When you say pressed your 'advantage'...?"

"Yes, all right, I did come on a bit strong, but she didn't have to beat me with her sandal. That was completely uncalled for."

"I'm surprised she managed to scar you with a sandal. If I remember rightly, she wore delicate little golden slippers with ribbons and stuff."

Pan looked slightly embarrassed and took a long draught of his coffee and finished the last of his biscuit before replying. "It turns out that my reputation may have preceded me. She texted her son Eros as soon as I started chatting her up, and he showed up and beat the crap out of me. It was not a good day."

Janus chose not to mock Pan for this revelation, although he was sorely tempted. "So why do you want to see her now? Can't you put something together without her help?"

"I could but, let's face it, no-one knows what males want or need more than Aphrodite; she was known as the Mount Olympus bike at one time. Why do you think I tried it on with her?"

"So basically, she's the female you, and even she wouldn't sleep with you willingly?" Janus had rethought his plan not to mock Pan; he still had a modicum of respect for females, goddesses or otherwise. Unfortunately, Pan wasn't listening, having started on yet another chocolate biscuit. He was just reaching for a fifth when his phone bleated.

"What the bloody hell was that?" Janus looked startled.

"I just got an email; I think it's from Aphrodite." Pan unlocked his phone.

"No, what was that noise? Did you set bleating goats as your ringtone?"

"I sure did. Sexy, right?" Pan grinned. "Excellent, Aphrodite says she'll meet me…oh hang on, she won't meet me on my own after what happened the last time." His face fell. "Will you come with me?"

"I don't know Pan, that means phoning Zeus to get permission and arrange transport. I really don't feel like listening to him shouting at me for twenty minutes. Honestly, I have better things to do."

"Like what?" Pan was well aware that Janus' plans for the rest of the day involved watching day-time television for "research purposes."

"Look, tell you what, I'll text Zeus, and that way you don't even have to talk to him. You go and trim your beard so that you look nice for Aphrodite and leave everything else to me."

Janus crammed the last of the biscuits into his mouth and headed back towards the kitchen, careful to put the empty wrapper in the bin, and washed his hands. "Ok, but make sure you do get permission, Pan; I really cannot deal with one of Zeus' hissy fits." When he returned to the living room, Pan was avidly texting.

"Do you think you'll pop in and see your Dad when we're up there?" Janus knew Hermes vaguely. All the gods were aware of each other's existence on some level, but they were a very cliquey lot, and he and Hermes just didn't move in the same circles.

"You've got to be kidding. Why would I want to go and see him? He made my childhood a misery."

Janus hadn't really heard much about Pan's early years and was curious.

"Why what did he do?"

Pan put down his phone and tucked his legs up underneath him on the sofa.

"Where do I start? Firstly, he's a flash git who was always showing off. Grandma told me that, on the day he was born, he stole Apollo's cattle, and everyone thought it was really precious…apart from Apollo, obviously; when he eventually found out, he was furious. She also told me that he invented speaking, but I think the old bat was just losing it at that point." Pan's eyes were downcast, and he was picking at a loose thread on his cuff. Janus could see that Pan was upset but couldn't really understand why.

"Well, that doesn't sound so bad. I mean, it's not great to see your Dad showing off all the time, but it could have been worse."

"That's not really it." Pan was silent for a moment. He took a deep breath and continued with his story. "It was my tortoise; his name was Kallistos."

Janus wrinkled his nose "Why would you call a tortoise 'most beautiful'?"

Pan turned on him in a fury. "Because he was beautiful to me, that's why; he was my friend and I loved him."

Janus was shocked at the strength of the reaction. "OK, I'm sorry Pan, I didn't mean to upset you. What happened to him?"

When Pan spoke, it was in deadened tones and his black eyes were glistening with unshed tears. "My Dad happened to him. As, I was saying, Apollo eventually found out about the cows and went absolutely apeshit. My Dad knew that he'd get his arse kicked, so he decided to create a new musical instrument and write a song praising Apollo. He couldn't be bothered to go and chop down a tree like any normal god, oh no! He killed Kallistos, and then scooped out his insides before using him to make the first lyre." Pan started quietly sobbing, and Janus patted him, comfortingly, on the shoulder. "Well at least now I know why he's been acting out all these years," he thought. "Poor little sod."

"I wouldn't mind if Apollo had kicked my Dad's arse, but he didn't. He thought the song was wonderful and swore to be his best friend for ever more. The Bastard!" Pan spat out the last two words and then collapsed, sobbing, on the sofa.

Janus got up to put the kettle on again and hoped that there'd be enough brandy left to get Pan through the evening.

## Chapter 10

All the while that Pan and Janus had been planning and dealing with Pan's daddy issues, Hades had been up in his bedroom sulking and bemoaning the fact that no-one wanted to be his friend. Being a god, and having very few scruples, he had no problem listening in on their conversation and, after hearing Pan's revelation, he decided to go downstairs to join them. If anyone knew about daddy issues, he did.

As soon as Pan heard footsteps on the stairs, he pulled himself up into a sitting position and quickly rubbed his eyes, wiping away all traces of tears. He turned as Hades entered the room. "Oh great, that's just what I need," he thought.

"Hi, Hades. Janus is just making a cup of coffee if you want one." Pan felt relatively safe in making this offer as Hades never drank coffee, preferring caffeine-free infusions. He disapproved of stimulants in any form.

"That would be great thanks." Hades took a seat next to Pan. Janus had heard the exchange and was standing at the kitchen door with his mouth open.

Hades glanced at him. "What? I fancy a coffee," he muttered.

"OK, no problem, another coffee if you would be so kind Janus; a special one like mine I think." Pan beamed and winked conspiratorially at Janus.

"Well, I'll be damned," Janus said to himself as he reached for another mug and the brandy bottle.

"Yes, probably…..eventually." Hades called out before turning his attention to Pan. "You know, you're not the only one who had a bastard for a dad. I never told you about mine, did I? Cronus he was called, and he was a bloody nightmare."

"You were listening?" Pan's eyes narrowed as he looked accusingly at Hades.

"Pan you know what a god's hearing is like; I couldn't help it." There was enough of an apology in his tone to appease Pan and, besides, he was curious to hear what Hades had to say. The Underworld was a separate domain, and Pan knew little about Hades or what he did there, other than what he heard on the grapevine which was basically, "Miserable bastard, best place for him."

"Ok, go on then tell me. What was the problem with your dad?"

Janus had come back into the living room with three mugs and another packet of biscuits that he'd found in the cupboard. He took a seat in the worn leather armchair and looked expectantly at Hades who blew on his coffee before taking a tentative sip.

"Mmmm, that's not bad." He took another sip. "Quite warming. Anyway, as I was saying, you're not the only one who had a bad father. Mine ate me." He put his mug up to his lips once again as the other two just stared at him.

"When you said he ate you….?" Pan was far more liberal-minded than the average god, but even he was shocked.

"He literally ate me as soon as I was born – me and Poseidon; swallowed us whole apparently. If it hadn't been for my younger brother, Zeus, kicking the shit out of him when he was old enough to do some damage, I'd probably still be there now. I say, this coffee really is extremely good, it's perking me up no end."

Pan had been stunned into silence, but Janus' curiosity overcame his shock. "But why Hades? Why would he eat his own sons?"

Hades had almost finished his coffee and was looking more cheerful than Janus had ever seen him. "What? Sorry. Oh, that was Grandpa and Grandma's fault really; they were always prophesising things, and they told Dad that we'd eventually raise an army against him, so he ate us." Reaching forward, he helped himself to a biscuit. "Is there anymore coffee going?"

Janus took the empty cup and stood up. "Were they right, your grandparents, with their prophesy?"

"Oh yes, they were always spot on. We did raise an army *and* we overthrew him but, personally speaking, I wouldn't have got involved if the bastard hadn't eaten me. It was no fun sitting around in digestive juices for twenty years, I can tell you. Especially as I only had Poseidon for company. Honestly, you've never heard anyone bang on about fish as much as he does; he nearly drove me round the bend."

Janus shook his head and went out to make more drinks; he was tempted to forgo the coffee completely and just pour out three brandies, but he didn't want to spook Hades now that he was opening up to them.

Pan was still sitting in stunned silence, but then, suddenly, he threw himself sideways and wrapped his arms around Hades. "I never knew. I thought I was the only one to suffer at the hands of my father like that. I'm so sorry, Hades; I know what you've been through."

Hades patted him on the head absentmindedly; he was feeling slightly woozy but so happy that he was finally on the receiving end of a little affection. He had thought that he would find intimacy and happiness with his wife, Persephone, but, rather than woo her, he'd decided to kidnap her, and she hadn't taken it at all well. Hades had figured that she would grow to like it in the Underworld, but she had complained constantly that it was too hot, and she couldn't sleep with all the screaming. In the end, he was quite glad when Hermes came to rescue her. Unfortunately, she'd had pomegranates for breakfast that morning, and under the rules of the gods (which were bizarre at the best of times) she was now obliged to spend every winter in the Underworld. Over the millennia they'd reached an understanding; they both understood that their lives would be a lot easier if they were never in the same room together.

When Janus saw the happy smile on Hades' face, he made a decision. "We're going to see Aphrodite in a couple of days, why don't you come with us, Hades?"

Pan broke free of his hug "That's a great idea, Janus; we'll all go together, make a day of it." He and Janus grinned at Hades who looked a little confused; he couldn't remember the last time he'd been invited somewhere unless it was to "go to hell." He'd also never really understood the insult as he lived there.

"Why do you need to see Aphrodite?"

It took Pan and Janus about half an hour to explain their plan to turn the human males back into true believers, and at the end of it, Hades was beaming. He put his arms around the shoulders of his fellow gods. "I'm in!"

## Chapter 11

Hebe and Vesta had spent all afternoon in a little coffee shop away from the town centre, so that they could avoid bumping into the gods and to give Vesta time to sober up. She'd come round in the taxi when Hebe slapped her face two or three times, an action Hebe regretted immediately as Vesta had promptly vomited in her lap. Had it not been for Hebe's incredible beauty and effortless ability to charm human males, they would have had to walk home. As it was, the taxi driver found a relatively clean cloth and a bottle of water and Hebe was able to repair most of the damage to her leather trousers. Vesta was mortified and apologised repeatedly, but she was, at least, feeling a little better and managed to stay conscious for the rest of the ride.

After her fourth cup of black coffee, Vesta was almost back to her normal self, that is to say that she was, once again, demure and composed. However, her experience in the bar seemed to have given her a new grit and determination.

"I've been thinking about the gift that you have Hebe, and I believe I've thought of a way that we can profit from it and maybe attract some new believers."

"Tell me more. Anything we can do to get Zeus and Saturn off our backs is fine by me." Hebe would consider almost anything to show the gods that goddesses were useful for something more than being animated decorations at a drinks party.

"Well, I've read quite a lot of human magazines in the past few months. I like to read them when I've finished the housework and I have a quiet moment to myself, and it seems to me that human males almost worship what they call models. They are all thin and beautiful, and they show off clothes, make-up, perfume, even extraordinary things like dishwashers." There wasn't a dishwasher at Number 23, and Vesta was deeply enamoured of what she perceived as a wonderful human invention. If we were to use your talents on some ordinary woman around Brighton, I think that, maybe, we could start our own modelling agency. We wouldn't have to pay them very much in the beginning, I don't think." Vesta spoke shyly; she was unused to putting forward her own ideas, unless it was to instruct someone on how to get an ambrosia stain out of a toga.

Hebe looked thoughtful for a moment. "I think you're right about human males worshipping models; in fact, any beautiful female, but how will that help us? We need them to start worshipping us again not just increase their obsession with the female body."

"Just think about it. Look at how human males are with you; they become your slave if you smile at them. I know we can't create goddesses, and the women you transform won't have your beauty….stop looking smug Hebe, I'm just stating a fact, but they could have enough to enslave your average human male. Males have commanded and guided civilisation for too many years; it's time that females had some power. I'm not saying that beauty *should* give women power, we can't change human nature just like that, and it will take time. However, if it can empower some human females, really empower them, they can help us change the dynamic. If we can get human women to start thinking of themselves as goddesses that will put the word back in their vocabulary which can only help us."

Hebe was impressed with Vesta's speech; it was obvious that she'd put a lot of thought into the idea, but she still had her reservations. "You do realise that it will be like being back with your virgins again if it works?" Hebe's interest was piqued, but she was concerned that Vesta would retreat back into herself and revert to old habits.

"Oh, bugger, I didn't think of that." Vesta's hopeful expression faded but then suddenly she brightened, "Wait, hang on a minute. There's no reason for the models to have to take a vow of chastity is there?"

Hebe laughed, "No, I didn't mean that; I just meant that you'd be surrounded by women again."

"As long as I can still go back to my hearth at night, I think I can learn to live with it." Vesta winked and Hebe was quite taken aback; an afternoon in a bar with vast quantities of alcohol had really brought Vesta out of her shell.

"So how do we make this work? It's all very well creating beautiful women, but what do we know about running a modelling agency?" Even though it had been her idea and she still had a fair amount of alcohol in her system, Vesta was full of self-doubt. Although, as a goddess, she had been worshipped and revered by her virgins, it wasn't the same as being told, "You're a fascinating woman" or "That robe really brings out the blue in your eyes." The ego of a goddess is no different from that of any other creature; if it is not fed regularly, it becomes dry and fragile.

"How hard can it be? It's just a question of finding gullible men who want to pay a fortune for a beautiful woman to represent their product." Hebe, having been blessed with stunning good looks was not short on confidence; her ego had been fed so regularly and so well that it was in danger of becoming obese. "I'll find out who's in charge of a couple of the cosmetics companies we deal with at Boots and just invite them out to lunch."

"You think that they'll agree to see you, just like that, do you? These are important men we're talking about." Vesta was sceptical.

"They will if I email them with a copy of my Boots employee of the month photo." Hebe grinned and winked. Vesta sighed and wondered if she should start drinking again; her initial burst of enthusiasm was beginning to wane.

Hebe pushed back her chair and stood up, eager to embark on their new venture. "Come on, let's go and find some make-over candidates. This should be fun! At least, unlike at work, I won't have to call them madam and tell them they're beautiful when they look like the back end of a chariot."

Vesta rose reluctantly, having witnessed Hebe's lack of tact and diplomacy and the effect it could have; nevertheless, she followed her out onto the street. There was a loud shout behind them, as the owner of the coffee shop realised that two of his customers had just left without paying. Hebe turned around and smiled. "Never mind, it's on the house." Brian Gibbons had never given away a free cup of coffee in his life, let alone six but he would happily have handed over the keys to the café for another of Hebe's smiles. Fortunately for him, she had already forgotten the incident and was deep in conversation with Vesta.

"Right, I think what we're looking for are women who could do with a bit of a lift, maybe they've fallen on hard times or are in bad relationships."

Vesta was curious, she hadn't even considered what personality type they'd be looking for; she was quite impressed that Hebe had first considered women who needed some help with their lives. "Maybe she's finally learning to think of someone other than herself," she thought. Out loud, she said, "That's very commendable Hebe. What made you think of that type of woman?"

"Because they'll be grateful and easier to manipulate; don't forget, the aim of all this is to get the humans worshipping us again." Hebe frowned at Vesta's naivete. "I know that you have that whole mothering thing going on and want to take care of everybody, but we have a job to do. You're going to need to toughen up a bit."

Vesta threw back her shoulders, determined not to be seen by Hebe as weak. "What about her?" She pointed out a woman of about 40, who was sitting on the pavement outside a chip shop. She was clearly drunk and, wherever she was living, it was obvious that there were no showers. Her clothes were ragged and filthy, and her long straggly hair looked as though it hadn't been combed, much less washed, in at least a month. "Even Hebe's going to struggle with this one," she thought. Although Vesta was determined to be tougher, she had been annoyed with Hebe's blatant disregard for the humans' well-being and certainly wasn't going to do anything to make her life easier.

"Yes, good idea." Hebe's smile was forced, but she'd never been one to back down from a challenge, so she walked over to the woman. "Good afternoon madame, I wonder if I could have a moment of your time?" The woman looked at her with glazed eyes, and she swayed slightly before leaning over and vomiting copiously on Hebe's Christian Louboutin's. Hebe looked down at the woman, who was grinning inanely, and then at her shoes.

"Vesta, have you got a tissue?" Although Hebe spoke quite calmly, Vesta could see the muscles in her perfectly sculptured jaw working as she ground her teeth.

"Just the one?" Vesta grinned as she fished a tissue out of her pocket and handed it over.

"If you have more than one, it would certainly be helpful." Hebe's patience was wearing extremely thin, but pride would not allow her to admit defeat. Having wiped the worst of the mess from her shoes, she stepped behind the woman and, putting both hands under her oxers, lifted her to her feet. "Come on, we're going to get some coffee into you, and then we're going to have a chat." The woman tried to resist and struggled in Hebe's grasp, but Hebe was on a mission and she was a lot stronger than she looked. As the goddess of eternal youth, she knew a thing or two about keeping fit. Plus, carrying around trays of nectar and ambrosia for hours at a time did wonderful things for the biceps.

"Come on Vesta, we're going back to the café."

"But what about her things? We can't just leave them on the street." Vesta looked down at the woman's pitiful possessions: a grubby sleeping bag, a carrier bag containing half a bottle of cheap vodka, a bag of cheese and onion crisps and a dog-eared book called 'Kick Your Addiction.' "Never mind, I don't think anyone will touch them."

The café owner was reluctant to admit the drunken woman, especially as she was his second drunk of the day, but another smile from Hebe, and he was pulling out chairs for the three of them and insisting that they try his Welsh rarebit. Hebe graciously accepted for all of them and also ordered a coffee for the befuddled woman and a pot of tea for herself and Vesta. An hour later, the woman, whose name was Sue, had sobered up enough to listen to their proposal, and the café owner was in paroxysms of delight after Hebe had declared that his was the best Welsh rarebit she'd ever eaten. When he'd made the suggestion, she'd had no idea what Welsh rarebit was, so she was extremely relieved when he arrived with three platefuls of cheese on toast and had, therefore, been feeling magnanimous.

"I'm sorry, you want me to be a what?" Sue's jaw hung down, revealing blackened and broken teeth. She knew that she had a bit of a problem with drink, but she figured that Hebe and Vesta had to be on something much stronger to even consider making such a suggestion.

"A model. It's really quite simple; I'll teach you how to move elegantly and to pose, and then a photographer will take your picture." Hebe smiled reassuringly.

"Yes, I know what a model is." Sue did not appreciate Hebe speaking to her as though she were a five-year-old; she hadn't made the best decisions in her life, but she was far from stupid. "What I mean is, in what possible universe could I ever be taken for a model? I mean, look at me." She indicated her flabby body and nondescript face with an impatient wave of her hands.

Vesta could sense that Sue was about to leave and decided to interject before Hebe started patronising the poor woman again.

"I know it sounds a bit odd, but it's what Hebe does; trust me, she's a miracle-worker. Not only that, but we're just starting out as a modelling agency, and we're looking for women who are a little more 'girl-next-door.'" Vesta smiled reassuringly.

"I guess I could be considered that if you lived next-door to an abattoir." Sue was not convinced, and in her increasingly sober condition, was wondering if she were the subject of an elaborate practical joke. "Thanks for the coffee and the cheese on toast, ladies, but I think I'll be on my way." She stood up and started backing towards the door.

"Let me show you," Hebe cried out. She was determined not to fail with their very first subject. "What have you got to lose?" She was fishing around in her handbag looking for a face cream sample, something she could use as a prop as she would in Boots.

"No, don't." Vesta put her hand on Hebe's arm and whispered, "We want her to believe in miracles, don't we?"

Hebe brushed off Vesta's hand and called out to Sue once more. "Sue, really think about it. What have you got to lose?"

Sue stopped before she got to the door. The memories from her old life came flooding back to her. She saw sharp images of herself from five years ago when she'd been attractive, married, and had a good job. In every image she was smiling and happy, but then they became darker. When cancer claimed her husband, she started drinking heavily to mask the unbearable pain of his loss, and her smile was replaced by a bitter, drunken sneer. At first her employers had been sympathetic but, over time, she'd alienated colleagues and had eventually lost her job and then her home. For the first time in five years, Sue saw an image of herself as she was now; she needed no mirror. She could see the disgust and pity in the eyes of the few other customers who were watching her. Slowly, she turned around and walked back to the table where Hebe and Vesta were sitting patiently. "OK, show me what you've got, you're right I've got nothing left to lose."

Hebe stood up and looked deep into Sue's eyes. She saw the pain that the alcohol had previously hidden behind a mask of belligerence, and she determined to do her best work yet. She looked around the little café to make sure that no-one was watching them and then gently laid her hands on Sue's sunken cheeks. At once, the skin became clearer and her cheeks plump. Her greasy, lank hair arranged itself into luxurious curls, her lips filled out and her hooded, bloodshot eyes, widened. Her features arranged themselves into perfect symmetry and her body appeared to deflate and then, immediately, shudder and shimmer until a magnificent, sensuous figure was revealed. Sue hadn't lost any weight, but her body was firm and her curves in perfect proportion. Finally, Hebe stepped back to admire her handiwork.

"We'll need to get you some new clothes of course but I think that went really well." Hebe reached into her bag and pulled out a small vanity mirror which she then handed to Sue. "What do you think Sue? Sue?" Turning to Vesta, Hebe asked, "Do you think she's all right?"

Sue had taken one look at her face in the mirror and had fallen onto the floor of the café in a dead faint. Vesta peered at the unconscious woman anxiously. "Yes, I think so," she lowered her voice and spoke in a whisper, "It was probably just a bit of a shock for the poor woman; you need to remember that humans are fragile, Hebe."

Brian, the café owner had heard the crash from the kitchen and came running over to their table hoping that he wasn't about to stumble across another case of food poisoning. His business was still struggling to recover after a nasty incident with an elderly lady and a dodgy prawn. "Is she all right?" he poked Sue gently on the shoulder and she began to come round.

"Does she look nauseous to you? She doesn't, does she? No, she'll be fine." He helped Sue back into her seat. "What happened to the old bag lady, and why is this stunner wearing her clothes?"

Hebe flashed Brian a smile, ensuring his question was immediately forgotten, and thanked him for his concern before she sat down facing Sue.

"So, what do you think Sue? Have we got a deal? Will you come and work for us?"

Sue's eyes filled with tears. "You've made me beautiful; you've given me my figure back and you want to pay me to be a model – what do you think?" She started laughing and crying at the same time. Hebe looked curiously at Vesta. "I don't remember saying anything about paying her."

"We'll talk about it later." Vesta turned to Sue who was still sniffing and hiccupping and said "Let's get out of here and see if we can find you somewhere to put your head down for a few days, and then we'll take you shopping for some new clothes."

"Oh fabulous, I love shopping."

Hebe was already flinging on her coat and grabbing for her bag which she'd dumped under the table.

Sue stayed seated looking at Vesta and Hebe with awe and wonder in her eyes. "I don't know what I've done to deserve this, but you two are like my guardian angels."

"Close enough," said Hebe, winking, surreptitiously at Vesta.

The two goddesses grabbed an arm each and they walked Sue from the café and towards a brand-new future.


**Chapter 12**

Janus had left Hades and Pan snoozing side by side on the sofa and retreated to his bedroom; he needed to talk to himself and this was the only place he could get any peace. So as not to terrify the humans, he was forced to hide his second face when he was outside the house, but here, he could reveal his true nature. He settled himself on the uncomfortable wooden chair he'd placed before his desk and contemplated the room. It was slightly tatty; it certainly had none of the luxury that he was accustomed to, and the wallpaper was a depressing shade of brown with faded yellow flowers, but it was his and he could relax. Pan and Hades shared a room, reluctantly, as did Hebe and Vesta (when she wasn't in residence in the fireplace), so this was his sanctuary.

He felt his shoulders relax and his arms and legs grow heavy as he allowed his shield to drop away.

"It's about bloody time, I must say; I was beginning to think that you'd forgotten about me." Janus' second face was revealed, and it was not happy. His eyes blinked rapidly as he tried to get used to the light.

"Sorry about that, it's been a busy few days." Janus felt whole again but he'd forgotten what a whinger his second face could be.

"It's all right for you; you're the primary face. I'm shut away most of the time, I've got no-one to talk to, and I haven't a clue what's going on. What have I missed?"

Janus explained their plans for bringing the human males back into line and increasing their worshipper numbers to his other face.

"Well, I guess it's a solution, but it seems to me that you're only looking at the problem using historical data. Don't you think it would be a good idea to consider the problem using statistical probabilities?"

When Janus was at home and not in his bedroom at Number 23, he was worshipped as the god of past and future. Unfortunately, he had lost many of his followers when Buddha had come up with the idea of everyone living for the present moment, rather than dwelling in the past or imagining their future. He'd debated the matter at length with the Buddha himself, but he hadn't been able to shift him from the premise that humans function much better when they're not worrying. Buddha argued that people cannot cope with the regret they feel when they reflect on their past mistakes and fear the future as it is an unknown quantity.

At one point, during the discussion, Janus had lost his temper and insisted that humans weren't happy unless they were worrying about something, and he'd asked why he shouldn't benefit from their neurosis. Buddha just sat smiling gently in a state of complete calm and said, "You will not be punished for your anger; you will be punished by your anger." Janus told him to piss off and stormed back to the Capitoline Hill in high dudgeon. He was even more annoyed when he looked at the bi-century Deity Ratings and realised that the humans were far happier following the Buddha with his live-in-the-now philosophy than following himself and the other ancients. None of them really liked to acknowledge it, but there was a great deal of professional rivalry between deities.

"I've applied the usual algorithms, but any data related to humans is inconsistent and unreliable, and, in order to get them worshipping us again, we need to restore their mindset to where it was a couple of millennia ago."

"Well then, what the bloody hell did you wake me up for?" His second face was clearly not pleased.

"I just wanted to talk it through. I got a bit carried away when we were all discussing the idea downstairs."

"Then we need to consider potential human emotional, intellectual and spiritual development moving forward. It's possible that males will become redundant in the future if a way is found to genetically engineer sperm." Janus' second face was becoming more animated by the second.

"It's also possible that artificial insemination will develop to such a degree that offspring can be carried in machine made wombs. Have you considered that?" His eyes lit up. "Or….or…the humans might lose the plot completely, and there'll be a huge war and they'll all die."

Janus sighed. This was the problem when you had a second face that considered all future possibilities. "Yes, but let's assume that the human race continues with both males and females and their development continues on the same trajectory as it has for, let's say, the last thousand years."

His second face was quiet for a moment. "OK, well, based on that hypotheses, I still think that my idea that the human race will die out is completely valid. If we take into account the possibility that I am, in fact, wrong, there's a strong chance that they will start to worship Google, if they don't already, and whatever you try to do will be utterly pointless."

"You're really not helping you know." Janus was becoming irritated with his second face. "Why on earth would they worship a company? It doesn't make sense."

"Think about it – Google gives them everything they want; it educates them, directs them, lets them see the whole world without leaving their homes. It enables them to store their hopes, dreams and memories all in one place, and it's always one step ahead of them. What can we offer people?"

Janus thought hard; what had they offered humanity in their heyday? His second face could be right about Google, and he was quite certain that the company would encourage it. "Maybe they're already encouraging it." He was now feeling somewhat threatened, "I mean, why did they call their storage 'the cloud' if it weren't to subtly manipulate human thought? Bugger!" He thought even harder about the gods' contributions to humanity back in the day.

"Well, um, we looked out for them, didn't we?" He had broken out in a sweat trying to think of something positive that he and his fellow gods and goddesses had done for the humans in the past.

"Did we?" His second face revealed his scepticism. "Or did we just turn ourselves into beasts or swans and seduce them for our own carnal pleasures? Zeus was famous for that."

"Look, you're supposed to be the forward thinker. Where are you dredging all this up from?" Janus tried frantically to think of an example of gods benefiting humans as much as Google had. "Anyway, hang on. What about the human couple Philemon and Baucis? Zeus and Hermes stayed with them and rewarded them for their hospitality. Huh! What have you got to say to that smart arse?"

His second face remain placid. "Rewarded them? Seriously? Zeus turned their cottage into a temple and forced them to work as priest and priestess. You know that they had to give up their cheese-making business? Not much of a reward in my opinion. Incidentally, you do realise that you're arguing with yourself?"

Janus was starting to get a headache. "Look, let's get back to the point. Do you think it's a good idea for me to visit Aphrodite with Pan and Hades and will 'Panacea' help the human males rid themselves of their insecurity and turn them back towards the gods?"

Janus' second face considered for several minutes before he responded. "The overriding desire of the human male is to procreate in order to ensure the survival of the species so anything you do to ensure that they don't fail in their desire will be appreciated. However, there are already such products available to them, so you will have to find a way to offer additional 'miraculous' benefits that will encourage them to believe in 'superior' beings. Once that thought has been established, it will be a case of reaffirming this belief on a regular basis and rewarding them for their faith. Then you'll need to ensure that word spreads…..shouldn't be too difficult I wouldn't have thought." Janus obviously couldn't see his second face, but he thought that it sounded incredibly smug.

Janus put his head in his hand; he was regretting ever having started this conversation. "Right, OK, well thanks for your help, I'm afraid I'll need to hide you again now, but we'll talk again soon."

"Why? What did I do?" His second face was indignant.

"Nothing but I need to go to the chemist; I've got the mother of all headaches coming on."

He closed off his second face and walked downstairs. Hades and Pan were still in the living room, but they were wide awake and watching Judge Judy on the television. Janus watched for a moment as the Judge snarkily explained to the defendant that painting a giant, pink arse on your neighbour's car is no way to settle a dispute over boundaries. He could feel himself being dragged into the ridiculous, but somehow compelling, dispute, so he cleared his throat and announced.

"I've been thinking guys. It's my belief that we need to offer the human males something more than 'Panacea' if we're going to enslave....I mean encourage them to worship us again." He didn't think it was necessary to point out that his second face had had the idea; after all, they were one in the same god.

Hades picked up the remote and turned down the sound on the TV.

"Oi, I was watching that!" Judge Judy was one of Pan's favourite shows.

Hades ignored him. "All right, what did you have in mind?"

Janus took a deep breath. "'Panacea' will only address one of their insecurities; there is another, perhaps a greater one that we could help them with." He was rather hoping that one of them would understand so that he didn't have to explain further, but both Hades and Pan were looking at him with blank expressions; in Pan's case it could have been because he was trying to follow Judge Judy with the sound turned off. Janus ploughed on.

"You see, apparently human men have an issue with...um size..." He trailed off with a hopeful expression on his face.

"The size of what?" Hades looked confused and Pan perplexed as he continued to watch the TV and tried to work out what had been stolen from whom.

"Their...um...well...manhood."

"Seriously?" Pan had torn his eyes away from the television and was staring incredulously at Janus. "Well, that's not anything they've inherited from us. I've certainly never had any complaints in that department; I don't know about you two." He grinned, winked and turned his attention back to the plaintiff who had just thrown a punch at the defendant.

Hades and Janus looked at each other, their communication silent but understood by both.

"Oh, never mind, just forget it. I'm going out to get some paracetamol." Janus walked out of the living room and grabbed his coat before heading out into the warm night air.

Pan looked at Hades and raised his eyebrow.

"I have no wish to discuss the issue." Hades turned the volume back on the TV before going out to the kitchen to make a cup of coffee. When it was ready, he added liberal amounts of brandy.

**Chapter 13**

After their success with Sue's "make-over," Hebe and Vesta decided that, if they were going to pursue their idea of a modelling agency, they really needed to find premises. There was no way that they would be able to run a business from Number 23 without the gods finding out what they were up to. What's worse, if the gods did find out, they would interfere, so that evening, they decided to start looking for business premises to rent. When they'd come home, they'd seen that the three gods were watching back-to-back episodes of Judge Judy and were unlikely to be moving any time soon. Confident that they wouldn't be disturbed, they sneaked upstairs and darted into Pan and Hades' room. Pan's laptop was lying open on their small, metal desk, so Hebe unplugged it and carried it through to the room she shared with Vesta. They closed the door and settled down to do some research.

"We need somewhere with a decent address if we're going to attract the best clients." Hebe was currently looking at 7000 sq. ft. triplex in Lockview.

"I agree, but where are we supposed to get the money from? Your salary from Boots certainly won't cover it, and I can't siphon off any more from the house-keeping without the guys noticing." As the homemaker, Vesta was given money by each of the others every week which she used for food, drink and cleaning products. Although the gods didn't work, they were each given an allowance from Zeus to cover "business expenses" while they were living among the humans.

Zeus had assumed that they would look after the two goddesses and therefore hadn't thought to give them any money which was why Hebe worked in Boots and Vesta took care of the house. It had caused quite an argument before they'd left, but Zeus had stood firm, saying that based on his experiences, the goddesses would forget the task at hand and spend all their time shopping if they were given an allowance. Zeus' wives and mistresses had worked their way through a considerable fortune, it was true, but only to make up for the fact that he neglected, cheated on, used and patronised them all on a regular basis.

"Don't worry about that; we'll come to some sort of arrangement with the owner." Hebe was resolutely self-assured. "What do you mean you can't siphon off any *more*? Is that why we've been living off bloody pot noodles and baked beans on toast lately?"

Vesta had the grace to look slightly guilty. "Well, coal's not cheap you know, and if I can't keep the fire burning every night..." She looked down at her hands that were clasped firmly in her lap.

"We really need to find you a man or, failing that, a god." Hebe looked at her with a mixture of annoyance and pity. She did feel sorry for Vesta, but she was sick to death of beans on toast. "What I wouldn't give for another taste of ambrosia," she thought wistfully. She made a note of the agent's phone number for the office space and then started idly scrolling through Pan's emails. Most were from women, desperate to know why he hadn't called them or from companies advertising "adult services." She was about to return the computer but then something caught her eye.

"Vesta, look at this; Pan's been emailing Aphrodite; I wonder why?" Hebe turned the laptop so that Vesta could read the email.

"It looks as though he's trying to arrange a meeting with her." Vesta scrolled through the other emails in the thread. "See here, he's going to see her this week, and apparently he's taking Hades and Janus with him. Why haven't they said anything to us?"

"I don't know, and I don't like it. What could they possibly want with Aphrodite? Do you know her? Great fun on a girl's night out. The last time we went out, she hooked up with this human called Adonis; you should have seen the body on him! Anyway, we had one amazing party and then all woke up three days later in a field surrounded by sheep; it was hilarious." Hebe's eyes were bright with remembered pleasures.

"I've heard of her." Said Vesta sniffily. Although she was learning to become more liberal in her thinking, millennia of being surrounded by virgins with only a phallic flame to serve as male company, had left her with an innate disapproval of sexual adventuring. "I believe her husband was furious with her and rightly so in my opinion."

"Hephaestus? Yes, he wasn't best pleased, but what did he expect? He'd spend all day and most of the night at the forge banging iron. He couldn't blame her for doing a bit of banging of her own. He was good-looking and had muscles where most gods don't have places, but he was so dull." Hebe pulled a face; she'd been given a very stiff talking to by Aphrodite's husband which had resulted in a mild case of narcolepsy.

"So, he neglected her a little, we've all been there, it doesn't mean that she has to cheat on him with all and sundry." Vesta's face was the picture of piety and Hebe remembered why she got on her nerves but then Vesta said, "Ohh, I've just had a thought. Do you think they're all meeting up for an orgy?"

Hebe burst out laughing, snorting in a most unladylike manner. "Bloody hell, where on earth did that thought come from, Vesta?"

Vesta grinned shyly. "Well, I might have been surrounded by virgins for most of my life, but that doesn't mean that I was blind and deaf. For most of the gods and goddesses I knew, an orgy was just a dull Thursday evening."

"Yes, I suppose you're right. Things did get a little out of hand once the ambrosia and red wine started flowing, but to answer your question, there is no chance of those four having an orgy."

"Why, I didn't think Aphrodite was all that fussy." Vesta was automatically jealous of any woman who hadn't lived in pious seclusion with a bunch of virgins.

"She's not." Hebe was nothing if not honest. "But Pan already tried it on with her and got a nasty sandal-related injury for his troubles. Aphrodite might be a bit loose with her affections, but she still has standards."

"Well that's something in her favour, I guess," Vesta conceded. Although Pan was exceedingly popular with the female human population, he was considered a disgusting, randy old goat back home.

"She had a lot of things in her favour, not least that she took her pleasure like a god. Do you know, I never understood why there should be different moral standards for gods and goddesses," Hebe said, thoughtfully. She'd never really reflected very much on her life as a goddess, although she had always resented being at the beck and call of the gods. However, living amongst the humans, she'd begun to realise how little freedom she really had.

Vesta thought for a moment before replying. "I'd never really thought about it, but you're right. I don't think the gods ever wanted us to be equal to them. Look at the way that Zeus carried on. He'd chase after anything in a toga, but he forced *me* to take a vow of chastity – me, his own sister!" Vesta wondered why she hadn't done more to take control of her own life; she'd become such a creature of habit over the millennia.

"I know! As far as the gods are concerned, we are just second- class citizens. Even Hades, Pan and Janus order us around all the time *and* expect us to take care of their every whim and fancy." Hebe actually did nothing to help Vesta take care of the gods at Number 23, but she resented their expectation that she would if asked.

The two goddesses were becoming more indignant by the minute.

"I'm going to ring that agent and arrange a visit to see the office space as soon as possible." Hebe picked up the phone. "Once we start making our own money and pick up some new worshippers, we'll be free and successful goddesses in our own right." She had a look of grim determination as she drummed her fingers, waiting for the phone to be picked up at the other end.

"Yes, hello, I am interested in the commercial property that you have to rent in Lockview…..that's the one. Sorry, I didn't catch your name." Hebe was using her most charming and seductive voice, and Vesta rolled her eyes as Hebe winked at her. "Thank you, Simon; it's lovely speaking to you too…three-thirty tomorrow afternoon? That would be wonderful.

Thank you, Simon. I can't tell you how much I'm looking forward to meeting you."

Hebe put the phone down. "There you are, that's all sorted. Now, I don't know about you, but I'm going to bed. We need to be nice and fresh for tomorrow." She yawned and stood up. "Oh, by the way, can you remind me to have an illness in the morning so that I can get off work early? I thought that we could meet up around one and have a spot of lunch before we go and look at the offices."

Vesta was surprised; Hebe didn't normally worry about leaving work early. "Yes, of course, but can't you just walk out when you feel like it as your normally do?"

"I could," Hebe replied shortly, "but the other girls don't seem to like it, and I don't want them to hate me any more than they do already." She got up to return the laptop to Pan's room.

Vesta didn't comment, but in her opinion, leaving work early was definitely not the primary reason why the other shop girls hated Hebe. It had far more to do with her extreme lack of tact. "Mind you, at least it seems as though she's finally learning some empathy." She stretched her arms above her head and got to her feet. "I think I'll turn in as well. Just one thing, we're not telling the guys about this, are we?"

"Definitely not! We should keep this to ourselves until we've made a big success of it, and then they'll have to rethink their ideas about goddesses. You'll be working now as well, so they'll have to make their own bloody dinner and figure out how to use the washing machine!"

They giggled conspiratorially.

"Oh wait," exclaimed Vesta. "What am I going to tell them? How will I explain that I won't be there to take care of them?" She was worried. Having spent so much time caring for the gods, she'd never considered how they'd manage without her.

"They're not children, Vesta. They're millennia old gods and quite capable of taking care of themselves. Besides, you know as well as I do that, if there isn't a meal prepared for them, they'll just go down to the pub." Hebe yawned and climbed into bed. "Stop worrying, this will be an adventure."

Vesta turned out the light and lay down. "Yes, I suppose you're right." She wasn't convinced. She'd once seen Janus and Pan spend ten minutes trying to figure out how to get the cord back into the hoover when she'd left in plugged in and blocking the television. She then remembered that they'd given up and gone down the pub. "Hebe's right," she told herself, "I'm worrying over nothing."

## Chapter 14

The next morning, they all had breakfast together. Hebe and Vesta were careful to keep subjects neutral. They needn't have bothered as, first thing in the morning, the gods did little more than grunt and try to work up enough energy to chew.

"Vesta, do you think I could have another slice of toast if it's not too much trouble?" Hebe called out to the kitchen. "So, what are you guys up to today?" She turned to the gods with a bright smile. All three of them looked at her suspiciously; she was being polite, and it wasn't even 8 o'clock. They then looked at each other, all realising that the truth really wasn't an option.

"I'm going to the library. To do research," Janus ventured.

"Oh great, I'll come with you," said Pan, eagerly.

"Me too!" Hades chimed in.

Hebe looked coolly at each of them in turn.

"OK, Janus, I can understand why you would go to the library; you're an educated god after all, and Hades, well yes, you don't like talking to people, so at a stretch, I get it, but Pan? Seriously?"

"What? I can read?" Pan was considered intellectually challenged by many of the other gods and Hebe's comment stung.

Vesta walked in with a stack of toast and a fresh pot of tea. "Pan, for as long as I've known you, I have never seen you pick up a book. Magazines, yes, perhaps the racing pages, but never a book. So what's going on?"

Pan managed to look slightly embarrassed although the others all knew he was faking it.

"I read in a magazine that the library is a great place to pick up human females, so I thought I'd tag along, all right?" He affected the air of someone deeply offended, but again, he was fooling no-one.

Hebe helped herself to a slice of toast. "So, what sort of research are you going to be doing? Did you have any particular books in mind?" She slathered on butter and marmalade and then looked at them expectantly.

The gods hadn't been prepared for questions, especially this early in the morning, and Hebe could see that they were fumbling for an answer. She could have been helpful and prompted them, but she decided against it. Instead she glanced at Vesta who had just sat down at the table, and they both stared. Hard.

"We've prepared a list of the titles that we need, haven't we?" Hades kicked Pan under the table.

"A list? Oh yes, right, the list; I've seen it, it's a good list." Janus rolled his eyes. Pan was great for getting you in to trouble but rubbish at getting you out of it. Hades suddenly stood up, his chair teetering backwards. "I think we should be going, there might be a queue, and we don't want to waste any time."

Janus and Pan also leapt to their feet and mumbled, "Need to go, no time to waste," as they followed Hades out of the living room, towards the front door. Hebe and Vesta smiled at each other as they heard the door slam.

"Well, that's got rid of them. What do you think?" said Hebe. "Should we have another cup of tea, or shall we go and get ready for our meeting?" In the end, Hebe had decided that there wasn't much point going in to work for a couple of hours. She phoned Tim in human resources and told him that she had "female problems," and she wouldn't be coming into work. Tim had only met Hebe once but that was enough. He spluttered, "No problem Hebe, I'll tell the bosses for you. I hope you feel better soon." He'd intended to ask Hebe out for a drink, thinking it may be easier over the phone than face to face, but he was too late; she'd already put the phone down.

"I think we should probably get ready but what am I going to wear?" Vesta was as unsure about her wardrobe as she was about most other things. When your love interest is a flaming phallus, fashion is not high on your list of priorities. It was not as if she would receive any compliments about her choice of attire from her paramour. Firstly, their relationship was purely physical, and secondly, a flaming phallus doesn't have a mouth which, from Vesta's point of view, was disappointing in more ways than one.

"Don't worry, I'll find you something, come on." Hebe stood up.

"What about the breakfast things." Vesta frowned as she looked at the dirty plates and toast crumbs all over the table. "I'll need to clear up before we go."

Hebe grabbed her by the hand. "This is far more important; I'll give you a hand to clear up later." She had to virtually drag Vesta upstairs, and a short fight ensued when she told her she was going to do her hair and make-up as well. Vesta thought that, having seen Hebe at work before, she'd learned enough to take care of her own hair and make-up. In the end Hebe grabbed her by the shoulders and forced her into a chair. "If we are going to do this properly, we need to look our best so stop being such a damn virgin about everything!"

Vesta was so shocked by Hebe's outburst that she sat placidly and allowed Hebe to give her another make-over. Several hours later, they were both ready.

"I almost don't recognise myself," Vesta was turning this way and that in front of the mirror, carefully examining her immaculate hair and flawless make-up. "But are you really sure about this dress? It's rather short."

Hebe sighed. "It's just above your knee, Vesta. You're not revealing anything significant, and it's very flattering on you; you can keep it if you like."

Vesta smiled shyly and moved to hug Hebe but then stopped herself; she'd been without physical contact for so long that it felt unnatural. "Thank you, Hebe, you've done a great job."

"I know." Hebe grinned, and picking up her handbag, headed out the door. "Come on, if we don't hurry up, we won't have time for lunch."

Vesta took one last look at herself in the mirror and followed Hebe; there was a definite spring in her step.

"Hey, I've just had a thought," Vesta called out to Hebe's retreating figure. "What are we going to call ourselves? We can't have a business without a name."

Hebe stopped dead in her tracks, which was unfortunate as Vesta was right behind her. "Oops, sorry." Vesta held out her hand to Hebe who was inelegantly sprawled at the bottom of the stairs.

"Don't worry, my fault." Hebe recovered her left shoe and pulled down her skirt so that it was, once again, within the bounds of decency. "You're absolutely right, Vesta. I hadn't even thought about that; what are we going to call ourselves?"

Vesta smiled shyly. "Well, I did have one thought, what about 'Virgins.'"

"It's a great name, but I think Mr. Branson might have something to say about it I'm afraid," Hebe explained, gently. She was pleased that Vesta was starting to come out of her shell and didn't want to discourage her.

"Who?" Vesta really didn't get out much.

"Seriously? No, you know what, never mind. Come on, we'll think of something on the way." She opened the front door and they both hurried outside.

By the end of the afternoon, they had signed a contract, at a heavily discounted rate with a young male estate agent who would be in serious trouble when he got back to the office. Hebe had led the negotiations and had also charmed the still bemused young man into tracking down some office furniture and installing it for them.

"Thank you so much for all your help, Simon. You've been absolutely wonderful, and I was so impressed when you moved all that furniture; you must spend all your time at the gym." Hebe grasped the young man's bicep and Vesta thought that he might faint. Hebe's charm could be quite overwhelming for the uninitiated. With her hand still on his arm, Hebe guided Simon towards the door and, once there, opened it for him.

"Interesting name for a business, 'Goddesses.' How did you come up with that?" Simon was desperately trying to keep the conversation with Hebe flowing.

Hebe looked over at Vesta and they both grinned. "Let's just say that when our creative juices are flowing, we have no limits; we are like goddesses." Hebe smiled lasciviously at the young agent who was licking his lips frantically in an attempt to stop himself from drooling.

Vesta could see that Simon was extremely reluctant to leave so she walked over to join them. She shook his hand and thanked him once again, promising to let him know if they had any problems. Unfortunately, the young estate agent just couldn't bear to leave Hebe's presence. He put his hands on the door jambs so that he could spend another moment in her company, but Vesta had had enough, and she shoved him forcefully and then shut the door behind him. There was a loud scream and several thuds as Simon tumbled down the stairs that were positioned just opposite their new office door.

"Sorry!" Hebe yelled out. "Right, let's have a tour of the building and see whom we can recruit. There must be loads of women here just dying to become world-famous super models." Hebe strode confidently out of the office, ignoring the whimpers that emanated from the floor below and knocked on their neighbour's door. Vesta leaned over the railing and made sure that Simon was still moving before joining Hebe. Their neighbour turned out to be the head office of a nationwide cleaning company – Spotless UK.

As Hebe approached the young woman at the reception desk, Vesta gazed around in awe. There were samples of cleaning products everywhere, and she felt her fingers itch; her default state of "homemaker" was threatening to overtake her.

"Vesta, come and say hello to Sally." Hebe's voice shook her from her reverie, and she wandered slowly over to the receptionist as if she'd just awoken from a pleasant dream. She had a sleepy smile on her face and her eyes were slightly glazed. She was unaccustomed to the high heels that Hebe had made her wear, and she stumbled slightly, knocking over a display of Spotless Handywipes: Erase Your Stains.

"I'm so sorry," she exclaimed as she frantically began picking up packs of Handywipes, trying to restack them on the display stand. "Ooh look, these have vinegar in them. I imagine they're simply marvellous for cleaning glass. I'll have to buy a couple of packets; the windows at home have been looking distinctly dingy lately." She happily carried half a dozen packets over to the slightly bemused receptionist.

"Vesta, focus!" Hebe's voice was stern as she glared at her companion who was still looking around excitedly at all the products on display. "This is Sally, and I've just been explaining to her about our new agency; she's going to come to the office later this afternoon for a make-over….Vesta!"

At Hebe's sharp tone, Vesta tore her eyes away from a display of Spotless Easywax floor polishers. "That's wonderful! I'll be sure to make some tea." Hebe realised that Vesta was still completely distracted, but she ploughed on regardless.

"Sally was just telling me that they have fifty women who work for the company, and many of them are looking for new career paths, so I've told her that we'll be holding an open day at the end of this week." Hebe absolutely radiated enthusiasm that she hoped would rub off on her colleague. Unfortunately, Vesta had spotted a stand of Spotless washing-up gloves – "elegance in rubber" – and had rushed over to take a closer look. She was carefully reading the product description when a middle-aged woman with a wispy brown bun and unflattering round spectacles joined her.

"Aren't they marvellous?" she enthused. "Quite the best product we have in stock in my opinion; I'd be lost without my rubber gloves." Vesta sensed a fellow devotee.

"I couldn't agree more. I'm rarely happier than when I'm sliding my hands into rubber. I'm Vesta, nice to meet you."

The woman gave her a slightly odd look, but nevertheless took the proffered hand and shook it briefly. "Gladys. Pleased to make your acquaintance. Are you with a supplier? Can I show you our full range?"

"Ahem!" Hebe's fake cough rang out like a shot across the office space.

"No, actually my colleague and I have just opened up an office next door." Vesta smiled and the woman, managed a sidelong glance at Hebe who was looking slightly pacified.

Gladys was less interested in Vesta now that she knew that she wouldn't be making a sale but was polite enough to enquire about their business.

"What is it you do?"

"We've just opened a modelling agency, called Goddesses, which will promote forward-thinking and intelligent businesses using real women who are proud of their beautiful flaws," Vesta carefully recited Hebe's mission statement.

"That sounds promising; it's about time that we had less of those skinny minnies in the magazines." As a middle-aged, somewhat rotund woman, Gladys thoroughly approved of the idea of "real" models.

"Why don't you pop round to the office when you've got a minute and we can have a chat?" Vesta's face was open and friendly, and Gladys had the impression that she was totally sincere, but she was, nonetheless, sceptical. "I can't see anyone wanting to put me on the cover of a magazine."

Hebe glided over to them, a big smile on her face. "She does love a challenge," Vesta thought as Hebe held out her hand in greeting.

"Gladys, is it?"

Gladys looked a little stunned as Hebe turned on the full force of her personality. "Yes, that's me." She gave a short, self-conscious laugh.

"Well, Gladys, you'll be amazed what we can do with some make-up and a little bit of magic. You come over later, and we'll have a nice cup of tea and a chat. All right?"

Gladys buckled under the weight of so much charm and nodded helplessly.

"Excellent. Come on, Vesta. We need to get on the phones and get some business coming in."

They waved cheery goodbyes to Gladys and Sally and went back out into the corridor to find some more human females in need of a make-over and a new career.

## Chapter 15

Hades, Janus and Pan had stopped off in a local café to finish their respective breakfasts before heading back to Olympus for their meeting with Aphrodite. Janus had argued that they should just wait until they got there so that they could dine on ambrosia, but Hades had insisted it would just spoil them for when they had to go back to eating sausage and chips in the human world.

"Hades will you stop looking at the humans like that? You're making them nervous." Hades had once had a staring competition with Medusa, and she'd lost, so people generally felt more than a little uncomfortable when he turned his gaze upon them. Hades had always maintained that Medusa had been so embarrassed by this defeat that she vowed to give up turning people to stone, but Perseus, who was trying to make a name for himself, cut her head off, so she never had the chance to turn over a new leaf. As a result, Hades had no way to prove his story.

Hades was unrepentant and continued staring at the humans; he was trying to ascertain which ones he would soon be welcoming to the Underworld. Janus nudged him, breaking his concentration. "What? I need to think about stocking up for when I get home. You know I had to leave Persephone in charge while we sort out the humans, and her record-keeping is abysmal; I'll probably have to do a complete audit when I get back. The souls of the dead do have a tendency to wander off every now and again if you don't keep an eye on them. So it would be as well if I have a few spares to take back home."

Pan put his head in his hands; Hades' singlemindedness never ceased to amaze him. Janus, however, decided to see what he could do to ease the situation.

"Hades...Hades look at me...that's better. Look, you do get that the Underworld is full of the souls of the *dead,* don't you?"

"I do, yes." Hades looked mildly affronted. "I've ruled it for long enough; I should know how it works."

"Yes, indeed but, the thing is, the humans you've been staring at well, they're not actually dead, are they?" Janus was using the same voice that he used for Pan when he was explaining that goats didn't have the same sex appeal in the human world as they did at home.

"No, they're not dead," Hades conceded. "Yet...But what's the point of being a god if you can't do a bit of forward planning." He turned his gaze towards a young man with a shaven head and swastika tattoos on his neck and made a note in a small black book, he took from his pocket, without once moving his eyes or blinking. The young thug began to sweat and gulp convulsively. The teenage girl with him looked concerned for a moment but then got up to leave as the thug mouthed "mummy," and a small damp patch appeared on the front of his ancient jeans.

"I think we'd better be going." Janus grabbed Hades by the scruff of the neck as Pan went to pay the bill. "We'll meet you outside."

Hades and Janus bickered all the way to Mount Olympus.

"Trust me, Janus, it would have done that young human good to have been given a glimpse of the Underworld."

"I have no doubt you're right, but our job is to bring humans back to us, to renew their faith in us, and we're not going to do that by scaring the crap out of them!"

"It always worked in the past; the odd lightning bolt or flood here and there used to work wonders for reinforcing the humans' faith." Hades was beginning to lose his temper.

"Yes, it worked when we had followers who needed a bit of proof that we exist, but we don't have any followers anymore, so all you've done for that particular human is to force him into a change of underwear. Not only that, but a lightning bolt is now considered to be a weather phenomenon, so throwing them at the humans would just be a waste of good lightning bolts. Furthermore, Zeus said that he's getting low on stock, and you wouldn't want to piss him off, would you?" Janus was known, amongst the other gods for his air of quiet reflection, but Hades was getting on his nerves.

"We're here," Pan declared, grateful for the chance to interrupt and change the subject. He wasn't averse to the odd argument himself, but Hades and Janus' non-stop bickering was wearing in the extreme, and he had to be at his charming best if he were going to win over Aphrodite. He smoothed his hair, breathed into his hand to make sure he didn't have goat breath and knocked on her front door. Hephaestus, Aphrodite's long-suffering husband, answered the door. "What do you three want?" He'd experienced enough of his voluptuous wife's philandering ways to greet fellow gods with at least the minimum of suspicion.

"Morning, Hephaestus. How're things at the forge?" Janus, the eternal diplomat, jumped in before Pan could ask to see the god's "better half."

"Can't complain. Thanks, Janus. I'm just heading back there now; Pegasus has slipped a shoe, and Ares wants to talk to me about restocking the armoury. If you've come to see Aphrodite, I think she's in the shower; you can wait in the living room if you like." With that, he strode down the path towards the forge, leaving them to fend for themselves. He was a god of few words and had little interest in any discussion that didn't involve horses or weapons.

"He could have offered us a bloody drink," moaned Pan as they all traipsed into the large, white villa.

They arranged themselves on the huge leather sofas scattered around the palatial room and waited for Aphrodite to arrive. Forty-five minutes later, Pan had dozed off, and Janus and Hades were busy ignoring each other.

"Gentlemen, I do apologise for having kept you waiting." A mellifluous voice floated into the living room and was closely followed by a vision in a periwinkle blue toga. The three gods leapt to their feet and bowed gracefully before the goddess Aphrodite.

Pan was the first to speak. "Lady, your beauty is quite beyond measure. I am enraptured, your slave for eternity." He moved to take her hand, but Aphrodite swayed her voluptuous body to the left and out of his reach.

"That's enough of your nonsense Pan; don't think I'm going to fall for that old crap."

Pan looked crestfallen for a moment but then remembered the reason for their visit and moved away so that Janus could make his greeting.

"We are agreed that Pan is a scoundrel and a villain, but in this, he is right; you have never looked more lovely." Aphrodite smiled slightly and held her hand out for Janus to kiss, before turning to Hades.

"And you here as well, I see. What drags you from the Underworld, Hades? The reason for your visit must be of great importance if you have deserted your army of condemned souls."

"Our quest is indeed most important fair lady." Hades wasn't a big one for flowery compliments. "We have been tasked to recruit new followers from amongst the humans so that we, as gods and goddesses, may once again flourish."

Aphrodite raised a delicate eyebrow. "You mean Zeus is skint?"

The three gods glanced at each other and then replied in chorus.

"Basically, yes."

The goddess indicated that they should all re-take their seats. "And what is it that you want from me? I have been given no such task and live in great luxury as you can see; I have no need of human followers."

Janus smiled at her as she indicated her boredom by plucking at the folds of her toga. "That is indeed good to hear. Now, down to business; perhaps we could discuss the reason for our visit over a cup of ambrosia?"

The other two gods sat forward with eager looks on their faces. They'd both learned to enjoy various human beverages, especially the ones containing alcohol, but nothing beat a cup of ambrosia.

Janus continued. "Maybe you could ask one of your many slave girls to bring a flask." Aphrodite was starting to look a little uncomfortable. "A large flask I think, seeing as there are four of us."

He could almost see the cogs turning in Aphrodite's mind, but Janus said nothing and surreptitiously raised his hand to indicate to the others that they should remain silent.

At last, she spoke. "Oh, all right, fine." She rose to her feet, magnificent but slightly embarrassed. "I don't have any ambrosia, and all the slave girls have buggered off because I couldn't afford to keep them in sandals any longer. Maybe, some new followers would be helpful."

The gods realised how much it had taken for Aphrodite to make such an admission; all those who lived on Mount Olympus were known to be fiercely proud. Janus held out his hand and Aphrodite joined them on the sofa. "Any human male that beheld your great beauty couldn't help but be besotted with you, but as you know, under normal circumstances we cannot reveal ourselves to humans, so we have had to come up with another plan. If you will permit, Pan will explain our idea."

Aphrodite looked across at Pan who was doing his best to look charming. She sighed deeply. "Oh all right."

Pan explained the problem for human males and the gods' solution. "It's called 'Panacea,' and it will ensure that no human male will ever again have to suffer the indignity of," he paused and considered his words carefully, "a drooping flower."

"You are doing the human race a great service, Pan; I can see that this would be a terrible affliction for any male, but how can I help?" Aphrodite was now leaning forward and had stopped sneering as she regarded Pan. In fact, she was looking rather eager.

"We can produce a potion that we know will be effective, but we need to consider the female perspective, and as you are much experienced in the ways of men and their psyches, we thought that you could help."

Janus and Hades stared admiringly at Pan; he was showing rare diplomacy, and Aphrodite was starting to look quite coquettish. The smile she turned on Pan was radiant. "Your potion will need to include something that allows men to look beyond the physical so that their relationships with human females will be far deeper and, therefore, more intimate. In my experience, human males show great enthusiasm and ingenuity during the seduction phase, but this wanes once they have had their…pleasure." She ran the tip of her rosy pink tongue across her full lips.

Hades rolled his eyes. "Pan, I think you've got a bit of drool on your chin."

"What?" Pan rubbed at his chin with the back of his hand before glaring at Hades. He hadn't forgotten Aphrodite's rejection of him, and Hades had just humiliated him mid-seduction.

Aphrodite's tinkling laugh rang out around the enormous room. She turned to Janus.

"You see how easy it is for a male to be rendered insensible by beauty, yet if I were to acquiesce to Pan's advances, he would forget me in minutes." She raised a quizzical eyebrow at Pan.

"Not minutes," he said defensively. "Hours. It would definitely be hours."

"Do you see what I mean?"

Janus rolled his eyes at Pan. "Yes, my lady, I quite understand, and I think that you are absolutely right in what you say. What do you think we should add?" He handed her a list of the ingredients that they'd prepared, and she looked down it carefully before replying. Janus continued. "Can you also think of something that would…ahem…increase…um…" He faltered.

Aphrodite raised one delicate eyebrow, "Dimensions?"

Janus slumped in relief, "Yes, quite so."

Aphrodite turned her attention back to the list. "I think that this will be most effective, but I would also add Mugwort as this will calm the males long enough for them to see beyond the obvious physical attraction of the females. Also, lemon balm, as this will give them clarity of thought and mental focus." She handed the paper back to Janus and rose to her feet. "As for 'dimension,' may I suggest adding some kelp meal? It is a natural fertilizer, so its purpose is to help things grow."

She directed a loaded smile at Janus. "Now, you must excuse me as I have an appointment with a human shepherd who caught my eye a few days ago."

The three gods rose. Pan could not help but ask, "And will you be using Mugwort and lemon balm on him?"

Aphrodite laughed. "Heavens, no. The last thing I want him to have is *mental* focus. You can see yourselves out, can't you?" With that she left the room.

The three gods stood without moving for a moment, surprised and happy that they had achieved their aim. Pan was the first to move towards the door. "We never did get a bloody drink, did we? Come on, let's head back to Brighton and the nearest pub."

## Chapter 17

In a bid to feel a part of their fledgling business and make herself useful, Vesta had decided to organise the office. She had prepared files for each of their new models and a list of contacts for Hebe. Business cards were on order as was a gold embossed sign for the front door. There was an advert for a receptionist in the local paper, and she'd arranged a selection of fashion magazines on their large coffee table. She was also busying herself making endless cups of tea and coffee for the stream of women pouring in. Vesta had worked her magic on Gladys and Sally, and when their friends and colleagues had seen the results, they'd immediately beat a path to door of Goddesses.

A week later and Vesta was interviewing their latest candidates while Hebe charmed potential clients.

"Signor Romano, how delightful to speak with you. Your voice is more charming than I could possibly have imagined," Hebe purred into the phone and then giggled as a senior executive at one of Italy's biggest fashion houses told her that she sounded like an angel. There was a good chance that he might not have been quite so charming had he not seen Hebe's photo, but one never knows with Italian men. "You're so kind, Signor….Alessandro? Thank you, Alessandro. Please call me Hebe; I am sure that we are going to be great friends." While she listened to the besotted man confirm, in poetic Italian that they would, indeed, be *great* friends, Hebe's fingers flew over the keyboard of her computer as she emailed profiles of the latest models from Goddesses. Word had spread about Hebe's miracle make-overs, and they were now having to turn hopefuls away until they had secured more clients.

"Grazie, Alessandro, grazie. Now, I've just sent over some files for you to have a look at; I am sure you won't be disappointed in our goddesses."

She waited patiently, saying nothing, but ensuring that her breathing was audible.

"Yes, you are quite right, some of our models are more mature, but your brand is for *all* women isn't it? *All* women want to be wearing your magnificent creations and feeling beautiful, so we need to be marketing to *all* women. Your current models are quite stunning, but I don't think that there are many potential customers out there who can really relate. I'm sure that your sales statistics will confirm that a great many of your customers are not as young as they once were."

Hebe's voice was still and soft and flowed like warm honey, but there was a core of steel; she wouldn't back down until the signor agreed that all women were gorgeous in their own right and should be celebrated as such by the fashion industry. She didn't have to wait long; the signor would have said anything to please Hebe, and he was soon gushing that all women were a thing of beauty regardless of their age or size. He further commented that he couldn't understand why their industry hadn't focused on this potentially large client base sooner.

"It's strange you should make that point, Alessandro, as I was talking to Pascal over at Vestiti de Lusso only this morning, and he agreed with me that, where the super-luxury brands lead, others will follow."

Hebe listened for another couple of minutes. "Yes, exactly, it's powerful men like you, Alessandro, who set the trends. How many of my models did Pascal hire? Hold on just a moment would you?"

Hebe covered the receiver of the phone with her hand and whispered to Vesta, "Got him." Vesta replied with a thumbs up and a huge grin.

Hebe returned her grin and then turned her attention back to Alessandro. "Pascal hired Gladys, Helen and Stephanie for his runway and Sally and Mildred for the photoshoot next week in Paris. You know, I really shouldn't be telling you this, Alessandro." She giggled flirtatiously. "So, you'll take all five? That's wonderful news; you've made me so happy. If you email me the details, I'll arrange for the girls to join you in Milan, and we simply must have dinner very soon so that I can thank you for your business *personally*."

She put the phone down five minutes later after having listened to Alessandro wax lyrical about his favourite Italian restaurant and insisting that she confirm a date and time for their meeting.

"I need to go to Milan next Thursday; can you make a note in the diary please, Vesta?" Hebe sighed, between using her powers to create potential supermodels and her charm to entice clients, she was feeling tired. Worse, she was realising that, although their little business was making great strides and plenty of money, they weren't really doing anything to reclaim their lost followers.

"Vesta?" Hebe called across the office and Vesta looked up from her filing; her last interviewee for the day had just left, and she was busy updating personnel files. "Why did humans start worshipping us in the first place? I realise that we're all-powerful, magnificent beings so there's no reason why they shouldn't, but how did it all start?"

Vesta leaned back in her chair. "Well, I never got it from the horse's mouth; you know Zeus, he's not really the kind of god that you can have a philosophical discussion with, but Juno had some thoughts on the matter."

"I always liked Juno; she was never stuck-up like some of the other, older goddesses. Anyway, go on." Vesta had Hebe's full attention.

"Juno thought that humans worshipped us for two basic reasons. One, they needed to have some sort of context for their own existence – where they came from, why are they here, that sort of thing; and, secondly, they needed to have an explanation for everything that they don't understand."

"What do you mean exactly? It seems to me that many of them understand extraordinarily little." Hebe retained a deep cynicism about human capabilities.

Vesta was more compassionate. "Take death, for example. Humans just can't handle it; they understand that it will be the end of their life, but they can't imagine what it would be like to not exist. Therefore, they think of ways to explain it that makes the whole thing more palatable for them; the idea of spending eternity amongst the gods is much more appealing than the idea of crumbling into dust."

"They wouldn't think like that if they'd met Hades. I would have thought that crumbling to dust would be a darn sight more enjoyable than spending eternity in his company," Hebe scoffed.

Vesta laughed. "Yes, but they don't know that do they? All they know is what they've experienced and what they can imagine or what other people can imagine for them."

Hebe thought for a moment. "So, all we need to do to get our followers back is to explain something they don't understand and give them context for their own existence?"

Vesta nodded. "I guess so but how do we do that?"

Hebe frowned. "I'm not really sure to be honest. Let's start with what they don't understand and go from there."

Vesta ran her hand across her forehead and pushed away a stray lock of hair. "The problem with that is finding something that *none* of them understands; explaining how email works would seem like a miracle to some of them."

"All right, well what's really important to them that they don't understand? We must be able to come up with something, surely." Hebe had little patience and was beginning to get frustrated.

At that moment, there was a knock on the door, and Sue sidled into the office. She had just come back from a casting call with Rococo Blaine and wanted to deliver the news, in person, that she'd been successful.

Hebe and Vesta both rose from their desks, took an arm each, and led her to the black leather sofa that graced the reception area. Sue was a little bemused but had become used to the somewhat eccentric ways of her two bosses. She smiled at each of them in turn and waited for an explanation. Vesta and Hebe looked very intense, and Sue couldn't help but wonder if she'd done something wrong.

"Sue. Dear Sue, it's lovely to see you." Hebe's default position, in any situation, was to go on a charm offensive. "I wonder if you could answer a question for us?"

Sue was still a little wary but also curious. "Yes, of course, what do you want to know?"

Vesta patted her hand. "Think very carefully; this is important. Is there one thing on earth that you really, really don't understand, however much time and effort you dedicate to attempting to understand it?"

Sue answered almost immediately, "Men."

"Are you sure you don't want more time to think?" Hebe had never had any problem understanding men or, at least, manipulating them.

"Love?" Sue didn't want to disappoint her bosses.

"Men and love? That's interesting; thank you, Sue," Vesta smiled encouragingly. "How did you get on at the casting today?"

"I got the job." Sue's grin was huge and lit up her whole Hebe-engineered face. "I've been booked as the new face of Rococo Blaine; you should have a confirmation email in your inbox."

Hebe clapped her hands and gave a most undignified squeal, and Vesta gave Sue a huge hug.

"I think you guys are on your way." Sue was almost in tears; her life had been completely turned around by these two women and she absolutely worshipped them. She determined to tell as many people as possible about her good fortune; she wasn't sure how many people still believed in miracles, but she was living proof, wasn't she? "I really need to see if I can track down an old photo from somewhere," she thought. It occurred to her that the media might be interested in her story. Although she was making money now and had a lovely studio flat to live in, it never hurt to earn a little more on the side.

## Chapter 18

A few days later, the five gods and goddesses were sitting down to breakfast. Vesta and Hebe were full of smiles and energy, and it was clear from their body language that they were eager to start their day. Pan, Hades and Janus, on the other hand, looked tired and slightly grubby. Hades' normally perfectly coiffed hair was dishevelled; Janus had a black smudge on the back of his neck and one of Pan's eyebrows had a large chunk missing.

"Honestly, I don't know what's the matter with you three at the moment; look at the state of you." Vesta was having to keep her hands busy with toast and jam to overcome her natural compunction to tidy them up. Unfortunately, once her hands were free, she couldn't resist taking a napkin, spitting on it and rubbing at the smudge on Janus' neck. He jerked away, flapping his hands at her.

"What are you doing? Stop that! I'm an ancient god, not a bloody toddler!"

Vesta stopped rubbing and sat down again, looking slightly hurt. They were all used to her mothering instincts, and it was unlike Janus to be impatient.

"Don't be so mean; she was only trying to help." Hebe's quick temper flared. "And she's right; what's the matter with you three, I've never seen you looking so tatty."

The three gods looked at each other, and it appeared to the goddesses that there was some sort of unspoken dialogue between them. Finally, Pan spoke. "We've been working, all right? We've been busting our balls to try to achieve what we were sent down here to achieve. Unlike you two who just seem to worry about how your hair looks and whether the kitchen's tidy."

Hebe picked up a jar of strawberry jam and drew back her arm, intending to launch it at Pan's head, but Vesta caught her wrist and frowned at her, shaking her head. "I am sure that Pan didn't mean anything by it Hebe. It's obvious that the three of them are feeling stressed; we should just leave them to get on with their day in peace. Come on, you can help me clear up." Hebe glared at the three gods but said nothing and, rising to her feet, picked up their breakfast plates and took them out to the kitchen. Vesta followed her.

"Keep your calm with them Hebe; we'll get our own back when they see that it's us who has regained our human followers. When Sue told us about her new contract with Rococo Blaine, I could feel her belief in us and what we're doing, and belief is only a small step from faith. Trust me, we are empowering women; we already have queues outside the door every day, and that's an indication of their belief in us. It's a small start, but we are beginning to make a difference."

Hebe bowed her head in acquiescence. "Yes, I know that you're right, but we need to find a way to reach a mass audience if we are going to get our full strength back. To be honest, I am starting to find it harder and harder to summon the power to change these women's appearances."

Vesta looked momentarily worried; her job had been to guard the sacred fires, and although she was worshipped as a goddess in her own right, she'd had no special powers to speak of and hadn't felt herself weakening. In fact, she'd only noticed one small difference since they'd arrived. "I know; I can see that you're looking tired. Being down here on Earth, the loss of faith is so much more obvious. Do you know, even my flaming phallus was looking limp last night?"

Hebe eyebrows shot up into her hairline and she opened her mouth to say something, but Vesta interrupted her. "I think what we need is to create more publicity. From what I've seen, the media controls the human minds to a greater or lesser extent so why don't we use them?"

"That's a good idea!" Hebe grinned broadly. "We could call a press conference to announce the new contract with Rococo Blaine and use that as an opportunity to speak to more women." She put her arm around Vesta's shoulders "You're a genius!" They quickly finished the washing up and then went upstairs to get ready to go to work. It hadn't occurred to Hebe that she'd never called a press conference and had no idea how to organise one, but she figured that as long as the journalist was male, she shouldn't have any problems. The thought never occurred to Vesta either, but then again, she had seen Hebe's charms at work and was sure that if Hebe wanted a press conference, Hebe would get one.

The gods ignored the whispering in the kitchen and leisurely finished their tea and wine. Pan, Janus and Hades had, in fact, spent the last three days perfecting the recipe for "Panacea," bottling it, setting up an account on eBay and trying to understand how to market it to humans. Before they'd come to Brighton, humans were just something to ignore, seduce, use as target practise or, in Hades case, terrorise. Trying to persuade and cajole them through direct advertising was not coming easily to them. Hades was having an especially difficult time as, having spent so many millennia in the Underworld, the subtleties of living humans were completely beyond his comprehension. His suggestion for the marketing campaign was, "Buy this or spend an eternity suffering interminable torment."

Ever the peacemaker, Janus had said, "I just don't think it's quite catchy enough, Hades, but good effort." Pan was far more blunt in his summation.

"It's bollocks. We'll do the marketing; you can do the packing."

An argument ensued during which the gods unleashed their diminished powers. What should have culminated in a battle of epic proportions, merely resulted in a smudged neck, the loss of half an eyebrow and messy hair. This was the greatest indicator so far that the gods were fading, and they'd doubled their efforts to get "Panacea" out to the male human population and, hopefully, regain at least some of their lost followers before they popped out of existence.

That evening Pan was to, inadvertently, change their fortunes as he had a chance encounter with a female executive who worked for a well-known shopping channel. He was so furious with Hades and Janus that he'd told them he wanted to spend the evening alone. In reality, he wanted to find a human female to seduce but saying he wanted to be alone sounded far more dignified and dramatic. Not even bothering to grab his coat, he slammed out of the house and strode to the nearest pub. His black shirt and ripped jeans were absurdly flattering on his muscular frame and he turned several heads, both male and female, during the short walk. He would usually have flashed a smile at his admirers, but he desperately wanted a drink.

He ordered a glass of red wine and cocked his leg over a bar stool. He looked mean and moody, and it wasn't long before he caught the eye of a lone woman sitting at the bar. She was slightly too rounded for his taste and her make-up looked as though it had been applied with a trowel, but she had a "come hither" smile, and Pan was feeling in need of comfort. He first asked the barman to send her a drink, and when that was accepted, he wandered over, swinging his lean hips and treated her to the full force of his personality. The fact that the executive, Charmaine Masters, had had a pet goat as a child that she'd loved dearly only helped his case.

"That sounds absolutely fascinating Charmaine. So, your show promotes new products on television to give exposure to start-up companies and entrepreneurs; what a wonderful idea." Pan had long ago perfected the art of pretending that he was deeply interested in what was being said to him. Charmaine took a long sip of her white wine and resisted the strange urge to scratch under his chin. Her wide blue eyes were locked onto his as she ran her fingers through her short blonde curls, exposing her long neck. Pan leaned forward and lightly brushed his lips against the pulse in her throat. Charmaine let out an involuntary sigh and leaned in closer.

"That's exactly what we do, yes, and it's my job to decide what we promote...oohh!"

Pan had taken her hand and was running his index finger lightly across her palm. He put his mouth close to her ear and whispered, "I think we could be a perfect match, my charming Charmaine." He smiled to himself as Charmaine gave a little gasp. He put his lips to hers briefly before suggesting that they leave the bar and find "somewhere more romantic" to continue their discussions.

Many very satisfying hours later he was feeling much more relaxed and excited about sharing his news with Janus and Hades, their previous argument forgotten. He gave Janus a call, and they arranged to meet up for a drink that evening. Once they'd ordered their drinks and were comfortably seated in a booth, Pan filled them in on what had happened the previous evening.

"Did she really have a pet goat?" Hades was becoming fascinated by human predilections.

"Yep," Pan nodded before taking a gulp of beer. "He was called Derek, apparently."

"And she was affectionate to the creature?" Hades was on his second beer and was becoming far chattier than was his custom.

"Definitely, she told me that she used to hug and 'pet' him (whatever that means) all the time." Pan enjoyed being the centre of attention and was happy to answer all of Hades' questions as long as they related to himself. Janus, on the other hand, was becoming impatient and wanted details of the arrangement that Pan had entered into with Charmaine.

"What did you promise this human female exactly?"

Pan was immediately defensive. "I didn't promise her anything. We spent a lovely evening together and, over dinner, I told her about 'Panacea.' She was impressed with the idea and said that we could go on her television show to promote it."

Janus was suspicious; he knew that Pan could be extremely economical with the truth when it suited his purpose.

"Did your discussion with her have romantic overtones at any point?" He kept his expression neutral, hoping that Pan's naturally boastful nature would incriminate him.

"Well, of course she was romantically inclined." Pan gave Janus a broad grin. "You know the effect that I have on human women; I honestly think that, by the end of the meal, she was quite besotted."

Janus smiled back, and Hades listened intently hoping to pick up tips on how to be successful with women; his job tended to limit his options.

"What did you say to her?" Janus persisted, maintaining his neutral smile.

"The same thing I say to all women, that they are perfectly exquisite, and that I won't be able to stop myself from falling in love with them."

Hades mouthed the phrase silently and hoped he'd have an opportunity to use it before long, while Janus slapped his palm to his forehead.

"So, you didn't make any promises? You just told her that you would definitely fall in love with her?" Janus couldn't believe Pan's egocentric stupidity sometimes.

"Well, yes, but I didn't mean it. You know me; I didn't mean it," Pan grinned nervously.

"But did Charmaine know that you didn't mean it?" Janus asked pointedly. Driving a point home with Pan was like trying to nail jelly to a tree – difficult and time-consuming with no guarantee of success.

Pan frowned and then looked mildly worried. "Oh, right, I see what you mean." His expression then cleared, and he grinned once more. "Not to worry, I'll break it to her gently once we've finished recording the show."

"Pan," Janus spoke through gritted teeth. "We need them to take the buyers' details and, more importantly, their money after the show has aired. Do you honestly think that any of that money will reach our pockets if you break the executive producer's heart?"

"Oh, right you are. No problem. I'll give her my full attention for as many hours as are necessary." He looked pleased with his concession.

Janus shook his head despairingly while Hades gazed intently at an attractive brunette who was sitting at the bar. He was mouthing "You are exquisite," over and over. The woman looked worried and was having a furtive conversation with the bar manager about the possibility of him having a psychopath in his establishment. The manager also looked slightly worried, but he squared his shoulders and walked over to the gods' table with a determinedly angry expression on his face. Janus stood up to greet him, and after a brief exchange, the two shook hands and the manager returned to the bar.

Janus then slapped the back of Hades' head to draw his attention from the poor woman he'd been staring at and jerked his head at the door, indicating that they should all leave as quickly and with as little fuss as possible. He quickly drained the last of his beer and said, "Another bar we won't be coming back to. Come on let's go home."

## Chapter 19

Rococo Blaine had been delighted with Sue and their campaign, which had been targeted towards "real women," had been a huge financial success. As a result, Hebe and Vesta found themselves inundated with requests for their models. Such was the interest in Goddesses that their fledgling company was even being championed by the media. Sue had approached a local journalist to publish her "human interest" story, but the journalist had refused since she had no photos from when she was living on the street and no-one would attest to her story. When she'd been homeless, she'd made a number of friends who were also living rough, but when she'd approached them, they either didn't recognise her or were too drunk to focus.

However, the journalist had been intrigued by Sue's story of the two 'miracle workers' and had published a small piece in the local paper along with a photo of Hebe and Vesta. The piece wasn't particularly well-written and probably would have sparked zero interest if it hadn't been for the photo. As it was, several Fleet Street journalists had been in touch wanting interviews. Vesta had responded by suggesting that they email their questions, but they had all been adamant that they needed face-to-face interviews.

Hebe had decided that the publicity would be good for them but had insisted that each interview would be no longer than ten minutes, and she would not guarantee any of them an exclusive. In order to pre-empt any unpleasantness, they'd hired a bouncer from one of the local pubs to escort the journalists from their office should they try to exceed the ten-minute time slot. Most left, albeit reluctantly, but one of them had to be dragged out by his ankles whilst declaring his love for Hebe at the top of his voice. They two goddesses felt certain that he would publish a bad review of their business, but as it was, his piece was professionally detached and extremely positive. This may have been a result of the bouncer bouncing his head on every step on the way out of the building while repeating, "Be kind to the nice ladies." The journalist took the hint but couldn't resist asking, "How do you resist that Hebe? She's exquisite, quite the most beautiful woman I've ever seen."

The bouncer, whose name was Baz stared at him for a long time before answering, "You don't know my wife, mate; if I so much as looked at another woman, she'd be wearing my bollocks as earrings." The journalist nodded and then hurried back to his office, sincerely hoping he'd never have cause to interview Baz' wife.

"Hebe, you'll never believe this!" Vesta looked up from her computer where she'd been going through their emails.

"What? Is it that executive from Black Carat Diamonds again? If it is, you can tell him I'm not going out on another date with him, not after the last time. He was all hands that one." Hebe's exquisite face darkened at the memory. "Mind you, it did confirm for me that a human male's tender parts are just as vulnerable as those of a god. As Aphrodite used to say, 'A swift, sharp knee under the toga will stop just about any god in his tracks.'"

Vesta cut her off before Hebe started ranting and raining down curses on the besotted executive. He had actually sent another begging email, but Vesta had deleted it after replying with details of their latest price increase.

"Hebe, calm down. It's nothing like that; we've been asked to go on a television show to explain the, and I quote, 'phenomenal success' of Goddesses. What do you think about that then? This could be a way to connect with more humans and gain some new followers. All the humans watch television after all."

Hebe looked surprised. "More followers? Have you seen our SEO stats? We've got over 200,000 followers on Twitter already."

"I don't mean those kinds of followers; I mean worshippers. You do remember how we ended up in Brighton, don't you? The little job for Zeus and Saturn that we need to do before we lose our powers and fade out of existence?" Vesta couldn't help the note of sarcasm in her voice; although she was happy with the success of Goddesses, Hebe seemed to be consumed by the business and had clearly forgotten its real purpose.

"Oh, right, yes of course, those kinds of followers." Hebe had the grace to look slightly embarrassed. "So, did you reply? When do they want us to come on? What show is it? I don't want to be on one of those soppy, 'sit on a pink sofa and pretend to admire the host' type of programmes."

"The email is from 'Modern Women.' Apparently, it's a day-time talk show that 'promotes successful female executives' and 'aims to further women's rights in the workplace.' What do you think?"

Vesta looked at Hebe expectantly; she was very keen to be involved in something that promoted women's rights after all the bullshit she'd had to put up with from the gods over the millennia. Since coming to live in Brighton, she'd begun to wonder how she'd ever been persuaded to seclude herself with her virgins. She didn't remember how it had even happened, but the way she felt now, she was sure it would have taken more than just "keep an eye on the sacred flame and don't let any of these young priestesses get up to any shenanigans." Then again, once the gods started pouring the ambrosia, you could find yourself agreeing to pretty much anything.

"I think the most important question here is: What are we going to wear?" Hebe grinned "Tell them yes, and then when we've finished here this afternoon, you and I are going to do some late-night shopping."

The two goddesses spent a happy couple of hours in the Churchill Square shopping centre trying on outfits in an effort to capture their "brand identity." (Hebe had spent a few minutes on Google earlier in the day researching "corporate speak.") They tried power suits, floaty feminine dressers and sweater sets but both of them felt that they weren't really capturing the essence of Goddesses.

"I don't really think this is appropriate." Vesta stepped out of the changing room wearing an outfit that Hebe had chosen for her - tight leather trousers and a transparent chiffon blouse in deepest blood red.

"Let me see." Hebe was wearing Vesta's choice, a softly draped jersey dress in palest yellow. It had long sleeves, a high neck and fell just below the knee. Hebe hated it. She looked at Vesta critically.

"Perhaps if we swapped outfits?" She'd already decided that she would buy the leather trousers even if Vesta deemed them unsuitable.

"No, it won't work. Look, we've tried on loads of clothes, and none of them feels quite right. You can say what you like about our togas, but at least they were acceptable for any occasion....assuming the brooch stayed fastened."

She was looking at her rear view in the mirror appreciatively; Vesta might have conservative leanings but even she had to admit that leather trousers do something wonderful for the derriere. She decided there and then that she had to buy them. She wasn't going to bother with the blouse though; although she had come a long way, she had to draw the line at clothes that showed her underwear.

She caught a glimpse of Hebe's face in the mirror as she contorted her body. "What? What are you thinking?"

"I'm thinking, my dear Vesta, that you might be on to something."

"What do you mean?"

"I think we should wear our togas on the TV show; they're the perfect representation of the Goddesses brand, and what's more, they'll remind humanity of a time when they worshipped something other than iPhones and Birkin bags." Hebe was visibly excited by the prospect of revealing her "true self" to the nation; however great she knew she'd look in whatever else she put on, nothing showed off her figure quite like a toga.

Vesta hesitated for a moment; she really was loving the way she looked in the leather trousers but then she acquiesced; Hebe was right. They grinned at each other before heading back into the changing room.

"I've decided to get the trousers," Vesta called out as she reluctantly divested herself of the soft leather.

"How funny! I've decided to buy a pair too. Can you give the sales assistant a shout and ask her to pull another pair for me?"

Vesta did ask the sales assistant; unfortunately, they were the last pair and a small but embarrassing scuffle broke out at the till as the goddesses fought for the precious item. It was only resolved when Vesta promised Hebe a single night with the flaming phallus. The woman at the till watched the back and forth exchange, both bemused and fascinated by the exchange.

"Here is your garment, madam, and thank you for shopping with us today." Her patter was automatic which was just as well as she was mentally reeling from the image of a flaming phallus. "Christ," she muttered to herself "that would have to sting."

Several days later, waiting until after the gods had gone out, the two goddesses prepared themselves for their television interview. They'd recently hired an assistant, Kelly, whom they'd trained in the finer points of the business i.e. how to charm the pants off anyone who called, how to calm down neurotic models (they may have started out as ordinary women, but they'd quickly picked up neuroses from other models on the circuit) and how the filing system worked. Hebe and Vesta felt confident that she'd be able to manage things in the office for a few hours.

"What do you think, hair up or down?" Vesta was looking at herself nervously in the mirror.

"Definitely up. I think with just a few tendrils escaping, like we used to do it in the old days." Hebe was running eyeliner along her lash line and her eyes looked like huge liquid pools.

"You do know that they'll do our make-up when we get to the studio? It said so in the email." Vesta's own face was bare of cosmetics, but her hair was now twisted into an elaborate coif, and she was pleased with what she saw in the mirror.

"What can a make-up girl do for me that I can't do for myself? She won't need to touch my face," Hebe scoffed. She slicked on a layer of lip gloss and declared herself ready.

"Have you checked the clasp on that brooch?" Vesta was worried; they couldn't afford to have a Janet Jackson moment on live TV. She checked, for the third time, that her own clasp was firmly closed.

"Yep and I've added Velcro to the toga's edges and the top of my bra; trust me, this baby isn't going anywhere. Are you ready?"

Vesta gave herself a final once over before picking up her bag and coat. Although she'd never given it a second thought when she was with her virgins, she felt slightly uncomfortable going out in a toga in broad daylight. They'd ordered a taxi which pulled up outside the house just as they were locking the front door. The driver's jaw dropped when he saw them both and then a wide grin spread over his face. "The boys in the office won't believe this when I tell them," he thought to himself. He was gay and in a very fulfilling relationship with a Portuguese interior designer, so the goddesses' charms were lost on him, but he admired anyone who had the guts to go out in a toga at 2 o'clock on a Wednesday afternoon.

"Off anywhere nice, ladies?" The cab driver couldn't help himself. "I have to say, I'm loving the look." He smiled kindly at Hebe in the rear-view mirror. She caught his eye and was surprised to see no drooling or glazed eyes; he just looked genuinely interested. "Perhaps I'm losing my touch," she thought.

"We're going to the television studios for a business event, but I'm sure we'd rather spend the afternoon with you." She flashed him her most brilliant smile.

"You going to be on television then?" The come-on and the smile were completely lost on Dan, the driver. He just seemed interested in what Hebe had to say.

"Umm, yes." Hebe was at a complete loss. She looked over at Vesta who was staring resolutely out of the window trying not to giggle. She could feel Hebe's discomfit and confusion.

"That's great; I'm sure you'll do an amazing job. A dear friend of mine is an actor; he does mainly theatre stuff, you know?" He didn't wait for an answer but regaled them with stories of his various "dear friends" and their exploits.

"Here we are ladies, right on time." Dan parked the taxi outside the studio. "That will be £25 please."

Vesta handed over £30. "Thank you and, please, keep the change."

"Very kind of you, my dear," Dan grinned happily.

Vesta stood up in the cramped space, knees bent, and tutted impatiently at Hebe who still hadn't moved. "Come on Hebe, get a move on."

Hebe shook her head as if she were trying to dislodge water from her ears. "What? Oh, sorry Vesta. Thank you, driver."

The two goddesses alighted from the taxi. Hebe kept muttering to herself, "I just don't get it; that's never happened before. Never!" As Dan pulled away, Vesta explained to Hebe that she thought he probably preferred men; she'd seen a picture of Dan and his boyfriend in a close embrace on the dashboard.

"Oh thank gods! I thought I was losing my touch! Phew, I was worried there for a moment; it was like I was *ordinary* or something."

Vesta pushed her into the TV studio, and before they knew it, they were seated on a stage, in front of an audience of women, with a number of cameras pointed at them.

"Welcome ladies, it's so good to finally meet the women behind Goddesses. For those of you who don't know, a few months ago, this was just a start-up modelling agency but now its clients include some of the biggest names in fashion." The chirpy presenter, a slender, slick blonde who had the air of a particularly skittish thoroughbred, was grinning at them maniacally.

"Thank you, Chelsea, it's wonderful to be here." Hebe inclined her head regally at the enraptured presenter and gifted her with a radiant smile.

"Well, I have to say, you two certainly know how to represent your brand; you are both definitely goddesses today. Wouldn't you agree, ladies?" Chelsea looked expectantly at her audience of businesswomen who obliged her by applauding vigorously. As Hebe had expected, the on-set make-up girl hadn't needed to do a thing to her face, but Vesta had spent an uncomfortable thirty minutes being plucked and painted. She'd complained throughout but couldn't deny that she was happy with the results, and she smiled confidently at the audience.

"So, please tell us as we're dying to know, how have you achieved such amazing success in such a short period of time?" Chelsea leaned forward eagerly.

Hebe inclined her head slightly as if preparing to share an intimate moment with the presenter; she was positively oozing charm.

"Really, Chelsea, it's simple. For too long, the fashion world has been dominated by men who *think* that they know what women want, who *think* that by bombarding us with images of perfect, teenage, airbrushed young women that they are giving us something to aspire to. Goddesses is about proving to the world that *all* women are beautiful. Our models are representative of women in 2020, and each and every one of them shines with a light that is in all of us, if we are just prepared to reveal it."

The audience of women was on its feet by the end of Hebe's little speech and was applauding her wildly as images of Sue and Goddess' other models were flashed up on the giant screen in the studio.

Vesta was slightly miffed that she was being left out of the lovefest and decided to contribute.

"We, at Goddess, understand women. We know that many of you are insecure about your faces and your bodies and that some men feed off those insecurities and put you down so that, eventually, you feel that your feminine power is all but lost. We want to give you that power back."

The applause grew even more intense; cheers erupted from the audience, and Chelsea just sat back in her chair happy to let Vesta and Hebe run the show; this was great television.

Vesta was now on her feet and had turned to face the audience of women.

"Yes, our models are beautiful, but they are real women, just like you – all of you. They put their *faith* in us, and they believed us when we told them that we could help them reveal their inner light."

By this time, Vesta could barely be heard above the cheering and stamping which was probably just as well.

"No more will women be chained by fear and insecurity; we will release our inner goddesses. We will not be Vestal Virgins dictated to by men, and if we want to ride a flaming phallus, we damn well will!"

Fortunately, Hebe had seen where Vesta was going with her speech and she used the bare minimum of power from her remaining stores to cut Vesta's microphone so the only person who heard her was Chelsea. The presenter had worked in journalism for a long time and considered herself to be unshakable, but she felt a blush creep up to her cheeks and she swallowed hard as she considered what Vesta had said. For a moment she was lost in her own imagination but then her ingrained professionalism took over.

"Well, thank you ladies." Chelsea turned to the audience trying to be heard over the deafening cheers. "We can certainly see how your company has become a force to be reckoned with. We are not just women, we are Goddesses!" The presenter punched the air, losing all her usual reserve; there was just something about Hebe and Vesta that brought out her innate feminine power. "I feel completely liberated," she thought before slumping back into her chair, letting the show go on without her as her mind turned, once again, to thoughts of a flaming phallus.

Hebe and Vesta met with many of the women who'd been in the audience after the show, and they were all enthused and inspired by the passion that the two goddesses had shown.

"I think it's simply marvellous," exclaimed Pamela Montcliffe-Dubois, a well-known socialite and staunch feminist. "Men have been holding us back for far too long and dictating what we, as women, should be. I saw one or two of your models at London Fashion Week and they were glowing. Neither of them were po-faced twigs, but they stood out. They seemed more….well….real." Her words tailed off as she tried to recall exactly what it was about the models that had grabbed her attention.

"I couldn't agree more, Pammy. We have been forced to measure ourselves against unrealistic stereotypes for far too long. Our spirits have been crushed by the patriarchy, and it's time that we stood up for ourselves. Down with men!" Amanda Montague was a long-time friend of Pamela's but was far more militant and much taken with wearing khaki and carrying aggressive-looking handbags.

Vesta looked rather alarmed at the last comment, she had her fair share of being oppressed by the gods, but she'd spent almost her entire life with a bunch of subservient virgins and was feeling somewhat overwhelmed by the animosity that was emanating from the women. Hebe saw the look and touched her arm gently before addressing Pamela and Amanda.

"Ladies, ladies, whilst I appreciate your sentiments and utterly sympathise with them, I think that we should be looking at less *aggressive* ways of promoting women's interests. I think that so much more can be accomplished by charm and grace that, let's face it, comes naturally to us than by sinking to the same level as men. We don't want to *oppress* men; we just want them to see us for what we are – goddesses who deserve to be worshipped every waking moment." Hebe looked each of the women in the eye. She was quintessentially feminine, but they could all see the steely determination that gave her such a forceful personality; Hebe was a born leader of women.

Amanda looked as though she were about to protest; she wanted to put her new-found kick-boxing skills to good use and testicles seemed like the perfect target. However, it was Pamela who spoke.

"Do you know, I think that you're right Hebe; if only all women had a little of your magic." She had a huge crush on Hebe and Vesta, the like of which she hadn't experienced since her prep school days.

"It's funny you should say that, Pam," Hebe rewarded her adoring look with a luminous smile "We were thinking of launching a new product called 'Light of Aphrodite'; it's a revolutionary face cream that works wonders. We gave a pot to each of our girls when they started working for us, and you have seen how radiant they look. I know it will sound a little trite because all great cosmetics brands promise the same thing, but it really does contain a little magic."

"First I've heard of it," Vesta muttered under her breath, but she allowed Hebe to continue, knowing that her companion's business acumen far exceeded her own.

Hebe laid her hand, gently on Pamela's shoulder, establishing an intimacy between them. "The only problem we have at the moment is funding. Goddesses has been hugely successful, as you know, but we're not cash rich as yet. I think I have a sample somewhere in my bag, perhaps you'd like to try it?"

She rummaged around and seconds later produced a tiny, black pot that looked as though it had been crafted from onyx. The lid was gold, and once Pamela unscrewed it, she could see a blob of dark green liquid, rich and slightly grainy. She looked quizzically at Hebe; the product didn't look like any face cream she'd ever tried, but she didn't want to offend Hebe by saying so.

"Try a little on the back of your hand," Hebe encouraged.

The other women had all gathered round Pamela as she took a miniscule amount of the green gunk underneath her fingernail and gingerly applied it to the back of her hand; it had rather an odd smell. For a brief moment, her skin seemed to glow.

"My God, that's amazing!" Amanda was staring at the back of her friend's 40-year-old hand; her skin, where she'd applied the cream, looked like that of a teenager. Pamela said nothing for a moment as she searched under her fingernail to find another small dab of cream to apply to her other hand but then she looked at Hebe in wonder.

"How much do you need? Honestly, I can let you have whatever it will take to get this into production; Daddy's got oodles of spare cash."

"Mine too. Don't leave me out; I want to be in on this as well." Amanda took the pot from Pamela, closely examining the contents and wondering if Hebe would mind if she tried a little on her own weathered skin.

Hebe saw the look and said, smoothly, "Amanda, please don't be shy; try a little and see what you think. I'd love to hear your opinion. And you ladies too." She signalled to the other women who'd crowded around herself and Vesta after the interview, "Please do try a sample."

Amanda dipped her finger into the little pot and then stepped back so that the others could try it. "Wonderful name," she said as she rubbed the cream on the back of her hand "Aphrodite was the most beautiful goddess on Olympus, wasn't she? Very clever marketing idea, you two; I can't imagine many women would turn down the chance to look like her." Fortunately, Amanda missed Hebe's fierce glare as she was admiring her newly regenerated skin. Vesta saw that Hebe was about to make a snide comment about Aphrodite and stepped in quickly. "Thank you Amanda, we thought that the name fit in well with the brand."

Each of the women dipped a fingernail into the little pot and then smoothed the green paste, reverentially on the backs of their hands. One of the women, Lady Sarah Buckley, was even so bold as to apply a little along her cheekbone. That side of her face tightened instantly, and her skin become beautifully clear and blemish free. Unfortunately, the other side looked like a mottled bag of water, so Hebe had to step in quickly and apply a little of the cream on the other side to even things up before the others noticed.

Hebe and Vesta signed up six investors that afternoon and would have more than enough money to launch "Light of the Aphrodite." The two goddesses promised to email contracts to their investors the following day before taking a taxi back to Number 23.

"Well, that was rather successful wasn't it? I wish that you'd told me about the new product, but I have to admit that little trick really sealed the deal. What was in that paste?"

Hebe had leaned her head against the window of the taxi and had closed her eyes, but she replied, nonetheless, "Swarfega."

"What?? Bloody hell, your powers are good." Vesta turned her head. "Hebe you're looking tired; are you sure that this was a wise move?" Vesta was aware of the effect that using her powers on earth was having on Hebe.

"We have to do something for *all* women if we're going to get them believing in us again, you know that."

"Yes, I know you're right, but I am worried what it will do to you. Pam and Amanda want to launch Light of Aphrodite globally. How much of your power will it take to transform enough Swarfega to cater to hundreds of thousands of human females?" Vesta pulled Hebe into a small hug.

"Don't worry about me, I've thought this through. Have you heard about the power of suggestion? It's a human thing – if they believe in something enough, their body will respond accordingly; I've been reading up on it. Lots of them are given what they call 'placebos,' which are really nothing more than sugar pills, to cure illnesses, and very often they work. All we need to do is make enough of the product to get women talking about it and believing in it, and they'll get the results that they're looking for."

Vesta was determined to research the subject herself when she got home. She had no problem with the concept, as belief was what had kept all the gods in existence for millennia, but she was unconvinced that the same could be achieved with tiny pots of Swarfega, however pretty the packaging. She couldn't resist asking, "What are you going to put in those pots, Hebe? Green gunk with no magic is not going to fool anyone, however much they believe."

Hebe rolled her eyes. "I'm not that daft; I'll use some Aloe Vera, turmeric, red clover and some chamomile to make a paste and then add it to a cheap skin cream with a bit of green food colouring."

Vesta was still not convinced but she knew that time was running out for them, so she said nothing.

## Chapter 20

Hebe and Vesta missed the gods by no more than five minutes. Pan, Hades and Janus had jumped in a taxi and were on their way to a studio in London to make their own television debut on the evening shopping show "Bon Buy."

"Are you quite sure you know what you're going to say, Pan? Don't forget that 'Panacea' is for men; your famous charm won't work on them in the same way that it does on women." Janus was highly sceptical about the television segment and was worried that Pan's performance could scupper their plans before they'd really got the product off the ground. "What do you think Hades?"

Having had seen Pan in action and having been amazed by his success with the human females, Hades was now Pan's biggest supporter.

"I think that charm like Pan's will appeal to all the humans, not just the women. What is it they say? 'The men will want to have what he's got and…and so will the women.'" He trailed off lamely, wishing that someone wanted some of what he had, but as it was a love of all things dark and various forms of emotional torture, he thought it unlikely.

"There, you see, Hades is behind me on this." Pan clapped Hades on the shoulder who promptly blushed although he had no idea why. "Why can't you be more supportive?"

"Because I know what you're like, if there are any women on the set, you'll be far more interested in trying to seduce them than promoting 'Panacea,' and our audience will be lost. I haven't forgotten the time that you dressed up as a sheep, of all things, just so you could seduce Selene, the sky goddess. She went on about it for decades, telling anyone who'd listen that you were a manipulative, unprincipled liar who'd do anything to get under a goddess' toga." Janus was getting more and more angry as he spoke and was considering taking over the presentation himself.

Pan's face was serious for a moment as he considered how to respond. He knew that he was capable of drumming up business for their product, but he also knew that he had to convince Janus. He began slowly.

"Yes, I know my reputation, but there is something that you don't know about me."

Janus and Hades looked at him with interest, Pan was not known for being unforthcoming about his exploits. In fact, he would tell anyone who would listen the full and frank details of his private life.

"As you both know, I like the physical pleasures and...how can I put this...I take them where I find them. As you know, I would often walk amongst the humans disguised as a goat herder and, well, some of the young shepherds were quite appealing....as were some of the goats..."

A look of hope shone in Hades' eyes which he quickly hid by faking a sneeze and a look of disgust shone in Janus'.

"Seriously? Is there nothing that you won't ravage, Pan? I mean, I can almost understand the shepherds if you were out in the middle of nowhere for a while but livestock?"

"It was only when I was in my goat form, Janus. You don't have to look at me like that and, you know what they say, don't knock it until you've tried it." Pan winked at him saucily.

"Don't talk to me, just don't." Janus turned away and looked out the window. Pan just shrugged and turned to Hades, putting his arm across his shoulders in a conspiratorial gesture. Hades allowed himself to snuggle into Pan's shoulder for a moment before pulling away, confused.

By the time that they pulled up at the entrance to the studios, the three gods were subdued; even Pan had lost some of his natural exuberance. Despite his debauched lifestyle and frivolous attitude, Pan had never lost sight of their reason for coming to Brighton. He knew that he was not popular amongst the other gods and was barely tolerated by the goddesses because of his licentious behaviour, so he thrived on the worship of humans. He also had a certain fondness for them that went beyond sexual attraction; in many ways, they were far more liberated than any deity that he knew.

Janus led them into the building. "We just need to remember why we're here and what rides on our success or failure. If we are to continue, we have to regain the faith of the humans and, to do that, they have to trust us and lose their primeval fears."

"No pressure then!" Pan muttered under his breath as they were taken to the green room. He couldn't resist making the flippant remark, but he wished that Janus could appreciate his desire to make a success of their product.

Charmaine had obviously been alerted to their presence, as she bustled into the room two minutes after they had settled themselves on the deceptively uncomfortable chairs.

"Pan, how marvellous to see you, and you must be Janus and Hades." She embraced Pan and then held out her hand to the other two gods in turn. "What wonderfully exotic names you have in your family, really quite delightful. Now are you prepared for your presentation, Pan? We have the product on set, and they should be ready for you in about fifteen minutes. Just relax, look at the camera but don't stare; don't speak too quickly; keep your breathing even and try not to stutter, OK? Marvellous! See you all later." She turned sharply on her heel and hurried out the door, slamming it behind her.

"Bloody hell! The woman didn't even draw breath. How on earth did you put up with her for a whole night?" Janus was still staring at the closed door with his eyes wide.

Pan grinned at him impishly. "Well, firstly, I didn't really listen and secondly, when it all got a bit too much, I found a few ways to keep her quiet. No-one can speak with their mouth full." He winked at Hades who blushed.

"What is the matter with me?" he thought to himself "The sooner I get back to the Underworld, the better." Although Hades had ruled his kingdom effectively and without compassion for thousands of years, he had surprisingly little in the way of self-awareness. In order to do his job, it was essential that he keep a very tight rein on any emotions. On the rare occasions that he had a strong feeling about anything, or anyone, it worried him, and he did his best to bury it. Had he been human, he would have been a therapist's dream; his mind was a veritable Pandora's Box of supressed emotions.

Precisely fifteen minutes later, the three gods were taken from the green room and onto the set. Pan was installed in front of the three cameras, and Hades and Janus were told that they could watch from the side lines.

"Do you think he looks nervous?" Hades asked anxiously.

Janus looked at him scornfully. "Of course he's not nervous, we're gods. What could we possibly have to be nervous about in the human world?" Hades refrained from commenting, but from his perspective, the humans held the future of all the ancient gods in their hands. If that weren't something to worry about, he didn't know what was.

Pan would never admit to feeling nervous, but he did find the lights and the cameras slightly intimidating. He picked up a bottle of "Panacea" and ran through the patter he'd prepared in his head while, at the same time, reminding himself why they were doing this. He'd had millennia of fulfilling his desires, and he had no intention of stopping because humans had stopped believing in gods. "They will believe, I will not be wiped out of existence while the possibility of pleasure remains." He said the words over and over in his mind as he waited for his cue.

"Five, four, three, two…" The silent cue came far more quickly than Pan was expecting, and for a brief moment, he was like a deer caught in headlights, but then he smiled and spoke directly to the camera as if he were conducting the most intimate of discussions. The harsh lighting of the studio seemed to enhance his natural good looks, and his dark, flashing eyes connected with the camera as if he'd been doing this his whole life.

"Bloody hell, the camera just loves him." Janus and Hades turned around sharply; Charmaine had appeared from nowhere and was whispering excitedly. Putting a hand on Hades shoulder, who tried desperately not to recoil in horror. She leaned forward, hanging on Pan's every word. Janus took a step sideways and, as Charmaine took his place, Hades glared over her head and mouthed furiously at him. "Why won't this wretched human female stop touching me and let me watch Pan in peace?" he thought to himself, but as Pan began speaking, he forgot all about her and let himself be carried away by those dulcet tones.

"We've all had the problem, guys; the girl of your dreams or the love of your life is ready for you, waiting impatiently for you to fulfil her secret physical desires and your equipment just won't function. We all know that feeling of shame; we've all seen the hurt and disappointment in her eyes. We know that look of accusatory confusion when our sweetheart questions our love for her." Pan looked down for a moment and, when he raised his eyes back to the camera, his pain was evident for all to see.

"Jesus this guy is pure gold!" Charmaine was ecstatic.

"Bloody drama queen," Janus muttered under his breath. He'd seen Pan mid-seduction many times and was unimpressed. Hades, on the other hand, was riveted by Pan's performance. "He's magnificent."

Janus opened his mouth to say something, but Charmaine shushed them both with an angry stare.

"Yes, there are other products that you can try, but 'Panacea' is made from all-natural ingredients. There are no side-effects, and you can use it as often as you wish without risk. Panacea comes in three strengths which we've called 'Apollo', 'Dionysius' and 'Zeus' so you can be sure to find the product that will be perfect for your requirements." He indicated the three bottles displayed in front of him. "You deserve to have passion in your life; the woman you love deserves the physical satisfaction that you so want to give her." Pan was building up for his big finish, and his beautiful dark eyes gleamed with mischief as he smiled his wolfish smile at the camera. "This, my friends, is what you have been waiting for, a product that will allow you to take your pleasure whenever...... and however you wish." Pan gave his trademark slow grin and a cheeky wink. Charmaine had to stifle a passionate gasp.

"Well, thank you, Pan, that was some pitch." A young male presenter had walked onto the set to join Pan and close the presentation. He clapped his hand on Pan's shoulder and shook his hand. "If you'd like to order 'Panacea,' and let's face it, guys, who wouldn't? Please call in using the number on the bottom of the screen, and don't forget to tell us whether you'd like Apollo, Dionysius or Zeus. We accept all major credit and debit cards, and we look forward to receiving your orders for this amazing new product." The two were seen chatting amicably as the lights faded and the cameras turned away.

Once she was sure that the cameras were no longer focused on the set, Charmaine rushed over to Pan and drew him into a passionate hug. There were a few raised eyebrows from her staff as she was known to be a tough cookie (or a complete bitch depending on who you listened to), but she was oblivious.

"Pan, you were quite wonderful. You smouldered, and the camera *adored* you, you…" Her tirade stopped abruptly as Pan kissed her full on the mouth; there were audible gasps from her team.

Janus rolled his eyes and looked over at Hades, expecting to see the same reaction. However, what he saw was a look of jealous rage. Hades realised that Janus was staring at him and quickly rearranged his features into their normal grimness before turning away and calling out to Pan.

"Great job, Pan. Charmaine, how will we know if we've sold anything?"

His comment served to disrupt the lip lock between Pan and Charmaine, and for some reason he couldn't quite fathom why that pleased him. He had thought that his fascination with Pan could be attributed to his desire to emulate him and his success with women, but he realised that it had developed into more than that. The realisation worried him; he had spent his entire existence ensuring that he did not form emotional attachments. "It's a mild obsession, nothing to worry about," he told himself. "Like that time when I was fixated on having a daily roll call in the Underworld. It won't last."

The daily roll call of all the dead who resided in the Underworld was universally agreed to be a complete pain in the arse. It couldn't be completed in a single day which annoyed Hades further, and whoever got the job of checking off names, invariably dozed off through sheer boredom and had to start again. On top of that, the lost and tortured souls who roamed the Underworld couldn't be trusted to form an orderly queue which meant that Hades' three-headed dog, Cerberus, spent several, fruitless weeks trying to round them all up.

"We're getting some numbers through now," Charmaine's voice roused Hades from his reverie.

"How are they looking?" Janus was trying to see over Charmaine's shoulder at the monitor that was delivering data at a steady pace.

"Well, it's only fifteen minutes since your broadcast, but I would say that you could have a hit on your hands, gentleman. This is showing that you've sold 100 units already; 40 units of Apollo, 25 of Dionysius and 35 of Zeus. I just knew, when I first spoke to Pan, that this product would be a success; didn't I say that to you Pan? In the bar, do you remember....? She was forced to stop talking again, much to the relief of Janus and Hades, as Pan, once again, clamped his mouth over hers.

Happily, one of the production assistants decided to brave her boss' wrath by announcing that there was a problem with the presentation in the next studio. Apparently, the product owner was virtually catatonic with nerves and was refusing to speak; Dan the floor manager didn't have another product ready and was tearing his hair out.

"Damn! Can't someone else deal with it?" Charmaine pulled away from Pan; her cheeks were flushed and her eyes bright with longing.

"Sorry, Boss. Dan asked me to fetch you." Charmaine knew that she couldn't risk upsetting her best floor manager, so she straightened her skirt, patted her hair back into place and followed the assistant.

"Call me," she yelled over her shoulder at Pan who had slumped in his chair; he wasn't sure what had suffered more – his lips or his ears.

"Let's get out of here you two. I've had enough of human females and television for one day. Apparently, they'll keep us informed of sales numbers by email." He stood up wearily and made for the studio exit. Hades walked ahead and held open the door for him.

"You're never going to see her again are you?" Janus asked as he picked up his coat and followed Pan.

"What do you think?" Pan flashed a grin. Janus rolled his eyes but chose to say nothing, he was watching Hades who was trying very hard to hide a delighted smile.

"At least if they email the figures to Pan, we'll have something to send to Saturn to let him know that we've haven't been idle these last few months. Have either of you heard anything from him by the way? It worries me when he's quiet." Hades looked back at the other two gods who both just shook their heads; they were ashamed to admit that they hadn't given Saturn or the other higher gods a second thought since they started project "Panacea."

"Let me have the report as soon as it comes through, Pan, and I'll drop Saturn a line," said Janus after a few moments.

"You should really," confirmed Hades, "he is your brother after all."

"I know, don't remind me," Janus opened the door to a black cab that had pulled to a stop in front of them and climbed in. The three gods sat despondently in the back of the cab on the way back to Number 23, each reminded of his obligations and duties. They were quite depressed by the time that they arrived.

## Chapter 21

Saturn was rather relived to receive the email from Janus, not because he was particularly interested in hearing news from his brother, but because he had something to show Zeus who was becoming increasingly difficult. His office door had been blasted open so many times by Zeus that there was an imprint on the wall behind, and he'd had to have it reinforced with iron bars to stop it from splintering.

Zeus was temperamental at the best of times and his dislike for humans was well known; for him, the thought of losing his powers as a result of their being too lazy to worship him was insufferable. Unfortunately, he forgot, or chose not to remember, that his extraordinary wealth had been accumulated by taking it from the humans. As far as Zeus was concerned giving was a one-way street, and he didn't feel that it was his responsibility to do anything to aid their race. If it hadn't been for his cousin, Prometheus, who gave humans fire, they probably would have died out millennia ago, and the gods along with them. Prometheus made the mistake of pointing this out one evening at a cocktail party hosted by his brother, Atlas. They'd all had far too much ambrosia and were taking turns doing impressions of Zeus which got more and more outrageous as the evening wore on.

"I'm so stupid," Prometheus slurred drunkenly, "I'm going to curse the humans so they'll all die.....and then I'll be dead...hiccup...but I'm too stupid to see it." He was so busy roaring with laughter at his own impression that he didn't hear a door splintering behind him as it flew off its hinges. Zeus was apoplectic with rage at the disrespect being shown to him. Prometheus, as intoxicated as he was, only realised that something was afoot when his friends all shuffled away, leaving him standing alone in front of Zeus.

"Hic! It was a joke Zeus. We were only [hic] having a bit of fun."

Zeus smiled manically at him, and Prometheus grinned back, sure that he'd been forgiven for his mockery. However, he began to have his doubts when he found himself chained to a rock with Zeus muttering "If it's fun you want...." then whistling to a giant eagle that had been expectantly circling the rock. For the next few years Prometheus experienced the agony of having his liver pecked out by the eagle, only to have it regenerate overnight so that the torture could begin again the following morning. It was during this period that he learned that Zeus could dish it out, but he really couldn't take it.

Saturn sighed as his door slammed open and his office was filled with bright, crackling light.

"Come in, why don't you?" he muttered under his breath as Zeus stormed into the room.

"Saturn, how are you? No, don't bother answering I'm not really interested. You have some news for me I hear." Zeus threw himself into a chair and looked at Saturn expectantly. As usual his thick, white eyebrows were drawn into a scowl and his powerful frame was bristling with barely supressed rage.

Saturn had been taught to respect his fellow gods and felt that he should offer Zeus a drink, but he was damned if he were going to share the last of his wine with this arrogant hothead.

"I have." He picked up a printed copy of the email that he'd received from Janus and handed it to Zeus "You can see for yourself."

"I don't have time to read all that, just tell me what he said." Zeus was too embarrassed to admit that he needed reading glasses. Seeing as he had the key for the cupboard where they stocked the lightning bolts and unleashed one every time something got on his nerves, this was becoming a serious worry for everyone.

Saturn replied through clenched teeth. "Well, it seems that Janus, Hades and Pan have developed a product to treat a serious problem that afflicts male humans, and it has been very well-received. They have drawn attention to themselves, and the humans, the males at least, are beginning to have some respect and admiration for them."

Saturn expected Zeus to roar out questions or orders; instead, he looked curious. "What problem are you referring to? Was it a problem I gave them?"

Saturn was not impressed by the pleased look he saw forming in Zeus' eyes. "No. It was nothing to do with you; it's a *plumbing* issue caused by stress and anxiety. Anyway…."

Zeus had leaned forward. "What do you mean a plumbing issue?"

"You know….plumbing…" Saturn nodded towards the front of his toga and looked meaningfully at Zeus.

"Oh….Oh!...Is it something that could affect the gods?"

It was on the tip of Saturn's tongue to assure Zeus he had nothing to worry about, but then he looked at his door and the shattered remnants of several of his favourite vases that were in the bin, having fallen foul of one of Zeus' tantrums.

"Basically, male humans sometimes suffer from a certain limpness in the genital region that is, apparently, caused by anxiety and stress. At the present time, I am not entirely sure if gods could suffer the same problem, but it is possible."

Zeus' faced blanched. "Limpness?" The word was a mere whisper.

Saturn was starting to enjoy himself. "Yes, you know, a…how shall I put it? A waning. A deflation." He held up his index finger and then let it slowly fall forward. "Obviously, like us gods, the human males enjoy taking their pleasure with the human females, so you can understand, I'm sure, this is a big issue for them. Apparently, after a while, some of them are rendered completely incapable." Saturn managed to keep the smile off his face, but it was difficult as he watched Zeus' shoulders slump.

"Incapable you say? So, what have they come up with? What is this product?"

"It's called 'Panacea' and they've been advertising it on television; they have something called 'shopping channels' apparently." Saturn's spirits had revived enormously.

"'Panacea'? Who came up with that stupid name?" Zeus was trying to rally and attempting to organise his eyebrows into a stern frown, but their heart really wasn't in it.

"I'll give you three guesses."

"Pan I suppose? Oh well, if it's bringing us attention and admiration again, I guess we can't complain. Where did you say it was for sale again? I should probably do some investigating of my own, just to make sure you haven't missed anything." His voice was gruff but there was an eager look in his eye that he couldn't disguise. He was inordinately proud of his manhood and couldn't bear the thought of it shrivelling up like a grape left for too long in the summer sun.

"On one of the humans' shopping channels; I can email you the link if you'd like? For research purposes." Saturn's response held a note of innocence but the broad grin on his face communicated his pleasure in his boss' discomfiture.

"Umm, yes, research, indeed. Send me the link…um….please." Zeus rose from his chair and walked stiffly to the door which he closed quietly behind him as he left.

Saturn was still smiling to himself as he drafted his reply to Janus, making sure to pass on the details of his meeting with Zeus. He then realised that he hadn't heard a word from the two goddesses and drafted a curt email demanding to know what progress, if any, that they'd made.

## Chapter 22

Hebe and Vesta were, in fact, making great progress. In the six months since they'd become businesswomen, they'd created a growing market for "real women" in the fashion industry, found a strong voice within the feminist movement and had just launched a skin care product that was being touted as the new "miracle cream." Their confidence was growing as was their presence in the media, so much so that they'd been unable to hide their success from the three gods. However, as "Panacea" had become the overnight star of late-night shopping, everyone's secrets were out. You would think that they would have been happy to share in their respective successes, but the breakfast table at Number 23 had turned into something of a verbal war zone.

"Of all the ways that we could help the humans and gain back our followers, I can't believe that you chose that! 'Panacea'! I ask you!" Vesta slammed a plate of toast on the table, not even flinching as a slice flew off and landed on the floor.

"Well what about you two? Models, face-cream and feminism; what a combination. You convince the human females that they're beautiful and then tell them that they don't need males and, what's worse, you try and make the males feel guilty for being attracted to the females. If the females don't want the male attention, why bother going to so much effort to be attractive in the first place? Why don't they just stay ugly?" Pan picked up the slice of toast from the floor, flicked off a piece of fluff and then liberally covered it with salted butter.

"You sexist pig!" Hebe had been learning some new expressions from their feminist friends, Pamela and Amanda. "Do you mean to tell me that the only thing that would ever attract you to a female is her face!?"

Pan looked at her thoughtfully. "Not the only thing, no," he said with dignity. "She'd have to have a nice body as well." He smiled provocatively, dark eyes flashing, so Hebe threw her plate at him.

"How dare you!" Hades was immediately on his feet and shaking his fist at a shocked Hebe. "You have no idea how much effort Pan has put into 'Panacea.' It was his concept; he came up with all the ingredients for the first batch, and he had to grovel to Aphrodite to get her help with the final product. He's worked really hard, and you should be thanking him not yelling at him. Watch the programme and you'll see; the camera loves him." He wagged his finger threateningly under Hebe's nose. "Just leave him alone." He turned and glanced briefly at Pan before storming out of the room, slamming the door behind him.

Vesta was looking at the closed door with her mouth open. "What's got into him?"

123

Janus had remained silent during the heated exchange; it was part of his godly makeup that he could see both sides of any argument and, although he supported his fellow gods, he could also understand the goddess' attitude. "I honestly don't know; he's been behaving oddly for the last couple of weeks."

"Perhaps he's missing Persephone?" Vesta posed the question partly out of curiosity and partly out of a desire to end the dispute with the gods. The same couldn't be said of Hebe who was glaring at a still grinning Pan, wondering what else she could throw at him. He'd caught the teapot with a deft flick of his wrist.

"No," Janus said slowly "No, I don't think that's it somehow."

"At least he's being supportive of Pan, that's a step in the right direction; he's normally a right unsociable sod who never says anything nice about anyone." Vesta flinched as the saltshaker went flying across the table.

"Supportive? Yes, that's one word for it I suppose," Janus replied thoughtfully.

Pan was still dodging the various culinary missiles being thrown at him. "Hebe, will you stop that? There's salt all over the place now." The lid had flown off the salt pot as Pan had caught it and his black hair was now liberally sprinkled with white. The distraction it had caused had dulled his reflexes and the pepper pot had hit him squarely between the eyes. Hebe, satisfied that she'd won the argument, went upstairs to apply her make-up.

"Do you think he'll be all right?" Vesta was looking concernedly at Pan who was slumped in his chair unconscious.

"Of course he'll be all right; he's a god." Janus gave Pan the briefest of glances before turning his attention back to Vesta. He was of the opinion that the five of them should be working together and not bickering amongst themselves if they wanted to be worshipped once again. Vesta was, despite her occasional violent outbursts, far more reasonable than Hebe, and he was sure that the two of them could come up with a plan.

"I can't help thinking that, although both our ventures have been successful, we would fare better if we could find a way to bring the human males and females together rather than driving them further apart. What are your thoughts?"

Vesta was very much enjoying her liberation from the gods' oppression and felt that females, goddesses and humans alike, deserved to be treated with more respect. Therefore, she wasn't terribly inclined to follow Janus' lead without careful consideration. However, she had also witnessed the horrific consequences when the gods had turned against each other. She'd never forgotten the terrible war of the Titans, not least because that was when Zeus was given his lightning and thunderbolts by the Cyclopes. He'd been bad enough before but armed with something that could fry and frazzle from a thousand paces, he had become unbearable. That said, she couldn't bear the thought of working with the gods to get back their followers, only to be recast into her boring, lonely and celibate role as guardian of the sacred virgins.

Janus watched her carefully, aware that she was trying desperately to come to a decision. He suspected that Vesta was of a calm enough disposition to be able to see both sides of an argument, and he hoped that she would eventually agree with him. Finally, Vesta spoke. "I do think that you're right, and I would be prepared to work *with* you, and I will do my best to persuade Hebe to do the same." Janus opened his mouth to speak but Vesta held up her hand to silence him. "However, I want something from you in return."

Janus was surprised; he was used to Vesta being subservient and compliant, and as a senior god, he was used to deference and respect. He frowned slightly. "Very well, what is it that you want?"

Vesta took a deep breath. "I want you to support me when we go back. I intend to tell Zeus that I will no longer be the guardian of the sacred virgins. I want my own villa, with a swimming pool and male attendants. I want a clothing allowance, a good supply of coal and a case of wine delivered to the villa every month on the new moon."

"I am not sure that we……" Janus stopped as Vesta held up her hand once again.

"I haven't finished. I will also be making my own decisions; no god will be telling me what to do, got it? If you want my help, then you can help me when we get back; I want your promise, Janus."

Vesta looked quite fierce, and Janus was taken aback. It was now his turn to consider. On the one hand he was certain that their plan to regain their followers would be more likely to succeed if they all worked together to bring the male and female humans together. On the other hand, Vesta's request would mean a major falling out with Zeus, if he were to support her. "Oh what the hell," he reasoned "Zeus has been getting on my tits for years; it's about time someone stood up to him and who better to do it than his little brother?"

"OK, Vesta, you have a deal." He smiled at her surprised expression and then held out his hand. They'd shaken on the deal; it was binding.

"Wass goin' on?" Pan slowly opened his eyes and looked around blearily. He had a splitting headache.

Vesta looked at Janus to respond, but he gestured for her to speak. Their brief discussion had given Janus a new respect for Vesta, and he was beginning to question whether the gods had shown the goddesses enough credit over the years.

Vesta spoke firmly and decisively. "We're all going to be working together from now on. There is too much division between the male and female humans, and we're going to close that divide and bring them all closer together."

Even with a pounding head and slightly blurred vision, Pan still managed to leer.

"Tha's great, 'm all for cumin togeth....." His head dropped forward, and he began to snore gently.

"Leave him to it." Janus rose from his chair. "Will you go and speak to Hebe while I run the idea past Hades?"

"Leave it with me. We're going into the office this morning, and she's always calmer when she's working, so I'll speak to her later. Failing that I'll take her out to lunch and ply her with alcohol until she agrees." Vesta faced Janus and, smiling softly, held out her hand. He shook it, surprised at how firm her grip was.

Several hours later, Hebe and Vesta were sitting in a smart restaurant being plied with cocktails by besotted waiters who figured that they could be in with a chance if only the two goddesses were drunk enough.

"Thank you but we'd like to order now," Vesta insisted as another round of vodka martinis arrived at their table. "We'll both have the mushroom tortellini with fresh truffles and a green side salad. Thank you." She forced their menus into the waiter's hands and pushed until he reluctantly walked away.

"What a great morning; did you see the forward bookings?" Hebe was looking content, self-satisfied and slightly squiffy. Vesta decided it was the perfect moment to pitch Janus' plan.

"I know; we really have become quite the success, haven't we? I do have one small concern though." Vesta spoke quietly and with enough deference in her voice that it was clear she was looking for Hebe's advice. Hebe, susceptible to flattery in any form, leaned forward. "What concern? Tell me."

"I can't help thinking that maybe we are losing track of our original purpose of regaining the respect and adulation of the humans so that they'll start worshipping us again," Vesta whispered, looking anxiously around her to ensure that none of the other diners were listening.

"I don't understand. We have huge respect from the feminists, which is no mean feat, let me tell you, and we are adored by all the women whom we've transformed. Not only that, but the human women are looking up to us because we are in the process of transforming the fashion and beauty industry. Have you seen the glossy magazines? It's all about 'real' women now and that's our doing." Hebe was confident in their success and was ready to dismiss Vesta's concerns. "Not only that but Light of Aphrodite is selling out fast; there is a goddess' name on thousands of women's lips. With the new Venus perfume and Athena cosmetics that are coming out next month, the human women will be talking about nothing but goddesses."

"Yes, I agree, we have made a huge difference in many women's lives." Vesta hesitated, choosing her words carefully, "But we are alienating quite a large portion of the human population with the position that we've taken."

"Who are you talking about? The stick-bean models who aren't getting booked now? The fashion houses and cosmetics companies that have been around for decades but still have none of our vision?" Hebe scoffed.

"No, I am talking about the human males." Vesta said gently.

"Oh," Hebe slumped back into her chair. She appeared to be mentally wrestling with something. "I got a bit carried away, didn't I?" She picked at the edge of her napkin; her eyes lowered. A flush came to her cheeks that was strangely unflattering, but it endeared her to Vesta.

She was not used to seeing Hebe downcast, much less humbled. "You did a bit, yes. To be honest, I think that we both did; it wasn't just you." She took Hebe's hand and smiled at her encouragingly. Hebe straightened her back and raised her head to look at Vesta.

"That's true; it's half your fault. So, what are we going to do about it?" Just like that, Hebe was back to her old belligerent self.

"Well, I wouldn't say half..." Vesta began, defensively.

"Look, it doesn't matter if it was your fault or not, the question is how are we going to fix it? I'm not having Zeus laying the blame at my feet if we don't get our followers back." Hebe took her hand from underneath Vesta's and folded her arms.

"What do you mean 'it doesn't matter if it was my fault'? It wasn't my bloody fault!" Vesta glared at Hebe but then remembered the discussion that she'd had with Janus and took a deep breath to calm herself. "Look, I spoke to Janus earlier, and we've agreed that we all need to work together if we're going to get our human followers back and that will mean no more bickering."

Hebe looked rebellious for a moment but then sighed. Uncrossing her arms, she put her elbows on the table. She was immediately forced to move them again as another besotted waiter arrived at their table with their lunch.

"There you are, madame." He placed a bowl of pasta and a plate of salad in front of Hebe. "And for you, madam." He stepped back slightly, grinning inanely at Hebe but didn't return to the kitchen. Vesta rolled her eyes and said "That's lovely, thank you. Anyway, as I was saying..."

"Black pepper, madam?" The waiter waived a large and distinctly phallic pepper grinder under Hebe's nose.

"Oh, yes please. So, what else did Janus say?" Hebe lifted her fork and prepared to dig into her pasta.

"Well, he seemed to think..." Vesta began.

"Parmesan, madame?"

"What? Oh, yes, thank you." Hebe put her fork down as the waiter slowly sprinkled the grated cheese over her tortellini. "Sorry, Vesta, you were saying?"

Vesta, who hadn't been offered a grind from the phallic pepper grinder was beginning to get annoyed. "Right, as I was saying..."

"Is there anything else I can get for you, madame?" The waiter was bowing low before Hebe, his eyes raised in hopeful adoration.

Vesta's patience snapped. "Oh, will you sod off and let us eat our bloody lunch?"

The young waiter flushed and immediately stood up straight before slowly backing away from the table, all the while hoping that Hebe would lift a finger to call him back. He managed to back himself all the way into the kitchen, where he sat in the corner and cried.

"Finally! As I was saying, Janus thinks that we should combine our strengths and work on a project together." Vesta took a grateful mouthful of her, now tepid, pasta.

"What sort of project?" asked Hebe with her mouth full; it really had taken an inordinate amount of time to get their lunch.

"He thinks that if we can persuade Pan to hook up with this female television producer he seduced, we might be able to get our own TV show, the aim of which will be to bring male and female humans together but also to give us a platform to recruit new followers. What do you think?" Vesta forked up some more pasta and waited for Hebe's response which was delivered in a matter of seconds.

"You mean that we'd be on television again?" Hebe's eyes lit up and a beatific smile spread across her face, causing a number of men in the restaurant to gaze at her adoringly, their forks paused half-way to their gaping mouths, food forgotten.

"Hebe, don't forget why we're doing this." Vesta's warning was clear, and Hebe dropped her smile.

"You're right, I'm sorry, I was getting a bit carried away again." She grinned sheepishly. "I'll try not to forget while we're doing all this."

Vesta forked up the last tortellini from her plate. "Don't worry, I'll remind you."

## Chapter 23

Later that evening the gods and goddesses had all made their way back to Number 23 and were busy thrashing out a plan. Hebe was wondering if an actual thrashing might be necessary if Pan didn't stop digging his heels in. She tried to remain serene as she pleaded with him.

"Pan, we need you to charm this female. We've all agreed that television is the best way to connect with the humans and bring them back to us." Janus, Hades, Vesta and Hebe were all sitting on the sofa, looking imploringly at Pan who was pacing the room.

"I can't. I can't *charm* her. She doesn't stop talking long enough for me to *charm* her." Pan was distractedly running his hands through his thick, dark hair making it stand on end. He was not used to being pressured to seduce someone; it was normally quite the opposite.

"You managed it last time," Vesta pointed out quietly.

"Yes, because it was a challenge, a conquest. You know damn well that I lose interest the minute that females succumb to my attentions," Pan was pleading with them to understand.

"Have you ever wondered why females don't hold your interest Pan?" Hades muttered.

"I don't know why...sorry, what?" Pan looked intently at Hades who dropped his eyes as a faint blush rose to his cheeks.

"I just think that you should examine your true *feelings*, that's all. Look, it doesn't matter, shall we move on?" Hades glanced at Vesta, his eyes begging for help.

Vesta picked on his cue but was perplexed by his comment; it was most unlike Hades to consider emotions, his own or anyone else's. She determined to have a quiet chat with him when they were alone. "I think Hades is right, it *is* something you should look at but maybe later. For now, we need this human female on our side, and she adores you. This is important Pan; Saturn is relying on us, and Zeus will do his pieces if we don't start getting some more followers soon. Please, do this for us, for all of us?"

Pan looked at each of them in turn, his eyes resting on Hades for a shade longer. There was something about the sombre, introverted god that was attracting his attention. The more time they spent together, the more he seemed to crave Hades' company. He wondered if he might finally be on his way to finding a friend. The thought cheered him.

"Right. Fine. I'll do it, but we're going to the pub first; I cannot spend a night with that female sober." He stormed upstairs to find Charmaine's number. After having placed a call, claiming a low battery on his phone as an excuse to cut it short, Pan grabbed his jacket and marched back downstairs.

"Come on, we're going to the pub, and we don't have much time. I've got to meet her in three hours," he yelled.

The other gods and the two goddesses leapt up from the sofa and grabbed their coats and jackets before following a rapidly departing Pan out the door.

Ten minutes later they were in an old run-down pub where they knew the barman was completely insusceptible to the charms of either Hebe or Pan. They had discovered, to their cost, that it was virtually impossible to hold a productive discussion when either of those two was being fawned over by all and sundry.

"I'm going to take a seat; you can each buy me an alcoholic drink of your choosing." Pan stomped off to the nearest booth.

"You can't blame him for being in a bad mood, you know; he'll be miserable going on another date with that wretched female." Hades signalled to the thoroughly uninterested barman.

"It's one evening, I'm sure he'll manage and, as he proved last time, he has his own special ways of keeping her quiet." Hebe had no sympathy; she had often tolerated insufferable lechery in order to get her own way.

"Oi! Is there any chance of getting a damn drink over here?" Hades yelled at the barman and slammed his fist down on the counter.

Janus and the goddesses looked at him aghast. "What has got into you Hades? You were always a miserable sod, but I never took you as the type who would yell at an aging, half-deaf barman." Vesta's reproach stung Hades, and he fired back at her immediately.

"You never took me as the type? I was Lord of the Underworld. I used to wait on the banks of the Styx to welcome new arrivals with red hot pokers. I used to make Charon, the boatman, give me half of his tips *and* make him clean out his own boat. Do you honestly think I'm going to feel bad about shouting at a barman who can't do his bloody job properly!"

"I do apologise, sir; my hearing is not what it was. What can I get you?" Albert, the barman, had shuffled over and was waiting expectantly with an apologetic smile on his leathery, wrinkled face.

"Oh, um, sorry, I didn't realise. Could I have five single malt whiskies please and take one for yourself.....and make them all doubles." Hades' words came out in a garbled rush.

"Right you are, sir." Albert wandered off to pour their whiskies.

"I don't want to hear it, all right?" Hades glared at his companions and then stood in rigid silence until their drinks arrived.

"Why don't you go and sit with Pan, and I'll bring the drinks over." Janus nodded at Vesta and Hebe who took his cue and joined Pan in the booth. He was still fuming, and his mood was not improved by the fact that he still didn't have a drink in his hand. He didn't even acknowledge the two goddesses, so Vesta and Hebe ignored him and began discussing more ways of getting back their human followers.

At the bar, Janus had draped his arm around Hades' shoulder and was talking to him quietly. He'd been thinking about what to say to him for several days. He couldn't be as blunt as he would like because he had no evidence to support his suspicions, but he had to make sure that Hades understood.

"Don't fall for Pan, my friend; he's not worth it. He doesn't *feel* deeply; his attachments are always intense, but they are short-lived because he's always looking for the next amusement. Sure, he's loveable and fun, but he'll break your heart, just as he's done to so many others."

Hades shrugged off the arm and answered coldly, "Thank you for the advice, Janus, I am sure that you mean well but, firstly, you are not my friend; and secondly, had you ever considered that maybe I would break his?" Albert had returned with the drinks on a tray, so Hades picked it up and walked over to the booth without a backward glance. Janus sighed. He felt sorry for Hades. Although he had ruled over the Underworld for millennia, in many ways, he was an innocent. He turned to join the others, but Pan was already calling out for more drinks, so he walked to the other end of the bar where Albert was sipping his whisky.

"Five more please, if you'd be so kind, and please, take another one for yourself."

A couple of hours later, Pan was feeling much better. All the other gods and goddesses were animatedly discussing their plans, and Albert was asleep behind the bar, snoring softly. Fortunately, there had been very few customers and, when they had ventured in, Janus got up from the booth, stepped over Albert, being careful not to wake him, and served them their drinks. He made sure to put the money in the till, including the price of a drink when he was told to "take one for yourself." He heard the door of the pub opening and looked up, ready to take his position as stand-in barman.

"Pan, it's her." Janus tapped Pan on the shoulder before, once again, getting up to make his way to the bar.

Charmaine entered in a cloud of perfume, silk scarves and hairspray. She was looking around the bar, searching eagerly, but she couldn't see Pan who was desperately trying to hide behind Hades.

"Don't let her see me," Pan whispered into Hades' ear. "I beg of you; I'll do anything if you keep me hidden."

Hades flushed at the feeling of Pan's warm, whiskey-flavoured breath against his skin and moved closer to him in an effort to hide him from sight.

"Stop that Hades," hissed Hebe. "He's got work to do. Pan go over and talk to her."

"Hebe don't make me; you don't know what she's like," Pan whispered urgently as he tightened his grip on Hades' shoulders. Hebe prised his fingers away and shoved him roughly so that he half jumped, and half fell from the booth.

"Oh, don't worry barman, there's my friend. Pan! Oh Pan!" Charmaine's strident voice rang out across the bar.

"I'll just bring your glass of champagne over then, shall I?" Janus was annoyed that Charmaine didn't even remember him and went on the hunt for a bottle of Asti Spumante.

Pan braced himself as Charmaine ran across the bar and launched herself into his arms, before attaching her lips to his with great enthusiasm. After several minutes, during which Pan tried to persuade himself that he'd had worse experiences, Charmaine finally pulled away from him and exclaimed "Oh, it is simply wonderful to see you, you handsome devil." She fluttered her eyes coquettishly. The effect was rather ruined as one of her false eyelashes had come loose as a result of her vigorous fluttering. Undeterred she carried on talking, "I was just saying to my dear girlfriend, Mindy, the other day, 'You simply must meet Pan; he is quite the most divine….' Who's that?"

Her voice which had been simpering and girly had turned to steel as she pointed her finger, accusingly at Hebe.

"Pan, who is she? I demand that you tell me. It was obvious that you were sitting with her before I came in." Before, he could reply, Hebe had risen from her seat and was holding her hand out to Charmaine. "I'm Hebe, it's lovely to meet you. Pan's told us so much about you."

Charmaine ignored her. "Pan, who is this *woman*?" She sneered as she looked Hebe up and down. "Is she your girlfriend, your wife? Tell me!"

"I will tell you if you'd only keep your bloody mouth shut for five minutes." Pan thought to himself. "She's a friend, well more of a colleague really. We're working on a project together…all of us…together." He gestured desperately at Hades and Vesta.

Charmaine was mollified slightly. "She's quite beautiful, I suppose. If your tastes run to very obvious beauty."

Hebe's eyebrows dipped alarmingly, and she opened her mouth to launch a verbal attack on Charmaine, but Pan held up his hand to silence her.

"Yes, my love, she is beautiful, but she doesn't have your charm, your energy, your capacity for love." He took Charmaine's hand in his, covering it with little butterfly kisses, before moving his lips to her neck and then to her ear. The others could guess what he was saying from Charmaine's sharp intake of breath and the flush that rose from the base of her throat to her cheeks. Pan was employing all of his considerable physical charms to calm Charmaine, so they would be able to use her for the next part of their plan. Unfortunately, his flow was interrupted by the sound of shattering glass.

"Oops! I guess I must be stronger than I look." Broken glass dropped from between Hades' fingers onto the table.

Pan broke free of Charmaine's clutches so abruptly that she sagged to the floor and landed heavily on her ample bottom.

"Hades, what have you done? Are you hurt?" Pan had taken Hades' hands and was examining them carefully.

"I'm fine as you can see Pan. I am a god remember, not one of these feeble humans." Hades' voice was deep and had a slight huskiness to it that Pan had not heard before. He looked up into the god's face and saw an intense light burning in his eyes; he was drawn in, and he felt a fluttering in his stomach that was new to him.

"Pan! Are you going to help me up? Your friend is quite obviously fine; I really don't know what you're making such a fuss about. I could have bruised my coccyx. My friend, Perdita, bruised hers and she was in agony for weeks. Weeks, I tell you!" Charmaine's voice droned on and on and she struggled to get to her feet.

Pan and Janus rushed over to help her up, wishing that they'd thought to put cheese in their ears before she'd arrived. It took several glasses of champagne and many outrageous compliments from the gods before Charmaine was amenable enough for them to explain their plan and make their request. Vesta and Hebe sat in stony silence with their arms folded across their chests. "Feminism is all very well, but I really hate women sometimes," Vesta thought to herself as she took a sip of her whisky and counted the minutes until she could be back at home in the fireplace.

## Chapter 24

Saturn was lying face down on a massage table that had been erected in his office, having his taut muscles kneaded by a rather attractive wood nymph when he heard the door to his office open. He was so relaxed that he was almost comatose and couldn't be bothered to turn his head to see who it was.

"Saturn!" The yell woke him from his reverie, and he opened his eyes, only to see Zeus' face directly below his.

"What are you doing down there?" The wood nymph was still working on a particularly stubborn knot and Saturn's voice was slurred.

"Talking to you, what the hell do you think I'm doing?"

"Yes, of course, how silly of me. What do you want?" Since their last meeting, Saturn had lost any fear that he'd had, and Zeus had taken to opening his office door rather than blasting it off the hinges. Their relationship had definitely progressed, but it was still far from perfect.

"I want to know if you've heard anything from Janus. It's just that I've noticed that the wine cellar in my villa has restocked itself. Either one of the other gods wanted to give me a thoughtful gift, or Janus and the others are getting somewhere."

Saturn leapt from the table, almost knocking the poor wood nymph to the floor and went hurtling out of his office.

"Hello young nymph," Zeus was still lying on the floor under the massage table and was now sporting a lecherous grin. The nymph smiled nervously before getting down from the table and scuttling, at high speed, towards the nearest potted plant where she promptly disappeared.

"Oh bugger." Zeus hauled himself upright and made his way to Saturn's desk where he flopped into a chair and put his feet up. A few minutes later, Saturn ran back into his office; his face was lit up with a huge smile.

"It's back! My wine is back! There's bottles and bottles of the stuff, about five hundred, that should last at least a month if I don't go too mad with it. Isn't it wonderful?" He was hopping from one foot to the other in excitement.

"Calm down; it's not like you've never had a full wine cellar before." Zeus rolled his eyes. He wanted to maintain his customary sangfroid, so he'd left it for a little while before sharing the good news with Saturn. He'd actually discovered his stock had been replenished yesterday, and after he'd stopped dancing around and laughing manically, he'd decided to celebrate with a young, very supple succubus. He'd been asleep ever since.

"I know, I'm sorry but I always used to take things like that for granted and when we didn't have them……Do you know I was down to the last inch of my last bottle of wine? I was drinking a teaspoonful a night." He frowned at the thought but then quickly perked up as something else occurred to him. "Have you checked your coffers? Is all the gold back too?" Not waiting for an answer, he tore open the drawer of his desk and pulled out his money bag. It felt rather light as he weighed it in his hands. He was disappointed but he quickly rallied, "Anyway, let's not worry about that for the minute and just enjoy the wine; did you bring a bottle by the way?" Zeus held out his empty hands. Saturn looked down at them and then at Zeus' face. "So, you wanted to know if I'd heard anything from Janus; let me check my emails."

"What do you mean, check your emails? Don't you check them every day?" Zeus demanded fiercely.

"I do have other responsibilities you know," Saturn replied with hurt dignity.

"Like what?" Zeus was nothing if not belligerent.

"Well, there's the personnel records, the filing...look, it doesn't matter. Right, there you are, there's an email from Janus and another from Vesta."

Zeus' thick white eyebrows shot up in surprise. "A goddess has emailed you? What's she doing writing emails? She should be tending the home and guarding her chastity."

"If you let me finish reading the damn thing, I'll tell you; stop interrupting."

Zeus was affronted and folded his arms defensively across his chest but refrained from making further comment.

Saturn had finished reading and had sat back in his chair, a slight smile playing around his mouth.

"Now that *is* interesting," he mused.

Zeus leaned forward eagerly, "What's interesting?"

"Who would have thought...?" Saturn wondered out loud. "Ow! What the hell did you do that for?"

Zeus had thrown a stapler at him, and it had hit him on his long nose.

"Just tell me what she said!" Zeus was unrepentant.

"I don't know that I will now; that hurt." Saturn was gingerly moving his nose from side to side.

"Don't be so feeble; you're a god! Now stop moaning and for the love of Aphrodite, tell me what was in that bloody email."

"Fine, you don't have to shout. She says that she and Hebe have started a business sourcing beautiful woman for jaded businessmen who want to advertise their products and that it's been extremely successful. They've also launched products which have been named for various goddesses and are selling out everywhere. Apparently, they've made rather a lot of money."

"Do you think it was them who sent the wine, as an offering to the gods?" Zeus looked pleased at the thought. Zeus appreciated adulation from everyone but especially goddesses. Like most bullies, he favoured victims whom he perceived to be weaker than himself.

"Don't be daft; how would they get it up here? Even Amazon isn't that good," Saturn scoffed, and Zeus looked momentarily embarrassed.

"What else does she say?"

"She says that they've gained a good following amongst feminists." Saturn had looked the word up on Google when he'd finished reading the email, having absolutely no idea what it meant. He was sure that Zeus would have no idea either. He looked at the ancient god expectantly, knowing that he would be in turmoil at the thought of having to admit that he didn't know something. He waited patiently.

After several minutes Zeus spoke. "That's excellent. They have followers. I'll make sure she's rewarded in some way…" He hesitated. "Feminists you say? I imagine that most of them will be males?" Zeus couldn't conceive of a world where females were of any real significance.

"Unlikely to be honest." Saturn replied, amused. He could see Zeus trying to work out how to phrase his next question to get the answer he wanted without having to admit that he didn't know what a feminist was.

Zeus opened and closed his mouth several times but didn't manage to form an actual word. "Oh damnit, I admit it, I don't know what a bloody feminist is!" He scowled and pouted furiously.

"They advocate for women's rights on the….on the…oh bugger." Saturn had forgotten the rest of the explanation and quickly turned back to his computer.

"You cheating bastard!" Zeus roared. "You looked it up on Google!" He slapped his hands onto the desk and stood up, glaring down at Saturn who had the grace to look guilty.

"Yes, all right I did. I didn't know what the word meant either. Right, there it is, I've found it again, "They advocate for women's rights on the grounds of the equality of the sexes."

Zeus dropped back down into his chair, a look of shocked horror on his face. "Equality? Humans believe that males and females can be equal?" He was ashen. "Tell me you're joking, please."

Zeus couldn't cope with this revelation. It had been bad enough when Saturn had explained to him that there was a possibility his equipment might stop working, but this, this was beyond shocking.

"Nope, not joking I'm afraid." Saturn saw the look of concern on Zeus' face and decided to play it to his advantage. "It will be interesting to see what happens when the goddesses return, won't it? I imagine that they'll be bringing back all sorts of new ideas."

"They bloody well will not!" Zeus was roused from his shocked stupor. "They'll bow to the will of the gods as they have always done; no goddess will command me." A small thunderclap accompanied his forceful declaration, and he had taken a thunderbolt from the pocket of his toga, ready to throw it at the next person who annoyed him.

Saturn smiled innocently. "How are Metis, Themis, Eurynome, Demeter, Mnemosyne, Leto, and Hera by the way? Sorry I should have asked?"

Zeus glared at him suspiciously; it was well-known that his seven wives plagued him with demands for fine clothes and jewels as a sop for their jealousy over his many mistresses. "They are all quite well, thank you. Anyway, don't change the subject; tell me more about these feminists."

Saturn thought carefully before answering. "It seems to me that human females have joined together, not to defeat the males but to compete with them as equals."

"Preposterous!" Zeus had spent millennia telling other gods, as well as humans, what opinions they should hold and firmly believed that a leader should dictate and not placate. As far as he was concerned, anyone trying to be his equal, male or female, would come to a sticky end (being struck with a lightning bolt tends to have that effect).

Saturn was genuinely curious, being far more liberal-minded than Zeus although, to be fair, this was not difficult.

"Why? Human females may, in general, be physically weaker than the males, but in many respects, they are far stronger. From what I've seen of human behaviour, it's a brave male who goes against a female when she loses her temper. Not only that but, in any species, there is nothing so vicious as a female when her young are being threatened." Saturn was on a roll, so he decided to torment Zeus a little more, just for the fun of it. "It's the same with us; don't you remember when Athena went up against Poseidon and won? And, if I remember rightly, she was a headache to you before she was even born."

Zeus had had a torrid affair with Metis, and before long, Metis was with child. Although he should have been delighted, an oracle of Gaea let slip that his first child with Metis would be a girl, but the second would be a boy and overthrow him. Zeus was furious. Unstable and paranoid at the best of times, he called Metis to him, using charm and flattery, and then, when he'd completely disarmed her, he swallowed her whole. Saturn wasn't there at the time, but he'd heard from one or two other gods that it was impressive but utterly nauseating at the same time.

Zeus was convinced that he'd solved his problem, but his unborn daughter continued to develop. Before too long she was born, while her mother was still swimming about in Zeus' digestive juices and, apparently, she was not happy with her lot. She had such huge tantrums that Zeus developed terrible headaches that caused him to cry out in unbearable pain. (This did nothing to help his already fragile temper.) Eventually, Hermes solved the problem by having Zeus' skull split in half and Athena, his daughter, emerged fully grown. Being a god, Zeus, of course, survived, but he'd had to go and have a lie-down for a couple of days. Athena had been a thorn in his side ever since, and he avoided her whenever possible; for some reason, he always felt a tension headache coming on as soon as he saw her.

Zeus hadn't responded, lost as he was in his memories, so Saturn carried on, determined to drive the point home. He was mentally driving a physical point home, somewhere in the region of Zeus' toga belt.

"Also, don't forget that the human females give birth to children; no human male would be able to tolerate that sort of pain. They also appear to be much better organised than the males; I've even heard rumour that they can do more than one thing at a time, although I don't know how true it is. Moreover, they live longer, have more empathy and are more sensitive and that can be an incredibly useful trait..." he paused for emphasis.

"Yes, yes, yes, I get the point, Saturn. You don't have to keep on." Zeus had leapt up from his chair and had begun pacing Saturn's office, twiddling the lightning bolt between his fingers. Aware that he'd been provoking Zeus, Saturn decided to try to placate him before he set fire to his office.

"Look, try not to worry; the human females have taken thousands of years to get to this point, so even if Vesta and Hebe do come back with some revolutionary ideas, we'll have time to temper them so that the goddesses don't try and usurp our position." He smiled encouragingly at Zeus who was still pacing.

"The other thing we have to consider is that Vesta and Hebe have managed to get back some followers for us, even if they are feminists, and that means that our wine cellars have been restocked."

The reminder that he, once again, had plenty of wine seemed to calm Zeus down, and he stopped his pacing. Turning to face Saturn, he asked, "What about the other email? What did Janus have to say for himself? Have the gods managed to get some followers as well?"

Saturn returned to his inbox – surprised that his office was still intact, as Zeus was, once again, fiddling with the lightning bolt – and opened the email from Janus. He read through it carefully before replying.

"It seems that they gained a number of followers with 'Panacea,' but he says that he, Hades and Pan are now going to be working *with* Vesta and Hebe. Apparently, they decided that it would better promote our interests if the males and females were encouraged to come together, rather than fight one another for supremacy. It seems that the feminist movement was starting to alienate many males and embitter many females, so much so that there was a great deal of enmity between them."

"I don't really see the problem," Zeus interrupted. He'd been overseeing the gods and goddesses for millennia, and in his opinion, if they were co-operating, it probably meant that they were plotting against him in some way. He believed it was always better to pit his subordinates against each other so that they were too busy to turn against him."

Saturn was also slightly perplexed as, it seemed to him, that human males and females had never been designed to get on with each other. They were certainly extremely successful at coming together to procreate, but other than that, he'd never really thought they had much in common.

"Well, I think in this matter," he began slowly, "we have to assume that they know what they're talking about; they have been living in the human world for quite some time now. Anyway, Janus says that they have been given a television programme on which they will be working with 'troubled' couples'." He put the word troubled in air quotes for emphasis.

"Why are you making rabbit ears with your fingers?" Zeus glared at Saturn. His naturally bad temper was rising to the fore again as he realised that he had very little idea what was going on.

Saturn sighed. "Why don't you have a seat? I'll open a bottle of wine, and we can talk it through."

"Yes, all right but explain the hand signals. What do they mean? What possible significance could rabbit ears have in a conversation?"

"It's to emphasise a word so that you know it's integral to the sentence," Saturn replied calmly, but he was thinking that one bottle of wine might not be enough.

"But why rabbit ears? Why not big flappy elephant ears if you want to *emphasise* something?" He put his arms against the side of his head and flapped them around wildly. Zeus was a very literal god and had little times for subtleties; he said and did as he pleased and damned the consequences. When his courtship of his wife, Hera, did not go according to plan, he transformed himself into an injured bird. She, being a kind sort of goddess, took pity on the injured creature and cuddled it to her at which point Zeus threw off his disguise and had his way with her. Not wishing to bring shame on herself, she agreed to marry Zeus when he asked. When it came to morals, Zeus was little better than a bull, rutting in the field (another disguise that he adopted from time to time when he was feeling amorous).

Saturn put his head in his hands, "Look, it's really not important; let me go and get the wine, and we can get down to business. I think I'll get a couple of bottles."

Zeus finally stopped going on about rabbits and elephants, so Saturn fled to his wine cellar, grateful for a momentary reprise. As it turned out, their discussion lasted the rest of the day and only stopped because they both passed out after working their way through a case of wine.

## Chapter 25

"I don't want to wear a bloody toga; it's too cold, and my knees look all purple," Pan was arguing with Hebe over her wardrobe choice for them all. "Can't I wear a jumper underneath or something…." He broke off as a huge yawn opened his mouth wide.

"It's the brand, Pan; we'll all be wearing them; brand recognition is hugely important." Pan tried to reply, but another yawn followed hotly on the heels of the first one.

"What's the matter with you Pan? Why can't you stop yawning?" Vesta was trying to fasten a brooch on Pan's toga, but his body kept sagging as he yawned, and it was making it somewhat difficult for her.

"It's Charmaine…..she is…..wearing me…..out." The last yawn was so big it looked as though Pan were about to swallow his own head. Hebe gently pushed Vesta aside, as she finally finished fastening the brooch, and slapped Pan smartly across the face.

"Oi! What the bloody hell was that for?" Pan rubbed his aching cheek, frowning but then realised he'd stopped yawning. "Thanks Hebe. Honestly, that bloody female only stops talking when she's got her mind on other things, if you know what I mean, and I swear, she's got the stamina of a pronghorn antelope. I'm a god so I can give her a run for a money, but I dread to think what she'd do to a human male; they're probably just bloodless, dried out husks after she's finished with them."

"Doesn't sound like you're having much fun at the moment, Pan, shame." Hades gave a twirl. "What do you think?" He'd had packed his own toga in his suitcase when he came to Earth from the Underworld, and it was absurdly flattering. One of the benefits of having the dead under your control is that, occasionally, you have a really good fashion designer turn up. He'd also treated himself to a bottle of outrageously expensive cologne and as he moved closer to Pan, he could see that the combination of musk and muscles was having quite an effect.

"Very nice Hades, you look quite…….handsome." Pan wet his lips and leaned forward slightly, hand outstretched, as if to test the material of the toga, but Hades moved deftly away and started a conversation with Janus about their prospective roles for the evening's show.

Pan shrugged and turned to Hebe who wanted to re-do his hair, but every few seconds, his eyes flicked to Hades who was more animated than Pan had ever seen him. He was complimenting Vesta on how beautiful she looked in her pristine white toga and then placing his hand on Janus' shoulder, listening intently to the god's advice. Not once did he look in Pan's direction. Pan knew, intuitively, that Hades was drawn to him; he'd had so many lovers over the years that he'd developed a sixth sense in these matters. However, each time he thought to pursue a relationship, Hades rejected him; he was never unkind or hurtful, but he seemed to have erected an invisible barrier. This had never happened to Pan before, and he was bemused and not a little intrigued. He'd been rejected, of course, and often violently, but never by someone who so clearly wanted him. Admittedly, he'd never set his sights so high before, Hades was Lord of the Underworld, after all. He sat down on a chair in a corner of the room, in quiet contemplation, watching as his fellow gods and goddesses preened and laughed together. Hades refused to meet his eye, and Pan felt strangely bereft.

Thirty minutes later, the gods and goddesses were installed on their brightly coloured sofas under the glare of the studio lights. There was no studio audience as some of the show had been pre-recorded, but still there was an air of tension. Suddenly the opening bars of a rocked-up version of "Love Will Keep Us Together" boomed across the studio, and

Hebe turned to face the camera, a bewitching smile on her face. The floor manager counted down 5, 4, 3 and then mouthed 2 and finally 1; they were recording.

"Thank you so much to everyone at home for joining us tonight. 'Couples' is a reality show which means that we will be dealing with *real* people who have *real* problems. We will be exploring what breaks two people apart and how they can be brought back together. I and my amazing team will be showing our lovely couple how they can rekindle the fire that first brought them together, and we will be helping them to effect the changes necessary to heal their relationships." Hebe indicated Vesta and the gods with a wave of her hand and a broad smile.

"Now, without further ado, I'd like to introduce our first guests, Sam and Natalie Coleman from Sheffield." Hebe rose from her seat and held out her hand in greeting to Sam and Natalie as they walked, nervously, onto the stage. The couple each briefly embraced Hebe and then turned to the sofa where they hugged each of the other gods and goddesses in turn before taking their seats.

"Sam, can you tell us what your relationship was like before 'Couples' intervened?" A photo flashed onto the screen at the back of the studio; Sam wore a deep frown and looked stressed, unkempt and deeply unhappy. Similarly, Natalie wore no make-up, sported an unflattering grey tracksuit and her deep-set eyes were dull with fatigue.

Sam smiled nervously at the camera but then turned his attention to Hebe. "Honestly, it was terrible. We were fighting all the time, and we'd lost interest in ourselves and each other. Before we heard about 'Couples,' we were talking about divorce because we couldn't see a way out. We couldn't even bear to be in the same room with each other." He grabbed Natalie's hand and grinned at her; she smiled back and rested her head, briefly, on his shoulder in an obvious gesture of affection.

"Let's take a look at Sam and Natalie's interview tape, shall we?" The video was queued, and they all knew that they could relax for a couple of minutes. The floor manager indicated that it was safe for them to speak if they wanted to, and one of the assistants rushed over with a jug of water and some glasses that she'd forgotten to put on the large coffee table that sat in front of the two sofas.

Natalie took the opportunity to speak. "I know I've said it before, you guys, but honestly, I can't thank you enough for everything you did for us. I thought our love had died, but now it's back, stronger than ever." There were smiles and muttered "you're welcomes" and "our pleasures," and then they were back on air.

Janus started speaking in his deep, mellifluous voice. "We can see from that video that you were in a tremendously difficult place; all communication between you seemed to have been lost. It must have been very painful for you both." The cameras zoomed in as Natalie's eyes filled with tears. Sam brought her hand to his lips, and she smiled at him, sniffing slightly.

"It was an awful time for us, Janus. You're right, but with the help we received from you guys, we're now happier than we've ever been." Natalie turned to Sam and kissed him gently on the lips.

"Well, shall we take a look at the first step on your journey?" Another video was queued that showed Janus talking intently to the young couple. As befits the god with two faces, Janus was an adept at seeing both sides of any given situation. The viewers would be watching as he broke down their barriers one by one, asked them to recall their happiest moments together and then address each of their issues in turn without anger or recrimination. There were more tears from Natalie, and even Sam seemed to well up, but he quickly swiped at his eyes with the back of his hand to cover his emotion.

During the hour-long programme, videos were played of Vesta helping the couple to introduce their own personalities to their home, but in such a way that the end result was completely harmonious.

"It's very important that your home is a reflection of you both and of your love for each other; it's not just a place to live." Vesta's calm manner and her obvious love for interior design encouraged Sam and Natalie to see their two-bedroomed flat in quite a different way; it was now their love nest.

They were both given a make-over. Hebe used their new products, Light of Aphrodite and Athena Cosmetics, ensuring that the labels were clearly visible to the camera. While she was applying the concoctions, she flexed her powers just a little. When she was done, Natalie was delighted with her appearance and thrilled with the newfound confidence that the shiny hair, clear skin and bright eyes gave her. Hades was appointed to spruce up Sam's appearance, and everyone was shocked when he made a superb job of it, not least of all, Hades himself. Life in the Underworld had not called for much creativity beyond devising new tortures, but life among the humans seemed to have unleashed his artistic side.

"Oh my God, you look amazing!" The delighted couple cried in unison when their new looks were revealed. Sam swung Natalie around in his arms, and she squealed with happiness as Hebe and Hades looked on, smiling indulgently at the young pair.

The final video was of the couple's session with Pan. With unaccustomed tact and discretion, he talked them through the problems in their love life or lack thereof. There were a few moments when Natalie blushed uncontrollably and Sam looked distinctly uncomfortable, but in the end, they spoke openly and honestly with Pan and each other. As he'd been instructed by Hebe, Pan had also made sure that a bottle of "Panacea: Apollo" was prominently placed in the shot. The following day, they'd had another meeting with Pan, during which they confessed that they'd rediscovered their passion for each other. Both smiled widely at the camera, highlighting both their joy and also the black smudges under their eyes. "So how did 'Apollo' work out for you, Sam?" Pan asked cheekily. Natalie gave a little giggle, but Sam, who'd thoroughly embraced the concept of openness and honesty, replied "Let's just say, I've never had so much exercise while lying down." He smirked playfully as Natalie slapped him on the shoulder, and then they both burst into fits of self-conscious laughter.

When each of the videos had been played, Hebe asked both Natalie and Sam for their feedback on the experience.

"Honestly, Hebe, what you did for us was like a miracle. We both thought our relationship had reached the end of the road," Natalie said earnestly.

"For me, you guys really *are* gods and goddesses, and I worship you." Sam dropped to his knees and bowed up and down, laughing out loud as he did so. "Seriously, though, you put love back in our lives, real love and real passion." He winked at Natalie, as he climbed back on to the sofa, and she giggled. The programme played out with the happy couple and the gods and goddesses laughing together.

The second the music finished, and the floor manager signalled they were clear, Charmaine came hurtling onto the set and threw herself at a startled Pan. She'd worked in television for years, and she just knew that the show was going to be a huge success and the money would come rolling in. Charmaine might be a slightly crazy nymphomaniac with a repressed goat fetish, but she was a damned good businesswoman.

As Pan tried to extricate himself from Charmaine's iron grasp, the others walked back to the green room. Sam and Natalie said goodbye after more hugs and thanks, and the gods and goddesses were left alone.

"I think that went well." Janus relaxed back onto the sofa and put his feet on the coffee table but then remembered that he was wearing a short toga and put them back down again, crossing his legs.

"It couldn't have gone better in my opinion." Vesta had thought that she looked very fetching on screen and found that her self-confidence was growing in leaps and bounds even when faced with Hebe's startling beauty.

Hades was just about to give his opinion when, suddenly, the door to the green room slammed open and Pan dashed in, grabbed him by the hand and pulled him out of the door and towards the studio exit.

"Come on you lot, we haven't got much time. I told Charmaine I needed the toilet, but I wouldn't put it past her to come looking for me – even n there."

Vesta, Hebe and Janus looked at each other and then, as one, launched themselves from the room. They knew that they were relying on Charmaine but couldn't stand any more time in her company than was absolutely necessary. Besides, they'd signed a contract for twelve episodes of the show, and she couldn't back out without huge penalties, so they figured that they were safe from her wrath when she found out Pan had made a dash for it.

Pan was laughing uproariously as he dragged Hades along behind him. "Come on, we're going to the pub, and the drinks are on me."

Sometime later they were all happily drunk and basking in the aftermath of their success. Vesta and Hebe were congratulating each other on how well their makeovers had gone, while Janus was busy drafting a long email to Saturn. Pan was sitting close to Hades and had casually slung his arm across his shoulders; he was encouraged that, although Hades hadn't acknowledged the gesture, he had inched slightly closer.

"Are you quite sure that Charmaine won't find us in here?" Hades whispered into Pan's ear.

"Quite sure, I've never been to this pub with her; we'd have to be really unlucky for her to track us down here." Pan drew Hades even closer and bent his mouth close to Hades' neck.

Just then, the door to the pub flew open, and a strident voice yelled out "Pan! There you are! I've been looking for you everywhere!"

Hades tried to move away, but Pan held him closer still as Charmaine stormed across the pub. She took in the scene before her and was uncharacteristically silent for several moments; the closeness between Pan and Hades was unmistakable.

"Bravo! How progressive of you, Pan! Why didn't you tell me that you're bisexual? This will do wonders for our ratings! I should have guessed, a man with your *appetites.*" She gave Pan such a lewd smirk that, for the first time in his long, long, life, the ancient god blushed. "I simply must put out a statement to the press right away; diversity *is* the new talent, you know." She leaned across the table and kissed both Pan and Hades, first on one cheek and then the other. "Ciao, you two; have fun!" She winked and departed just as quickly as she'd arrived.

The gods and goddesses just sat and looked at each other; they were all completely speechless but for a number of different reasons. Hades and Pan were battling their complex emotions for one another while Janus was fearful that Hades would get hurt and their brand would suffer. Hebe was wondering how on earth she could have missed something that was so obvious to Charmaine, and Vesta was pondering how one went about getting a boob job.

"Does anyone want another drink?" Pan asked quietly. There was a chorus of "Yes!" It turned out to be a very late night.


**Chapter 26**

During the months that followed "Couples" gained an enormous following. Audiences could relate to their guests, as very few people can say that all their relationships, either with friends or loved ones, are perfect. It appealed to all generations as Charmaine ensured that they interviewed couples both young and old. The media loved it as it didn't just focus on heterosexual couples, and Pan and Hades were being courted as poster boys for the bi-sexual community since Charmaine's press release. Hebe and Vesta were photographed everywhere and by everyone and the "look" on the London catwalks for the summer season was "the modern toga."

Sales of "Panacea" had earned the gods a small fortune, and Goddesses was going from strength to strength. There was now a waiting list for Light of Aphrodite, and Athena cosmetics had been blissfully adopted by teenage girls as their go-to brand. The five gods and goddesses had become celebrities; moreover, they were rich celebrities. All in all, they were having the time of their lives, except for Janus who, with his ability to see both sides of any situation, was worried at the changes he was witnessing in his colleagues.

Pan had always been outrageous in his dress and in his behaviour, but now he was taking things to extremes, and Hades was following his lead. They had somehow made friends with the hot new designer, Alaska Bliss, and were happy to model her clothes, however 'out there' they might be. Janus had always worn a toga and enjoyed the feeling of airy freedom that it gave him, but he'd always thought of it as a very masculine mode of attire. Yesterday he'd seen video of Pan and Hades arriving at a fashion event, and they were both wearing long, wool dresses, gold plastic crowns and high-heeled boots. Their make-up had been artfully applied so that their eyes seemed enormous and their lips were glossy pouts. The crowd went absolutely wild at their arrival, and the paparazzi couldn't get enough of them, but Janus thought that they were becoming caricatures of themselves and were losing their godly dignity.

It was the same with Hebe and Vesta. Hebe had always been vain and self-absorbed, but Vesta had been a homemaker, a carer – chaste and unassuming. Now, when she wasn't dressed in her toga at promotional events, she wore clothes that appeared to Janus to have been sprayed on. Both of the goddesses were regularly gifted with jewellery by advertisers and sponsors, and Vesta seemed determined to wear it all at the same time. Several photographs had been taken of her recently which appeared to show a small star – the glare from her diamonds was so strong – dressed in designer clothes.

As they were due to begin filming a second season of "Couples" very shortly, they were being courted by advertisers. They'd each been given a brand new Aston Martin Vantage which Pan had described as "sex on wheels" in several media interviews much to Janus' embarrassment. However, the lavish gifts meant that they'd all had to learn to drive, and as a result, there were several driving instructors being treated for post-traumatic stress disorder. As celestial beings, they were pretty much indestructible which meant that they had no fear of death, and therefore, all drove the powerful cars at high speed with little regard for their fellow road users. They were collecting points on their newly acquired licences at an alarming rate.

The others encouraged Janus to join them when they went out on the town, but except for promotional appearances, Janus refused, preferring to stay in his room at Number 23. He liked the peace and quiet it afforded him, and he used his time to reflect on what he really wanted from life. As he could see both sides of any situation and could look both to the past and the future, this was somewhat time-consuming. He and his second face spent countless hours pondering their own future, that of the other gods and also of the human race. He found himself alternately euphoric at the thought of all the possibilities and depressed for exactly the same reason.

He was deep in thought when he heard a tremendous crash downstairs, followed by raucous laughter. He had become accustomed to his fellow gods' behaviour, so he didn't hurry but composed himself and slowly wandered down the stairs to see what was going on. Pan and Hades were so drunk that they were having to hold each other up, and Vesta and Hebe were both locked in tight embraces with what looked like male models. Not only that but their ever-expanding entourage had followed them into the house, and the little semi- was full to bursting. Couples were diving off into the kitchen, hoping for a moment of privacy; friends were talking at the top of their voices, desperate to be heard; and a young male model was trying to beat the crap out of an investment banker who'd told him he was "just a pretty face."

Janus surveyed the chaos and then closed his eyes slowly. He took a huge deep breath.

"Shut the FUCK UP!" Janus roared at the top of his voice. Had he been a human male, the crowd would have probably just ignored him, but when a god shouts you can't help but listen. The people standing directly in front of him were blasted several inches backwards and didn't regain full use of their ears for two days. Pan and Hades sobered up immediately, and Hebe and Vesta shed their two models like snakes shedding their skins. All four turned to look at Janus who still had a face like thunder. Pan took the initiative.

"OK, I think it's time that everyone was going now. Nice to see you all…put that bottle down, Darren. No, Sharon, you can't sleep here; no, Storm, I don't know where your coat is. Are you sure you had one with you? Look we'll sort it all out tomorrow; just go."

Pan ushered all their guests out the front door and closed it behind them. When he returned to the living room, Hades, Vesta and Hebe were standing in front of Janus with their heads bowed looking like naughty school children.

"Go to bed all of you, and I'll speak to you in the morning."

Janus looked formidable and the four acquiesced with barely a murmur. He followed them up the stairs, after making sure that the front door was locked, and once in his room, he typed a detailed and very angry email to Saturn.

## Chapter 27

The following day, Pan, Hades, Hebe and Vesta all woke very slowly and with terrible hangovers. As they opened their bloodshot eyes, they realised that something was not quite right; instead the comforting floral wallpaper of Number 23, they saw white, marble columns and high, vaulted ceilings.

"Finally, you're awake," Saturn's voice was cold and unyielding.

"How….how did we get back here?" Hades' words were slow and filled with dread; last night he'd finally discovered who he was, and it had been the best night of his long life. The human world had freed him, and now realising that he could be sent back to the Underworld, he was filled with unbearable sadness. He reached across to Pan, who'd been lying next to him on the luxurious, silk-covered chaise longue and took his hand.

"Janus arranged for you to be brought back; he will be joining us shortly."

"Janus? That back-stabbing bastard! How could he?" Pan's voice was quiet but full of bitterness. "We were…happy." He rested his head against Hades' shoulder, and to the shock of everyone in the room, he began to cry. He didn't sob, breathless sobs, just silent tears that ran slowly down his swarthy cheeks. Hades took him in his arms and gently held him until the tears subsided.

Vesta was on her feet and advanced towards Saturn without a trace of fear on her face.

"What we did in the human world, we did for you and for Zeus because you commanded it of us. As always, what the gods want, the gods must have, and damn anyone who gets in their way. In the human world, we learned what it is to have choices, to use our divine gifts for good and not for power or control. We learned to laugh; can you believe that? After all the millennia we have existed, it took time in the human world to know what it is to have fun!" Vesta stood so close to Saturn that their noses were almost touching. "You have taken that away from us without discussion or warning. Why?" As she uttered the final word, she poked Saturn in the chest. Hard. He stumbled backwards and almost lost his footing but steadied himself by holding on to the corner of his desk.

"I'll tell you why!" The doors to Saturn's office flew off their hinges, and a deafening crack of thunder announced Zeus' arrival.

Vesta turned towards the powerful god and said, disdainfully, "Can't you just use the bloody door handle like everyone else? You really are the epitome of the oppressive patriarchy, aren't you? Slamming around with your balls out trying to make everyone cower before you. Well, I'm telling you this, Zeus – it won't work, not anymore, not with me!"

Zeus opened his mouth and then closed it again; he really had no idea how to respond in the face of Vesta's fury. Like most bullies, he tended to back down when faced with someone who was not afraid of him.

Hebe joined her goddess sister. "I'll tell you another thing; we all experienced love in the human world, real love, not just physical love or blind worship. We saw that there's no need for dominance or tricks. Humans are not like you; they don't need to turn into bloody swans or bulls and then seduce someone through deception."

Zeus opened his mouth to speak but Hebe wouldn't give him the chance.

"We all found love there in one form or another. What do we get up here? Poor old Vesta is isolated in her temple, surrounded by her obsequious virgins who are really sodding dull, let me tell you. Hades was banished to the Underworld where he learned cruelty and pain, which is awful because he really is quite sweet once you get to know him." Hades smiled at her gratefully. "Pan was so messed up by the ways of the gods that he built a wall around his emotions, sure that no-one could ever really love him for who he is." Pan hugged Hades to him and smiled at Hebe, a smile full of pure joy.

"And what of me? I handed round ambrosia at your posh parties and looked beautiful. What a vacuous life! I was so obsessed with looks that I couldn't see beyond; I couldn't see the real beauty in people." Hebe's voice began to waver. "I've spent my whole life trying to please you...what about me? What about me, Dad?"

Hades pulled Pan up off the chaise lounge, and they walked over to join the two goddesses.

"She's right. We have lived and suffered, forced into our various roles by you, the ultimate puppet master, but no more. We have seen what is possible, and we will not give it up easily. Do you understand me.....brother? A dark light shone in Hades' eyes that had been born there from the punishments that he had ordered in the Underworld.

"Look!" Zeus began to speak, but Janus had marched into the room and interrupted him.

"Excellent, you're all awake. Saturn, could you arrange for some tea, and we can all sit down and have a chat."

Vesta turned on him furiously. "A chat!? We don't want a *chat;* we want explanations!"

Zeus stepped forward. "If I...."

"Could you ask if we could have some biscuits with the tea as well, Saturn, and maybe some ambrosia, if it's not too much trouble?" Janus nodded his thanks to Saturn.

A bolt of lightning flared across the room and a small statue of a cat playing with a ball of wool exploded.

"Will you all just SHUT UP and let me get a sodding word in edgeways?" Zeus stamped his feet and thumped his fists on Saturn's desk.

"Of course, Zeus, there's no need for all that, why didn't you just say?" Janus asked politely. His fellow gods and goddesses nodded in agreement.

"I did bloody say...oh never mind. Look, we bought you back because you were all getting a bit too carried away. I know you were having fun, but you were risking disgrace in the human world. You have brought us new worshippers, and our fortunes are restored, but we will lose it all again, if the humans realise that you are just as flawed as they are. Human love is fickle, and we want our followers to pass on the message to future generations; we can't afford to have fifteen minutes of fame and then it all be over."

It was then that they all realised *why* Zeus had been in charge for so long; for all his bluster, he was actually pretty switched on.

"You're right." Vesta was the first to speak. "We were carried away with it all, and we would have lost a lot of the followers we'd gained if we continued down the path of drunkenness and wild parties. We were so flattered by all the adulation that we got caught up in the world of celebrity and I don't think it bought out the best in any of us." She looked at Hades, Pan and Hebe, and they all nodded their heads, looking a little shamefaced. "So, what happens now?"

Janus spoke, and his explanation was almost an apology. "I have arranged for a press announcement. The humans will be told that we were all travelling by private helicopter to an event in St. Tropez when a freak storm caused the helicopter to crash in the ocean. Nothing will be found, and no doubt the conspiracy theorists will wonder about it for years to come. A portion of the money we accumulated on Earth had been put into a trust for underprivileged children, and the rest will be used to ensure our businesses will continue without us."

"So, we're back, and life will go on as it did before?" Pan asked bitterly.

Zeus smiled at him and, for once, Pan didn't feel threatened. "Not quite as before, Pan. We've seen what it was like to live as gods when our believers lost faith in us, and it wasn't much fun. We're going to be making a few changes around here, and I am appointing you five as heads of the Transformation Committee. You can take all that you learned from the humans and apply it up here. I know I've been a cantankerous old sod, and I promise you all, from now on things will be different."

Hades stepped forward and shook Zeus' hand, "There's one more thing."

"Why does that not surprise me?" Zeus smiled wryly. "What is it?"

"Pan and I will be getting married; that's if he'll have me. Pan?"

"Yes. I can't say anything else, just yes." Pan beamed through his tears and embraced Hades.

Zeus looked shocked but then said, "Oh, why not? Any excuse for a party!"

## Chapter 28

There were quite a few changes in the lives of the five gods and goddesses after they returned to Mount Olympus. As joint heads of the Transformation Committee, it was their job to turn the other gods and goddesses away from the old ways and introduce more modern ways of thinking. Their efforts were greeted with suspicion from the gods and elation from the goddesses who, thanks to Hebe and Vesta's lectures on feminism, had finally realised how oppressed they'd been over the years and exactly who was responsible.

Vesta was an excellent seamstress, having had little else to do but sew when she was in the temple with her virgins, and she spent many, happy hours transforming togas into pantsuits. Aphrodite clung to her beautiful, draped silks but most of the other goddesses donned their pantsuits and took to marching in the streets, demanding that the gods give them equal rights. None of them had ever been enslaved – they were immortal deities after all – but they'd been led to believe that they didn't have the same right to voice their opinions as the gods. With newfound freedom, they castigated the gods at every opportunity and made it perfectly clear that they would no longer be bossed around.

The gods themselves had been used to having the goddesses at their beck and call and weren't quite sure what to do, so they relied on the fall-back plan which involved giving Dionysus a call and getting him to deliver vast quantities of wine to the harbour. They then packed up their fishing gear and disappeared for as long as it took the wine to run out. Two days later, the wine had been drunk; they'd shared their moans and woes and were hung over and belligerent. It hadn't helped that they'd all been given a massive bollocking by Poseidon for throwing their empty wine bottles into the sea. Normally, he was all for a good party, but no-one had thought to invite him, and one of the bottles had hit him on the back of the head whilst he was riding the surf. When he was in a really good mood, he transformed the spray on the water into dolphins and rode on their backs; the flying bottle had ruined his fun.

"Get out and bloody well stay out!" Poseidon stood on the backs of the spray dolphins and raised his hands above his head before thrusting them forward in the direction of the gods' boat. The water surged and a fifty-foot wave carried them back to the shore. The ride back had been fast and choppy, and the gods were soaked to the skin by the time the boat came to a halt on the golden sand.

"Oooh, look, it's a wet toga competition. Give us a twirl boys!"

Ate, goddess of mischief happened to be walking along the beach with Aphrodite and Hebe when the boat was washed ashore. In the past she had played tricks and pranks but had kept her distance from her victims. However, with her blossoming feminist leanings and the backing of her fellow goddess, she was quite happy to mock the gods to their faces. Aphrodite and Hebe were equally happy to join in and started catcalling the startled gods.

"Looking good, Apollo! Is that a bow in your pocket or are you just pleased to see me?" Aphrodite called out, winking at the embarrassed Apollo who was trying to peel the wet toga from his thighs.

The goddesses were in fits of laughter, and all the gods were starting to feel extremely uncomfortable as they tried to exit the boat with at least a modicum of dignity. Ares, the god of war, was getting flustered and hoped that he could sneak away without drawing the attention of the goddesses. Unfortunately, in his hurry, he tripped over one of the mooring ropes and sailed over the edge of the boat. His ever-present golden helmet flew off his head and he landed on the sand in a tangle of wet robes.

"Oh, nice entrance, Ares, been polishing your helmet I see." Ate had a leer in her voice that sent her fellow goddesses into further giggles. By this time, the gods were in a state of confusion, unsure whether to stay on the boat until their togas dried or to try to make a dash for it.

"Look at the body on that; give me a smile sweet-lips." Hebe was remembering all the cat calls that she'd received from builders when she was in Brighton and was thoroughly enjoying herself.

"Stand aside. Let me through." A booming voice could be heard above the frantic muttering of the gods. Hebe was readying herself for another jibe – "It must be jelly 'cause jam don't shake like that!" — when a god, the likes of which she'd never seen before, strode onto the front deck of the boat. He appeared to have been carved from a block of muscle and his rippling body glittered in the sunlight as tiny rivulets of water ran down his chest and across his rock-hard abs.

"Bloody hell!" Hebe's eyes were fixated on the magnificent god who towered over the others by several inches. "Who's that?"

Aphrodite shielded her eyes and looked up. "Oh yes of course, you haven't met him yet, have you? That's Heracles; he's quite something, isn't he?"

"You could say that." Hebe was transfixed. "Why haven't I seen him before?"

Ate had been listening to the conversation. She'd become bored trying to lift up the gods' togas so she could "rate their booty" as they descended from the boat and had joined her fellow goddesses. "His mother was mortal, so he didn't walk among us until recently. There was some drama or another, and he was given 12 labours to complete; I think it was some sort of penance but I'm not entirely sure."

"It doesn't matter, go on." Hebe was impatient to learn more.

"Right, sorry. Well, as I understand it, his final labour was to kidnap and master Cerberus, dog of the Underworld. When he succeeded, he was rewarded with immortality by Zeus and came up here to join us. Lucky us." She grinned at Hebe and was surprised to see that she was no longer staring at Heracles, she was looking down at the sand and her beautiful eyes were filled with tears.

"Hebe what is it?" Aphrodite put her hand on Hebe's shoulder.

"Cerberus is Hades' dog. He's had him from a puppy; he'll be absolutely devastated. I need to go and tell him before he finds out from anyone else. I'll see you later." With that, Hebe slipped off her golden sandals and took flight along the beach, her shiny hair flowing behind her. Heracles watched her, wanting to know more but unsure who to ask. He didn't really want to approach Aphrodite and Ate who were once again giggling and catcalling the gods, but he resolved to see Hebe again.

Unaware that Hebe was on her way to deliver some really bad news, Hades was busy having his first argument with Pan. He was throwing things into a suitcase with reckless abandon as Pan tried to reason with him.

"I never said that I wouldn't go. I just don't want to go right now, that's all."

Pan was trying to keep his temper but was finding it difficult. Hades was insisting that they visit the Underworld, as a couple, so that he could introduce Pan to Cerberus and show him around. Pan was, understandably, reticent as he had no desire to spend his time around a three-headed dog and countless tortured souls.

"Well I don't think you're being fair." Hades was standing in front of Pan with his arms folded. "You know I haven't seen Cerberus since we got back; he will have missed me, and I miss him. He's such a sweet soul; he loves to snuggle, and I know that he would love you too." His voice was wheedling now.

Pan was fairly sure that Cerberus would be far more likely to try to bite his head off than snuggle with him, but he knew that the dog was important to Hades, so he didn't mention it.

"The thing is Hades; I know that the Underworld is your home and Cerberus is your pet, but what would I do there? I've spent almost all my life outdoors, except when we were at Number 23, and I'm not sure I could stand being cooped up."

Hades pursed his lips and his eyes narrowed. "Cooped up? You wouldn't be *cooped up;* you'd be quite free to come and go as you please, Pan. In fact, why not just go now? It's quite obvious that you'd rather spend your time with a bunch of shepherds than with your boyfriend." Hades spat out the last word and then turned his back on Pan. He was hurt that this god, whom he loved, didn't want to see his home, but he was damned if he was going to admit it.

"Hades, come on, don't be like that." Pan reached out to put his hand on Hades' shoulder, but he twisted away.

"Don't touch me!"

"Fine. I won't. Honestly, there's just no talking to you when you're in this mood." Pan looked over his shoulder as he heard the sound of delicate sandals slapping on the cold marble which covered the floor of the atrium. "Hebe, what's the matter? Are you OK?"

Hades turned as he heard the concern in Pan's voice, and he was shocked as he saw that Hebe was in tears. He immediately joined Pan at her side and they both took a hand each, trying to comfort the distraught goddess.

"Hebe, please, tell us what's wrong," Hades' voice was low and his eyes compassionate. His obvious concern for her made it even more difficult for Hebe to tell him what she must.

"Oh Hades, my dear." She sobbed even harder, and Pan and Hades looked at each other, wondering if they should call Vesta. Hebe tried to pull herself together, and after a minute or two, her crying stopped. She took a deep breath and looked Hades in the eye; he saw the pain there and he was worried.

"Hades, I don't know how to tell you this.....it's about Cerberus..."

Hades immediately stiffened. "What? What's the matter? Is he OK?"

It took every ounce of composure Hebe possessed to continue.

"No, I am sorry; he's not....I am afraid Cerberus has been kidnapped. He was taken from the Underworld by Heracles on the orders of Eurystheus who laid down twelve labours for him in order to test his worthiness as a hero and potential as a god."

Hades was absolutely rigid with anger and any softness that had been in his face when he was worried about Hebe was gone. His black eyes flashed, and his jaw was clenched so tightly, it looked as though his face were made from marble.

"Whose candidate was he?" Pan asked Hebe without taking his eyes from Hades; he didn't dare attempt to touch him, but he would not let him out of his sight in this state.

"Candidate? I don't know, but apparently, it was Zeus who transformed him and gave him immortality."

"BASTARD!!!" Hades roared at the top of his lungs before darting over to his suitcase and picking up a golden helmet. As quick as a flash he clapped it on his head and disappeared.

Pan spun round on his heel. "Where'd he go?" He took Hebe by the shoulders and shook her. "Where did he go? He just vanished. I need to find him. I can't let him go while he's angry like that; he'll do someone a serious injury if they get in his way."

"Pan calm down. He took his invisibility helmet so you're not going to find him if he doesn't want to be found. Besides, you know very well where he's gone."

"To kick the shit out of Zeus? Right, well come on, let's go to Zeus' office, and we can both help him." Pan stormed across the atrium.

"Pan, wait. He won't have gone to see Zeus. He'll need to be somewhere familiar. If he's really upset, he will have gone back to the Underworld. If you care for him as much as you seem to, you'll follow him."

"Oh, bloody hell!" Pan hesitated for a split second. "Right I'm going after him." He made to leave the atrium again but then stopped and turned back to Hebe. "I don't suppose you've got any idea how to get there have you?"

Hebe took him by the hand. "Yes, I think so; I've been there a couple of times with Dad. Go and pack and I'll come and find you when I've thrown some things together."

"Right, OK, but hurry, won't you?" Pan turned to walk away but then he stopped. "How many pairs of pants should I take? Will it be warm down there? What should I wear? I'll need to look nice for when I see Hades. Do you think I've got time to have a quick haircut?"

Hebe just looked at him for a moment. "Pan. Go. And. Pack." She spoke slowly and deliberately. "And don't forget to bring some cash, we'll need to pay Charon."

"Sharon? Who the bloody hell is Sharon?"

"Not Sharon you idiot, Charon – the Ferryman. We have to cross the Styx."

Pan looked momentarily abashed. "Oh yeah, right, Charon."

Hebe rolled her eyes and then dragged him from the atrium. In her opinion, the less time that Hades spent on his own, back in the Underworld, the better.

She packed a little bag and left a scribbled note for Vesta, explaining where she'd gone and asking her to pass a message on to Zeus.

## Chapter 29

A little while later, Pan and Hebe were hurrying down to the River Styx. On its banks were the souls of the dead; a number of whom were wandering aimlessly, looking lost and confused whilst the rest had formed an orderly queue and were looking expectantly across the black waters.

"Why are some of them just wandering about like that?" Pan was curious.

"Those are the souls of humans whose relatives wouldn't or couldn't give them the money for their passage across the Styx. They'll roam around here for a while and then they eventually get the message and just pop out of existence. You ought to see the place after the humans have been at war; you can't move for all the lost souls. I came here with Dad once after the Great War; he kept telling me off for tripping over them and holding him up, but honestly, I couldn't help it." Hebe frowned at the memory but then she pulled Pan behind her and walked to the water's edge.

"Will he be long? I didn't have time to pack a picnic, and I'm getting a bit peckish." Pan was fidgeting. He was impatient at the best of times but worrying about Hades was making him ten times worse than usual.

"I don't know. Charon arrives when he senses souls here; there are quite a few milling about so he shouldn't be too long." Hebe sat down on her little case and paddled her toes in the water. "Why don't you come and sit down?"

"I don't want to sit down; I want to get to Hades. I miss him, and he needs me." Pan started chewing the edge of his thumb and paced back and forth anxiously as he stared at the horizon, searching for Charon's boat.

"Did you bring some cash like I told you to?" Hebe wanted to distract Pan in whatever way she could. He briefly flicked his eyes in her direction and said impatiently, "Yes, you told me the price was 1 obolus, so I bought 50; I'm hoping that if I tip Charon heavily enough, he'll put his foot down and get us there quicker."

"Pan, Charon is an ancient psychopomp; I don't think he'll be open to bribery somehow." Hebe spoke kindly, as if to a child.

"He's a what? A psycho? I'm not sure I want to get on a boat with a psycho. What's the reception like in the Underworld? Do you think Hades would pick up if I gave him a call?" Pan was already reaching for his mobile phone which he'd stashed in the pocket of his best toga.

"No, not a psycho you idiot, a psychopomp....an angel, if you prefer. Oh look, there he is now." Hebe waved at a vast, dark boat that was silently making its way across the river Styx.

Pan squinted. "He doesn't look much like an angel to me; he's filthy!"

"Shsh! He'll hear you." Hebe rapped him sharply on the arm.

The boat moved smoothly across the water, and before they knew it, it had ground to a halt on the soft sand.

Hebe ignored the queue of waiting souls and stepped forward to greet Charon. "Lovely to see you again." She shook his hand briefly. "This is my friend Pan. Listen, we need to go and see Hades, any chance you could give us a lift?" Hebe waved Pan forward and he held out five heavy gold coins. He'd decided to save the other forty-five in case the Underworld had a souvenir shop. Charon grabbed the coins with a huge hand that was encrusted with dirt and stashed them somewhere inside a threadbare loincloth that was black with grime. He pointed to the back of the boat and then turned his attention to the lost souls who each paid with a single coin.

Pan settled himself down on a bench, impatient for the boat to get moving. "You would have thought he'd be able to afford a decent toga, the money he's making, he must be raking it in!"

"Pan, shush! Please!" Hebe glanced at Charon, but he didn't appear to have heard Pan's comment. "He is one of the ancients; he has always looked like this, even when in his angel form."

"Yeah, OK. I get tradition and all that, but he's a scruffy sod, isn't he? I'll have a word with Hades when we get there, and we'll see about getting him a nice new toga or, at least, a nice pair of jeans and a clean T-shirt." Pan said in a whisper.

Once all the souls were loaded, Charon took his place at the helm and they set off for the Underworld. Pan tried striking up a conversation with the dead souls closest to them, but they didn't seem particularly chatty, so in the end he gave up, and they all spent the rest of the journey in silence. After a surprisingly short period, the entrance to the Underworld loomed before them: Vast, vaulted halls in dense black marble that appeared to absorb all light. The souls of the dead started shuffling their feet and arguing, in hushed tones, about who was going to go first. Charon carefully navigated through the halls that echoed with the cries of tortured souls, until he arrived at a small jetty where he docked the boat.

He watched in silence as the dead lined up before a panel of judges, whose job it was to decide the fate of those before them. The dead would either be sent to the Isles of the Blessed and spend the rest of eternity having subdued and respectable fun or go to Tartarus, where the only person having fun was Hades. Tartarus lay deep within the bowels of the Underworld and housed those humans who had really managed to piss off the gods at some point during their existence and would be subject to eternal punishment. Hebe and Pan joined the back of the queue as it snaked its way off the boat.

"I heard what you said," Charon's deep voice sounded in Pan's ear as he passed, and he turned around, shocked, expecting to receive a beating. "You're right; this loin cloth does nothing for my figure. Can you see about getting me some skinny jeans and a lovely rose-coloured T-shirt? I really think it would bring out my eyes, don't you?" Charon winked at Pan, blowing him a quick kiss and then quickly jumped back on his boat. "Well I'll be buggered," Pan thought to himself before rushing off to catch up with Hebe who was marching determinedly towards Hades' office.

As soon as they opened Hades' door, they saw him quickly reach for his invisibility helmet, but Hebe was too fast for him and she closed and locked the door behind her and then stood in front of it, blocking Hades' exit.

Pan strode towards the desk that Hades had been sitting behind when they'd entered, waving his hands wildly in front of him.

"Oi, that hurt!" Hades suddenly popped into view, rubbing his ear. "What are you two doing here? Can't you just leave me alone?" He put his invisibility helmet on the desk behind him and stood facing Pan, his arms folded.

"No, I am not going to leave you alone, especially not when you're hurting." Pan wrapped his arms around an unyielding Hades. "Hebe left a message for Vesta, and we've asked her to bring Zeus to the Underworld, on some pretext, so that you'll get your chance to persuade him to get Cerberus back for you." He felt Hades relax, just a little. "Not only that, but I am going to buy three bow ties, for each of his necks, so that he can wear them at our wedding." He drew back a little and looked into Hades' eyes; he saw the beginning of a smile there, and he felt Hades' strong arms snake around his body. At first tentatively but then with passion, their lips met.

"Right stop that you two, there'll be enough time for all that later on. First things first, we need to come up with a plan. You know how persuasive Vesta can be when she puts her mind to it, so Zeus could arrive any minute." Hebe sounded cross but, in reality, she was more than a little jealous of the relationship between Hades and Pan; seeing them so close, just made her realise how lonely she was.

Reluctantly, Hades broke the embrace. "You know what I'm going to do Hebe? I am going to beat the crap out of him until he agrees to get Cerberus back for me."

"And I'm going to help!" Pan punched the air.

"Yes, yes, all very macho but don't you think we can come up with something a little more subtle? Didn't we learn anything when we were at Number 23? We should play on Zeus' fears, exploit his weaknesses." She smiled encouragingly at the two gods who looked at each other thoughtfully for a moment.

"Nope, I still want to beat the crap out of him," Hades was adamant.

"Hold on a minute my love; I think Hebe may be onto something here. Didn't you tell me that Saturn put the wind up Zeus by making him think that he could be affected by the human affliction of 'drooping danglies'?"

"Yes, but what's that got to do with anything?" Hades was not following.

"Well, you have total control of Tartarus, don't you? You can manifest any torture by manipulating the minds of the dead who reside there, yes?" Pan was eager for Hades to like his idea.

"Yes. There's far too many of them to carry out the torture personally, and it all gets a bit messy if the tortures are physical, so we do it all through mind-control….it's quite clever really." Hades smiled despite himself.

"Where are you going with this, Pan?" Hebe was curious.

"If you let me finish, I'll tell you. We lure Zeus to Tartarus – we can tell him that a stunningly beautiful and very naughty human has just turned up there or something – and then Hades can play his mind games. We can convince Zeus that he's had an equipment failure, but that 'Panacea' will cure the problem and he can have a bottle as long as he releases Cerberus." Pan grinned, mightily pleased with himself.

"Yeeesssss," said Hebe slowly. "That would be a great plan if gods were susceptible to mind-control but they're not, none of us are."

Pan's face fell. He was desperate to help Hades and to impress him; he'd always felt a little intellectually lacking. However, much to his surprise, Hades was grinning from ear to ear.

"As a rule, you're right Hebe, but in Tartarus, I have complete control. It was granted to me when Zeus, Poseidon and I decided to go our separate ways. It's the same with the sea, that's Poseidon's domain, and if another god really pissed him off, he'd be within his rights to drown them."

"So, it will work?" Pan still needed confirmation.

"It will, my Pan; you're a genius!" The two embraced once more and then their mouths found each other.

"Ahem!"

"Sorry Hebe," Hades giggled. "Tell you what, why don't we have a glass of wine while we're waiting; I've rather gone off ambrosia since we got back from Brighton."

They worked their way through a couple of bottles of red while they were waiting for Vesta to arrive with Zeus.


"Vesta, is this absolutely necessary? I've already given the go-ahead for the bloody wedding. Why do I have to traipse all the way down here?" They could hear Zeus moaning as he and Vesta approached Hades' office. Hebe laid her hand on Hades arm. "Just stay calm, all right?" Hades nodded and then stood up to open the door of his office.

"Zeus, thank you for coming, brother. It's good to see you." He held out his hand to a bemused Zeus who shook it gingerly. Shaking hands was a habit that the gods had brought back from the human realm, and he didn't like it.

"Um, yes, ah, good to see you too. So, why am I here? Vesta told me you wanted to discuss something about the wedding. Don't know why you couldn't have sent a bloody email." Zeus' voice was gruff and impatient. "Hebe. Pan." He nodded curtly to the goddess and god in turn.

"I want to show you something; we've decided on the venue, and I'd really like you to see it." Hades smiled, his jaw aching with the effort.

"Down here? Why the bloody hell do you want to have it down here? It's gloomy." Zeus looked disdainful.

Pan could see that Hades had clenched his fists, so he stepped forward smoothly and took his hand. "This is Hades' home, and it's special to him, so it's special to me too."

Zeus looked slightly nauseous for a moment, but Vesta nudged him none too gently in the ribs, and he replied, "Yes, I see. Well then, let's take a look."

Vesta had no idea what was going on. Hebe's note had just told her that there was an emergency and she had to bring Zeus to the Underworld. She looked over at Hebe quizzically who winked at her and indicated the door with the slightest tilt of her head.

"Yes, let's go. I can't wait to see what you have planned!" Vesta took Zeus by the arm and they all traipsed from Hades' office.

"Follow me," said Hades. "We'll take the lift; it will be quicker."

The lift was a surprisingly modern affair in glass and steel, quite at odds with the black marble that seemed to cover the vast majority of the Underworld.

"Oh look, there's Charon." Vesta waved at the Ferryman who wiggled his fingers at her in greeting.

"What the hell is he wearing?" Zeus had his nose pressed against the glass wall of the lift as it plummeted downwards. "Where is his loincloth?"

"Oh Zeus," laughed Vesta, "you're so behind the times. I think he looks lovely."

Zeus was not impressed. "Gods should not wear pink," he muttered huffily.

The lift finally halted, and they all walked out into a vast blackness. The air had a thick, syrupy quality, and the only sound was the occasional scream or moan from the dead who resided there. Hades turned to Zeus.

"Now, I know it doesn't look much at the moment, but you have to imagine it with thousands of fairy lights, white silk chairs and arches with flower garlands." As he spoke, the dark cavern was illuminated and transformed into a beautiful, if somewhat macabre, wedding venue. The gods and goddesses looked around.

"I love it, it's perfect!" Pan was clapping his hands with glee; he had completely forgotten their reason for being there.

Hades was delighted. "Do you really?"

"Hades it's wonderful." Vesta and Hebe were looking around in wonder.

"Can I go now?" Zeus had taken one quick look, and for him, that was enough. He was a great fan of honeymoons but couldn't stand weddings, having borne the cost of seven of them.

Hades and the others had been skipping around delightedly, but when they heard those words, they all stopped, the smiles sliding from their faces.

"Are you feeling all right Zeus?" Hades said smoothly, a lizard smile on his face.

"Yes, fine thanks, I've just got better things to do with my time, that's all." He turned to go back to the lift.

"Don't go just yet. I've just taken delivery of a rather fine human who was a very naughty girl before she came to us." Hades snapped his fingers. "Come human female and bow before the mighty Zeus."

A woman stepped out of the shadows. She had raven black hair that fell to her waist and wide, startling violet eyes with long sooty lashes. Her breasts were high, her waist narrow and her legs long and shapely. She wore a wisp of silk across her hips and had a hematite tiara on her head which glittered wickedly under the fairy lights. Zeus gasped audibly. It didn't matter one iota to him that the human was dead.

"Master," the woman smiled seductively at Zeus, and he stepped forward, planning on taking her in his arms there and then, but suddenly he stopped, a confused and worried expression on his face.

"What do you think Zeus? She's a stunner, isn't she? We can give you two some privacy, if you like." Pan winked at Zeus and leered conspiratorially; the expression did not come naturally to him as it once had.

Zeus didn't reply, he was staring at the stunning young woman, a look of deep concentration on his face.

"Zeus? Are you all right?" Vesta touched the god lightly on the arm, but still he didn't speak. She turned to Hades, looking for some sort of answer. She was shocked at the look on his face, he was positively malevolent. He snapped his fingers again, and the young woman turned and walked back into the shadows, her hips undulating provocatively.

"What's happening to me? Hades? What have you done?" Zeus grasped at Hades' wrist.

"Me? Nothing?" Hades replied innocently. "Why, whatever is wrong?"

"I....I...never happened before...," Zeus mumbled quietly, almost to himself.

Vesta once again touched Zeus on the arm, trying to get him to focus his attention. "Zeus, what is it? What's never happened before?" She wasn't in on the secret, and she was becoming increasingly worried. The great god was still muttering and wouldn't look at her. As a last resort, she slapped him smartly across the face. She expected him to roar and turn on her; instead, he began to cry. She took him in her arms and mouthed at Hades over the top of his head as Zeus cried on her shoulder. "What have you done?"

Hades just looked at her with a nasty, spiteful smile on his face. Pan and Hebe were also smiling, but they both looked a little sheepish. They hadn't expected Zeus to react in this way.

"It doesn't work," Zeus' muffled voice floated up from Vesta's shoulder. She spoke very softly and gently. "What doesn't work?"

"My….my……equipment. I saw that lovely young thing and …. nothing…." Zeus once again buried his head in Vesta's shoulder and sobbed. Vesta tried to comfort him and, at the same time, glared at Hades, sure that he was responsible for Zeus' current plight.

"Zeus, my dear brother, don't upset yourself so. We still have some 'Panacea' left at Number 23 in Brighton. With your permission, Pan and I will go back to the human realm and get some for you. The problem will be fixed in no time."

Zeus looked pitifully at Hades. "Are you sure it will work? Isn't it just for humans?"

Hades slipped his arm across Zeus' shoulder and pulled him away from Vesta's embrace. "I am quite sure. Right, Pan?"

Pan walked forward, a smile played around his lips, but his eyes were black and hard. "No doubt at all."

Zeus looked from one to the other. "Well what are you waiting for? You have my permission. Go back to the human world and get me some straight away."

"Of course, brother, there's just one little thing you need to do for me first," Hades said silkily.

"Fine. What do you want? A bigger wine budget for the wedding?" Zeus sneered slightly, a touch of his old belligerence coming back.

"No, no, Pan and I have all that in hand. What I want from you is something altogether different." Hades' hand tightened on his shoulder, and Zeus winced. "Get me back my dog. I know that Cerberus was taken, thanks to you. Do this one thing for me, and I'll make sure that your *equipment* will be as good as new."

"You bastard!" Vesta's hand shot out and she slapped Zeus across the face once again, but this time there was anger and real power behind it, and Zeus stumbled. "How could you?"

Realising that he'd been duped, Zeus hung his head. "It was a bet; you know I can't resist a flutter." He looked up and smiled grimly at Hades. "I don't know what you did to me, but you've proved your point; I'll get your damned dog back. He'll be waiting for you as soon as you return from the human realm."

"He'd better be. If not, our whole world will know of your little *problem*." Hades spat out the last word.

"You think they'd believe you, do you?" Zeus scoffed at him; his tears forgotten.

"They won't have to take my word for it, dearest brother, we captured it all on video." Hades' smile was cold and malicious. "That human girl had a camera hidden in her tiara. Quite clever, don't you think?"

Zeus' face screwed up in fury, and he launched himself at Hades, but Pan moved like lightning to protect his lover and punched Zeus squarely on the jaw. The ancient god went down, and as he lay on the cold, black floor, his humiliation was complete.

Two days later, Cerberus was back in the Underworld, and Zeus was trying out 'Panacea' much to the delight of his seven wives and numerous mistresses.


**Chapter 30**

"I can't believe it's your wedding day. Truly, I am delighted for you both." Janus hugged first Hades and then Pan. He had been forgiven for dragging them all away from Number 23 and would be conducting the wedding ceremony. Vesta and Hebe had been asked to be "best goddesses."

"Thank you, Janus. We appreciate it and thanks again for agreeing to conduct the ceremony," Hades was humble in his gratitude, but he was showing a level of self-confidence that the others had never seen before, and it all stemmed from his love of Pan.

"Are you two ready?" Hebe had walked in with Vesta and they both looked stunning. The happy couple had asked that everyone attending discard their traditional togas for the day and create something elegant and fashionable, and the goddesses had risen to the challenge. Hebe's gown looked as though it were made from moonlight. (It wasn't but she had used moonlight to, as she put it, "jazz up" the delicate silk.) It was high necked in the front and then plunged almost indecently low in the back. Vesta, on the other hand, had decided on a deep red and orange velvet gown which gave the illusions of flames licking at her body. (There were certain old habits she just couldn't let go.) Since they had been back, Hebe had been insisting that they exercise every day, and Vesta now had the figure of a super model rather than a frumpy housewife.

"Oh, you look absolutely gorgeous! I could eat you!" Pan clapped his hands with delight.

"Us? What about you two? Those suits are incredible." Hades was wearing a suit of midnight black, that seemed to glow with a dark light and his lapels were covered with thousands of tiny fireflies (it had taken him ages to get them all well-trained enough that they'd sit still). Pan's suit was brilliant white and crackled with energy as he moved (he'd asked Saturn to pinch one of Zeus' lightning bolts and then crushed into thousands of pieces which were then applied to the suit. Both of them were wearing open-necked, pink shirts made of silk.

Janus announced that it was time for them to go and they all made their way to the shore where Charon, or Sharon as he preferred to be called now, was waiting for them. His boat was sparkling clean and bedecked with black and white ribbons. Pan and Hades' guests were all seated, waiting for them. Zeus, as usual, was moaning to Saturn. He couldn't decide which one of his wives or mistresses he wanted to bring with him, so he'd left them all at home and was hoping to meet someone new at the reception.

"I can't believe he charged us, and what is he wearing?" Zeus shook his head in disbelief as he looked at Sharon in his short shorts and pink shirt that he'd tied under his chest.

Saturn was not in the mood to put up with Zeus' complaints. His wife, Ops, had refused to come to the wedding as he wouldn't buy her another new gown, and now he was stuck with Zeus.

"Of course, he charged us; we're crossing the bloody Styx. Everyone has to pay, and you damn well know it, so stop moaning. As for what Sharon's wearing, he looks happy which is all that matters and is more than we can say for you!"

"All right, there's no need to get all snotty about it. Did you bring any wine with you?" Zeus looked hopeful.

"No! You can wait until you get to the reception, I don't want you getting pissed and ruining the ceremony."

Aphrodite was sitting next to Zeus with her husband Hephaestus.

"Will you two please stop bickering? This day is about Pan and Hades and their marriage. This should be a special day and all about love, not who brought the wine or who's wearing what."

"Shame, you didn't think like that when we got married. If I remember rightly, you sloped off with Poseidon half-way through the reception; we hadn't even cut the bloody cake!" Hephaestus hissed in a whisper.

Aphrodite was unrepentant. "What could I do, my darling? You've seen the size of his trident." She touched the tip of her tongue to her top lip and then smirked.

"You are shameless, I don't know why I ever married you."

"Of course you do, my darling." She put one hand on either side of her face. "You married me for this. That and my beautiful body." She looked directly into Hephaestus' eyes and laughed.

"You are beautiful on the outside and ugly on the inside; if the reverse were true, our marriage might have been a happy one," Hephaestus spoke with quiet dignity.

Aphrodite was shocked; no god or man had ever spoken to her like that. She had always naturally assumed that her face and figure would be enough to keep someone tied to her for as long as she wanted them around. She looked at her long-suffering husband with newfound respect. "Perhaps I should show him a good time tonight," she thought to herself. She put her hand lightly on Hephaestus' arm, but he shrugged her off and turned his back on her so that he could talk to Zeus. He wasn't usually one for small talk, but he knew that if he got onto the subject of wine or wood nymphs, the conversation would run long enough for them to get to the reception without him having to acknowledge his wife again.

Several minutes later, he was half listening to a diatribe from Zeus on the best way to entrap a wood nymph, when the wedding party climbed onto the boat. His eye was immediately drawn to Vesta. He had always worked in the forge; it was the place that he felt most at peace, and the flames on her dress ignited something in him. He looked at her face which was beautifully made up and radiant with happiness, and he made the decision, there and then, to seek her out at the reception.

When Pan and Hades boarded, Sharon started a rousing chorus of "Here come the grooms," and all the gods and goddesses got to their feet and clapped. The two gods raised their arms above their heads in salute and Pan yelled at the top of his voice, "Let's get this party started!" The moment was slightly ruined because Sharon pushed away from the bank with uncustomary vigour and Pan lost his balance and fell on the deck in a heap. Fortunately, Sharon had been so meticulous with his cleaning of the boat that Pan's white suit didn't have a mark on it when he clambered to his feet, looking slightly sheepish. All their guests laughed and cheered, and everyone was in high spirits by the time that they arrived in the Underworld. Hades had insisted that the dead not be excluded from helping out with the wedding, so he'd recruited several dozen of them to transport his guests to Tartarus in rikshaws. Once all the gods and goddesses were loaded, the dead took off at a run; Pan, Hades, Janus, Hebe and Vesta took the glass lift and arrived ahead of everyone else.

"Hades, it's wonderful! What a transformation!" Hebe was looking delightedly at the millions of tiny, sparkling lights that had transformed the dark and gloomy halls. There was billowing white silk and chiffon everywhere they looked, and there was a beautiful melody playing. It was both opulent and intimate. "What is that music? I've never heard anything like it."

"I told the tortured souls they could have the day off provided they formed an orchestra and a choir. I also gave them a couple of afternoons off so they could practice." Hades had the air of someone who thought he was being incredibly generous.

"A couple of afternoons? How did they manage to create such a wonderful sound in such a short period of time?" Vesta was amazed.

"Think about it. You're destined to be tortured for all eternity and someone tells you it will stop for the day provided you learn to sing and play musical instruments; you'd make damn sure you learned fast, wouldn't you?" Hades considered himself to be a great motivator.

"Isn't he wonderful?" Pan wrapped his arms around Hades and hugged him close. The others smiled indulgently; it was their wedding day after all, but secretly, they were all slightly uncomfortable. Gods and goddesses tended to be very open-minded about sex and were very courtly in their behaviour, but real love was a bit of a mystery to them.

"I don't care if you're already in purgatory, you'll really have something to cry about if I get my hands on you!" Zeus' voice boomed in the cavernous space as he hurtled past Pan and Hades, sandals flapping wildly. Saturn climbed down from his rickshaw and strolled over to join the wedding party.

"What happened?" Janus asked.

"He kept yelling at his rickshaw driver to go faster, so he did but then he overcooked it on one of the bends, and Zeus fell out. As you can see, he's not happy." Saturn, on the other hand, was obviously delighted.

"Oh Saturn, please can you go and fetch him?" Hades begged. "I promised the dead that there'd be no torture today, and I can't let Zeus break my word."

"Oh all right." Saturn shrugged and wandered off in search of Zeus who could still be heard yelling profanities at the dead rickshaw driver.

The rest of the wedding guests had assembled in the great hall and taken their seats on the huge, white thrones that had been provided for everyone. Janus spotted Saturn, dragging a still struggling and cursing Zeus by the scruff of his neck. As they reached the thrones in the front row, he slammed Zeus into his seat and told him to stop behaving like a spoilt child. Zeus was rummaging around in his robe looking for a spare lightning bolt and glaring murderously at Saturn.

"Gods and Goddesses," Janus' deep, clear voice carried across the hall. "Please be silent for the arrival of the groom and….the other groom." With that he walked between the two rows of chairs and he took up his place under a great arch on which thousands of white butterflies waited patiently.

"It's time." Hebe held out her arm to Hades, and Vesta held hers out to Pan. Watched by all their guests, they slowly walked down the makeshift aisle as the dead choir sang a spirited version of "Just Say Yes" by Snow Patrol. (Pan and Hades had discovered a shared love of human pop music.)

"This hardly seems appropriate music for a celestial wedding, who wrote this rubbish?" Zeus said under his breath.

"If you don't be quiet, I am going to dedicate myself to finding your supply of 'Panacea' and pouring it into the Styx. Do I make myself clear?" Word had spread. Zeus blanched and nodded vigorously, turning his attention to the happy couple as they stood in front of Janus. Vesta and Hebe kissed the gods' cheeks and then took their seats beside Saturn and Zeus.

"Dear fellow deities, we are here today to join this god and this god in celestial matrimony. Can I ask you all please to stand as Pan and Hades prepare to take their vows?" The gods and goddesses rose with much shuffling of feet and one, muffled coughing fit. It is universally acknowledged that coughing fits are most likely to arrive when there is a need for absolute silence.

"Do you Hades take Pan to be your husband, to love him and honour him, forsaking all others for as long as you both agree that it's the right thing for you both?" (Gods do not get sick and are immortal so that was the best Janus could come up with, based on what he'd seen on TV when they were in Brighton.)

Hades looked deep into Pan's eyes and smiled. "I do."

"Do you Pan, take Hades to be your husband, to love him and honour him, forsaking *all* others, including goats, for as long as you both agree that it's the right thing for you both?"

Pan reached out and took Hades' hands in his before saying, very solemnly, "I do."

Janus looked to Hebe, "Do we have the rings?"

Hebe rose from her seat and walked elegantly over to Janus to the sound of several appreciative murmurs. She handed two rings to Janus. One was encrusted with black diamonds that glinted wickedly and the other with pink diamonds that glowed with subtle fire. Janus handed the ring with the black diamonds to Pan and said: "Repeat after me. I Pan, take you Hades to be my husband, I promise to love you and share my life with you for as long as it suits us both."

Pan repeated the words and slid the ring onto Hades' finger. It was then Hades' turn; he spoke quietly but with a joy in his voice as he put the ring on Pan's finger.

"By virtue of the authority vested in me by Zeus, I now pronounce you husband and husband. You may kiss…..but no tongues." Living in Brighton had broadened Janus' horizons, but he was still a puritan at heart.

The two gods laughed and kissed very chastely to tumultuous applause from their guests.

"Where have they put the wine? I'm parched?" Zeus' voice carried over the noise of the applause and there were several raised eyebrows and a number of disapproving mutterings but Pan and Hades just laughed.

"He's right! Come on everyone, follow us, and let's go and have some fun." Pan led Hades from the vast main chamber into a smaller area, curtained off by white silk. There was a space for dancing, a vast buffet containing every delicious food imaginable, pots of chilled ambrosia and wine by the case.

"Now that's what I'm talking about," Zeus yelled delightedly, helping himself to a turkey leg and a bottle of Chardonnay.

Soon, all the gods and goddesses were busy gorging on ambrosia and wine and enjoying themselves enormously.

"Everyone, can I have your attention please?" Janus yelled over the noise of the assembled crowd. "It's now time for Hades' and Pan's first dance as husband and husband."

Pan led a self-conscious and blushing Hades to the dance floor. They entwined and moved slowly to the choir of the dead's rendition of "A Thousand Years." Everyone clapped and then the music changed to "Stayin' Alive" and all the gods and goddesses took to the dance floor; Janus did a very passable John Travolta impression.

Vesta, flushed from dancing, had moved to the side of the chamber and was helping herself to a glass of champagne when she heard a dark voice behind her.

"Hello, Vesta."

She turned sharply. Hephaestus was standing before her with a shy smile on his face. "You look quite beautiful today; your dress reminds me of the fire in my forge just before it begins to cool."

Vesta wasn't used to being chatted up and wasn't quite sure how to respond, but she could feel a smile creep to her lips and her cheeks began to glow. "That's inordinately kind, Hephaestus, thank you. Where's Aphrodite, is she not with you?"

"Oh she's about somewhere I think." He looked around the chamber disinterestedly. "She's over there." He pointed to his wife who had wrapped herself around the handsome Apollo under the pretext of dancing. Vesta looked over to where Hephaestus was pointing. "Don't you mind?" she asked quietly.

He looked thoughtful for a moment. "I used to, but to be honest, at this precise moment, I'd far rather be dancing with you than with her." He held his hand out to Vesta.

"But you're married." Vesta was confused. For her, Hephaestus was an extremely attractive god, and his connection to fire and the forge made him even more so, but he wasn't free. Hephaestus hadn't lowered his hand, and he was looking at her with such admiration in his eyes that Vesta couldn't help herself; she took his hand, and he led her onto the dance floor.

He was very respectful, carefully placing his hand on her waist and guiding hers to his shoulder, but as the song continued, he gradually drew her closer.

"Do you know, I've often admired you Vesta? I always had the impression that you were a goddess filled with great kindness and patience. I suppose that you learned that during the many years you spent with your virgins." Hephaestus was surprised to hear Vesta chuckle at his comment.

"I probably had that air because, when I had the chance to venture out and meet up with all the gods and goddesses, I was so bloody happy to have escaped the confines of the temple. Honestly, you have no idea how tedious it was. Although, to be fair, I had no real idea how tedious it was until I spent that time with the humans. Their lives are so short that they seem to want to fill them with as much as possible. It really brought it home to me that the years and years I spent in the temple were just wasted." Vesta looked up into Hephaestus' deep brown eyes. "Sorry, I'm talking too much. Tell me what's going on with you and Aphrodite. I always assumed that you two were happy together; she's so incredibly beautiful."

Hephaestus wasn't usually one to share, but he felt strangely comfortable with Vesta and was soon telling her all about the affairs that Aphrodite had had over the years and how the pain and humiliation had forced him to retreat inside himself.

"So now, I just spend all my time at the forge and take my frustrations out on the metal. Beating the crap out of something with a hammer really takes the edge off." He hesitated. "Sorry Vesta, I didn't mean to burden you with all my problems."

"That's all right; it's good to talk. The humans have a saying, 'a problem shared is a problem halved,' and I think that they may be right. Also, I can completely understand your sense of isolation. I felt that way for many years, hundreds of years." Vesta pressed herself against Hephaestus' broad chest and inhaled the scent of him. Her phallic flame had served her well over the years, but there was nothing like a good hug.

"And now? How do you feel now, at this moment?" Hephaestus' eyes bored into hers, and she felt a fluttering in her stomach that was new and not entirely unwelcome. "I feel….I feel…..not alone."

So intensely involved were they in each other that they hadn't noticed that they were slow dancing to "Living on a Prayer" and were almost knocked over by a drunken Zeus as he waved his arms over his head singing, "Oh yeah we're halfway there" over and over again.

"Shall we go and see if we can find somewhere quieter?" Vesta asked.

"Gladly." Hephaestus took her hand and they wandered away from the wedding reception and the noise of the gods and goddesses celebrating. They walked for a little while and then, suddenly, Hephaestus pulled her into a shadowed alcove. He wrapped his arms around her and bent his head, his mouth slightly open. Before his lips could reach hers, they heard peals of drunk, feminine laughter, and then "Are you taking me into the darkness, Apollo?" The lecherous response quickly followed, "I'll be *taking* you in the darkness."

Vesta could feel Hephaestus' body tense as Aphrodite and Apollo passed by their little alcove, quite unaware that they'd been seen. She spoke almost to herself. "The humans have something called 'divorce' for when their relationships break down. They go before a court and explain why their marriage has failed and then the judge grants their divorce and they are, once again, single and free to start new relationships….or not….you know..um." Vesta blushed, thankful that the shadows would hide her flushed cheeks.

Hephaestus looked thoughtful for a moment. "So I would get to stand before everyone and tell them why I don't want to be married to Aphrodite anymore?" His voice was hopeful.

"I don't think that you would be able to stand up before everyone, but you could ask Zeus to convene a court of twelve senior gods and goddesses, and they would then hear your case. Either that or you could just tell Aphrodite that you've had enough and leave. I mean that's what we normally do, isn't it." As immortal beings, the gods and goddesses often got fed up with each other, and it was extremely common for gods to move from wife to wife or mistress to mistress. As the goddesses were rarely independently wealthy, most of them just chose to put up with it; there was no such thing as a formal arrangement.

"I want people to know, and I want to hurt her as much as she has hurt me; what better way to do it than to shame her in public?" Hephaestus looked angry and Vesta regretted having raised the subject of divorce.

"Look, just think about it for a little while. You don't want to rush into anything that you might regret. You've spent so many years together." Vesta was trying desperately to calm him down in the hope that they might capture the intimate moment they'd shared earlier. Having seen Aphrodite's behaviour first-hand, she was less inclined to feel guilty about her almost kiss with Hephaestus.

"Yes, we've spent millennia together and she's been unfaithful for millennia which is probably why I am so utterly sick of the sight of her. As for rushing into things, that's something I should do more often. It's most unlike me to approach a goddess as I did with you tonight, but it's the best decision that I've made in a long time." He took Vesta's face between his large, strong hands and bent his head so that he could kiss her. She wrapped her arms around his neck and the kiss went on for a long, long time; even the drunk and raucous laughter that surrounded them didn't register.

Zeus had been having a marvellous time and was almost insensible with drink. Someone had started a conga line, and as it snaked past him, he noticed a delectable bottom in a pair of extremely short shorts, and he quickly grabbed the owner's waist.

"La, la, la, la, la, kick!" Zeus yelled as they took a tour of one of the vast buffet tables. Unfortunately, Adephagia, goddess of gluttony, couldn't resist the temptation to stop and make a quick turkey sandwich and half the conga line careened into each other. Zeus found himself sandwiched between the pair of short shorts and Poseidon (he didn't need to look round to know who it was, the smell of fish was unmistakable). Zeus was naturally lecherous, and the amount of wine he'd imbibed had robbed him of the few inhibitions that he had. He took the opportunity to run his hands over the delightfully high bottom in front of him.

"Is that a lightning bolt in my pocket or am I just pleased to see you?" he slurred into the ear that was resting deliciously close to his mouth.

"What kind of girl do you think I am?" Sharon dragged herself round, drew back her meaty fist and smacked Zeus straight between the eyes. Drunk as he was, he toppled backwards, out cold, and landed on top of Poseidon who did not take it at all well. "Will someone get this drunken oaf off me!"

A small fight had broken out, and Pan and Hades decided that it was time to call it a night. After one last dance, to "Beautiful" by James Blunt the gods and goddesses went home, and they all agreed that it had been a remarkably successful party. Hades decided that the dead could clean up the following morning, as part of their daily torture, so, he and Pan took themselves off to his vast bedchamber, arms around each other. Both were happier than they could ever remember being.

## Chapter 31

The following morning, Hebe was out walking. She was uncharacteristically glum. Although she'd enjoyed Pan's and Hades' wedding celebrations, she'd felt strangely lonely. When they were all in Brighton, she'd been admired wherever she went. She was irresistible to human men, but back home, she was just another beautiful goddess. She had danced with a few of the gods and been propositioned by several more, but for her, it held no excitement. She was so deep in thought that she failed to hear the sound of hoofbeats rapidly approaching.

"Good morning, lady!" The deep voice stirred her from her dark reverie, and she looked up to see an enormous black stallion standing before her, and on his back, was Heracles. Suddenly, she was furious.

"Don't good morning me you heartless bastard! Do you know what you did to Hades when you took Cerberus?" She put her hands on her hips and yelled at him. "Well? Do you?"

Heracles looked taken aback; such was his imposing strength that he was unused to anyone confronting him, much less a beautiful, if clearly very angry, goddess. He tried to maintain his dignity, but his efforts were hampered by his powerful horse taking him unawares and trotting off towards a particularly tasty looking bank of grass. Heracles almost lost his balance and was thrown forward across the stallion's neck.

"Bugger! Dobbin, stop messing about." He tugged at the horse's reins, but Dobbin had decided he was hungry and refused to move. Dismounting with what he hoped was a nonchalant air, Heracles looped the reins over a tree branch and walked over to join Hebe who was trying very hard to maintain her stern expression.

"Dobbin? Seriously? For that beast?" Dobbin stopped munching for a moment and looked balefully at Hebe before turning back to the lush grass.

Heracles cheeks flushed. "It was the name of the first pony I had when I was a human child."

"Oh yes, I had forgotten that you were human until you became Zeus' bitch and broke Hades' heart." Hebe's anger was back.

"I didn't become Zeus' bitch; it was Eurystheus who set me the tasks." Heracles flared, "And, for your information, I didn't hurt Cerberus. We had a wrestling match and I won, that's all. I took him from the Underworld, yes, but on the journey back, we got really close; he's actually a rather sweet dog. I would never do anything to hurt him."

Hebe relented slightly, hearing that Heracles had bonded with Hades' precious pet. "But what about Hades? He was distraught."

Heracles was standing on his dignity, annoyed that Hebe obviously thought so little of him, but with this comment his shoulders sagged, and he sighed deeply. "Look, I was upset when I found out how badly he'd taken it, and I begged Zeus to allow me to return Cerberus to the Underworld, but you know what he's like. For what it's worth, in my opinion, he completely deserved his punishment. Listen, I know that you're angry with me, but can we start again, please? I've been thinking about you ever since we came back on the boat, and you and the other goddesses were waiting for us on the shore. My brother gods were miffed that you made such fools of them, but I thought you showed real pluck." He smiled at the memory and his face lit up.

"He really is very attractive when he smiles," Hebe thought to herself. "Very well. I'm Hebe." She held out her hand expecting the god to shake it; instead, he bowed low and kissed the very tips of her fingers. A shiver went through Hebe's body. "Oh, bloody hell," she thought.

As Hebe and Heracles were getting to know each other, her sister goddess, Vesta, and Hephaestus were preparing for his hearing in front of twelve of the most ancient gods and goddesses. She had been unable to sway him from his chosen path, so she decided, instead, to support him. It had also presented her with an opportunity to promote equality for goddesses. When she and Hephaestus had approached Zeus with the idea, he had reluctantly agreed. "I can convene a court of the gods if that's what you want, but don't make a big deal about it. If you cut into my drinking time, I'm likely to find against you."

Hephaestus opened his mouth to thank Zeus, but Vesta got there first. "What do you mean 'a court of the gods'? Why not a court of gods and goddesses? A court is supposed to be representative of our society."

"That might be the case for the humans, but we do things differently," Zeus dismissed her with a wave of his hand.

However, Vesta was not to be dismissed, she grabbed Zeus' arm as he turned away from them and spun him around so that he was, once again, facing her.

"Don't you dare walk away from me when I'm talking to you! Just because we've always done something a certain way doesn't mean to say that we can't change. Human women fought for years to defeat the patriarchy while we goddesses have just accepted your dictates! Well not any more, buster. Things are changing around here, and it's about time that you changed with them. The court will be made up of six gods and six goddesses; do I make myself clear?"

Such was the force of Vesta's passion that Zeus was too taken aback to even consider launching a lightning bolt at her.

"And, what's more, you will allow those goddesses to have a voice and not just shout them down the way that you normally do. Got it?" Vesta poked Zeus in the chest.

"Now, look here missy, you can't talk to me like that," Zeus blustered.

"I can and I did. Just make sure you convene the court as I've suggested, or I and the other goddesses will dedicate ourselves to finding ways to make your life extremely difficult. Sisters stick together! Come on Hephaestus." With that, she walked away leaving a very bemused Zeus wondering what had just happened. Hephaestus gave Zeus a sheepish half-grin, shrugged his shoulders helplessly and hurried off after Vesta like a lost puppy.

Several days later, a court of six gods and six goddesses was convened for the purpose of considering a divorce between Hephaestus and Aphrodite. Someone had given Zeus a gavel and he was banging it enthusiastically on the heavy granite table in front of him even though nobody had spoken.

"Right, come on, let's get on with it. Why are we here? Hephaestus make your case."

Hephaestus gave Vesta's hand a quick squeeze and then rose to his feet. "Thank you, Zeus and honourable gods and goddesses. I am here today to request a divorce from my wife, Aphrodite, on the grounds of her habitual unreasonable behaviour...."

"What's he saying? Speak up, lad!" Uranus was the most ancient god on the panel, and his hearing was not what it used to be. He was a crusty, bad-tempered god who was well-known for his dislike of the young, presumably because they were enjoying all that he no longer could. Immortality was all very well, but in some cases, it just meant that you were old for an extremely long time.

Hephaestus looked flustered for a moment but then repeated his request in a booming voice that echoed around the impromptu courtroom.

"All right, lad; no need to shout! Now, what's divorce?" Uranus was becoming irritable, like all gods, he really hated it when he had to admit he didn't know something. Zeus leaned in and quickly explained the concept of a divorce.

"But why the bloody hell are *we* all here?" Uranus complained loudly. "If he doesn't want this wife," he waved his hand vaguely at Aphrodite, "and, frankly, I can't see why he wouldn't, why doesn't he just get another one?" Zeus leaned over again and began speaking rapidly.

"What do you mean it's a human thing? We're not humans!" Uranus yelled, furious. There was more muttering from Zeus.

"What do you mean you explained it all yesterday? I don't remember……a case of wine? Oh, yes I remember that…..in exchange for this? Yes, yes, all right but if I nod off, don't blame me." With that Uranus sat back and closed his eyes. Zeus cursed under his breath and instructed Hephaestus to present his case.

"Thank you, Zeus. The reason I am asking for this divorce is to make it known publicly that my wife, Aphrodite, has shamed me and herself by consorting with other gods with complete disregard for my feelings."

Eros, god of love and sex, leaned forward eagerly. "When you say 'consorting,' what do you mean exactly? Can you give us more details?" All the other gods also leaned forward.

"Stop that, Eros!" Nemesis, goddess of retribution, leaned across and slapped Eros smartly on the back of the head. "We are not here to listen to salacious gossip; we are here to determine whether Hephaestus has just cause to divorce Aphrodite."

"Well how am I supposed to determine that without knowing exactly what she's done to get him so riled up?" Eros rubbed the back of his head, looking hurt.

"Use your imagination!" Nemesis snapped.

"I knew I shouldn't have let the goddesses join in," Zeus muttered under his breath.

"What was that Zeus?" Nemesis raised her hand threateningly. In it was a small leather handbag that looked suspiciously like it was crammed with rocks.

"Nothing." Zeus said quickly. "Right. So, we've established that Aphrodite was unfaithful, and Hephaestus is not happy and wants a divorce. What have you got to say for yourself, Aphrodite?"

Aphrodite lounged languorously in her chair, a faint smirk on her face. She had continued her affair with Apollo and was more than satisfied with his performance. "I took my pleasures as we all do, and my dear husband had the right to do exactly the same thing, but he preferred to spend his time beating out his frustrations in the forge. All the time that he was working, I was neglected." She affected an air of hurt, but honestly, none of the other gods and goddesses were fooled.

"So, you don't think that Hephaestus should have the right to divorce you?" Zeus asked.

"Oh, I don't really care what he does; he can divorce me if he wants to. I have plenty of other *friends* to keep me company." Aphrodite turned to smile at Apollo who was sitting behind her.

Zeus banged down his gavel. "Good, well, that's that sorted. Aphrodite pack your things and be out of the villa by morning, and don't take anything that's not yours. Don't look at me like that; you know exactly what I mean. Don't think I didn't notice my stash of ambrosia going down after your visits," Zeus tutted as he got to his feet.

"But where will I go?" Aphrodite cried. She hadn't realised the full implications of agreeing to a divorce.

"Not my problem. Divorce granted. Hearing over." Zeus banged his gavel once again. "Fancy a glass of wine, Eros."

"What?"

"I said…..oh never mind." Zeus made a dash for the door.

Hephaestus gave an audible sigh of relief. "I can't believe it's over. After all this time, I am finally free of that cheating goddess."

Vesta took his hand in hers. "Do you have any regrets?"

"None at all. My future is looking much brighter with her out of it," he kissed her lightly on the lips, "and you in it."

"You bloody hypocrite!" Aphrodite's voice carried across the chamber. "You weren't *hurt* by me at all; you just wanted out of the marriage, so you could hook up with that simpering virgin." She looked at Vesta disdainfully.

Vesta immediately flared up. "Who are you calling a virgin?"

Hephaestus stepped in front of her and stood face to face with Aphrodite. "I did love you once, very much, but each one of your affairs chipped away at that love, and little by little, it died. I divorced you because I want to be happy, and I want to love. I can't do either of those things with you, and if you're honest, you'll admit that you feel the same way. We were not good together, Aphrodite, you know that. Go and be with Apollo, I think he will make a far better mate for you than I ever could."

He was surprised to see a single tear glistening in the corner of Aphrodite's eye. "My love for you did not die, Hephaestus, I just have so much love to give that one god is not enough for me. I hope you will be happy, and Vesta, take care of him. He has a good heart." With that she turned and walked away, taking Apollo's hand as she passed by him.

"Well I'll be damned! I did *not* see that coming!" Vesta came out from behind Hephaestus and stared at the rapidly departing Aphrodite.

"No," said Hephaestus thoughtfully "neither did I. I always thought that she messed around with the other gods just to hurt me, but now I'm not so sure. I just hope that she'll find happiness."

"Well, if Apollo has as much stamina as everyone says, then I'm sure she will." Vesta looked up at Hephaestus from under her eyelashes, a wicked little smile playing around her lips. For a brief moment he looked a little shocked but then burst out laughing.

"I think you and I will rub along together very nicely Vesta."

## Chapter 32

"I don't want to meet him. He stole my dog. He's mean!" Hades had his arms folded tightly across his chest, and his lips were pursed.

"Yes, I know he did, but look, Cerberus is fine, isn't he?" Pan gingerly patted the dog on each of its three heads. He was genuinely fond of the animal, but the week before, Cerberus had, in a gesture of affection, jumped up, putting his paws on Pan's shoulders. He was trapped under the slobbering dog for at least 20 minutes before Hades came to rescue him.

"Of course, he's fine. He's with me…I mean us but seeing Heracles again could set off post-traumatic stress; he's very sensitive you know." Hades bent down and hugged the great beast.

Pan was not convinced; he had personally seen Cerberus terrorise the dead when they tried to leave Tartarus, and it had not been pretty. "Listen to me, I spoke to Hebe, and she said that Heracles and Cerberus really bonded. I think he'd be pleased to see him again."

Hades jumped up. "So, he was trying to steal my dog's affection, was he? What a conniving git! I tell you Pan; he is not welcome here. I will not have that god in my home! He. Stole. My. Dog." Hades' voice rose to a screech which frightened the living daylights out of poor Cerberus who took shelter behind the sofa.

Pan sighed, "I'm sorry about this, Hades."

"Sorry about what?" Hades felt a stinging slap across his face. "Ow! What did you do that for?"

"You were getting hysterical," said Pan calmly. "Cerberus is perfectly fine; he's a three headed giant dog who's perfectly able to take care of himself. Hebe has been like a sister to us, and she has found love with Heracles, so we owe it to her to make him feel welcome. Now, why don't we have a nice cup of chamomile tea, and we can work out what we're going to wear. There's that beautiful gossamer shirt I had made for you that you haven't worn yet." Pan nudged Hades playfully. "You know how sexy you'll look in it."

Hades gave a little giggle and allowed Pan to lead him to their vast wardrobe. "All right, he can come, but he's not getting a drink."

"OK, fair enough." Pan sighed. Much as he loved him, Hades sometimes got on his last nerve. Even so, they spent a happy couple of hours trying on outfits and practising their catwalks.

"Will you stop fidgeting?" Hebe snapped at Heracles as they waited, at the shore of the Styx for Sharon to arrive with the boat.

"I can't help it; I'm nervous. What if Hades takes a swing at me? What if he takes me to Tartarus and won't let me leave? What if he sets the dog on me?" Heracles was nervously twisting the bottom of the shirt that Hebe had insisted he wear; it was blue with a fine, pale pink stripe and she'd paired it with some figure-hugging jeans. She didn't want Heracles to overshadow Hades or Pan, but she knew that they appreciated a well-dressed man.

"You'll be fine. Honestly, Hades is lovely once you get to know him; you'll just need to give him a little time, that's all. Oh look, there's Sharon." Hebe waved enthusiastically as the boat hove into view.

As soon as the boat came to a standstill on the sand, Hebe and Heracles climbed in. Hebe gave Sharon a hug. "You look wonderful, is that new?"

Sharon was delighted. "It is, I made the shirt myself." The shirt in question was white linen; it had a high collar and was slashed to the waist. Sharon had teamed it with a pair of lemon yellow, skin-tight, capri trousers that left little to the imagination. Heracles briefly shook Sharon's hand and then averted his gaze. He'd heard about the dour and silent Charon from some of the other gods, and he wasn't quite prepared for the ferryman. He was also not prepared for the appraising looks; he quickly crossed his legs and put his arm around Hebe.

"Will you calm down!" Hebe nudged him in the ribs. "So, how have you been, Sharon?"

"Can't complain." Sharon steered the boat out into the black waters of the Styx. "Hades has been a much better boss since Pan came on the scene. He even gave me this for ferrying all the guests across for his wedding." Sharon held up his wrist to show Hebe a bracelet made of tiny, black shrunken skulls that looked suspiciously real.

"Um.....lovely," Hebe wasn't quite sure how to respond. "It really suits you." She and Sharon chatted about fashion for the remainder of the crossing while Heracles chewed nervously at his thumb nail. As soon as the boat docked, Heracles jumped to his feet and strode off the boat, holding his hand out to Hebe. "Thanks Sharon, nice to meet you," he said politely.

"Nice to meet you too, big boy." Sharon gave him an exaggerated wink before turning to Hebe. "See you later love, have a good time, and say hi-di-hi to the boys for me." They hugged once more and then Hebe jumped gracefully from the boat and joined Heracles. As they made their way along the dock Heracles bent his head and whispered in Hebe's ear. "I thought the boatman of the Styx was supposed to be grim and imposing. I really thought the capri pants took away from the gravity of his position."

Hebe turned on him sharply. "Sharon has found *her* true self, and *she's* much happier for it! Now, come on, we don't want to be late."

They took the lift down to Hades' chambers, and as soon as the doors opened, they saw him and Pan waiting to greet them. Hebe rushed forward and pulled them both into a tight hug before waving to Heracles to come and join them. He walked over stiffly.

"Hades, before I say anything else, I must formally apologise to you for taking Cerberus. It was unforgivable to take such a beautiful and sensitive creature from his true master, and I am deeply sorry for any distress that I caused you or him."

Hades said nothing for a moment as he weighed the sincerity of the apology, but then his face broke into a broad and genuine smile. "He is sensitive, isn't he? I was just saying that exact thing to Pan earlier. Everyone thinks that he's such a beast, but he's an old soppy really." He put his arm across Heracles' shoulders. "Welcome to the Underworld, my boy. Why don't we all go and have a drink and some lunch. The dead have prepared some lovely finger sandwiches for us, and afterwards, we can have petit fours with coffee." They strode ahead, leaving Pan and Hebe to follow in their wake.

"Well, that went well. You've picked a good one there, Hebe. He seems very genuine." Pan linked his arm through Hebe's. "He's got a lovely arse too!" He laughed uproariously as Hebe slapped his arm and then giggled, "He has, hasn't he?"

**Chapter 33**

Some months later, all the gods and goddesses were once again back in the Underworld, this time to celebrate the marriages of Hebe to Heracles and Vesta to Hephaestus. It had become *the* venue after Pan and Hades' wedding, and the two gods now had a successful events business. The dead put up decorations, organised food and waited on tables; it turned out that, after all the hype, death was actually quite boring, so they were happy to have something to do.

"You two look absolutely stunning! Those dresses are *everything*!" Hades clapped his hands delightedly as Hebe and Vesta twirled in front of him. They were both wearing gowns of white organza, with tight bodices and long trains, and both had diamond tiaras tucked into their elegant up-dos. "The boys are going to just *die* when they see you!"

Pan added, "He's right. I have never seen the two of you looking so gorgeous; if I didn't have Hades, I could make a play for you myself." The famous leer curled his lip, but they all knew that it was just for effect; he had eyes for no-one but Hades.

Janus was conducting the marriage ceremony again, and he walked over to join the other four.

"Nice to see that you've played down the fashion a bit, we don't want you overshadowing the brides." Pan and Hades were both wearing severely cut, dark grey suits with white shirts and plain pink ties. At Janus' words they unbuttoned their jackets to reveal the linings; they were deep fuchsia pink and the inside pockets were picked out in diamantes. Pan laughed at Janus' expression.

"Don't worry, we'll keep them buttoned up until after the ceremony."

Janus rolled his eyes at the pair's extravagant taste before settling his gaze on the two brides.

"You both look quite ravishing. Are you ready?"

Vesta and Hebe looked at each other and grinned. "Janus," Vesta sashayed towards the god, "we were born ready!" She took Pan's arm, Hades offered his to Hebe and all four of them walked behind Janus to the back of the great hall where sat hundreds of deities, all anxiously waiting to get started on the wine. Heracles and Hephaestus waited at the other end of the aisle; both of them handsome and both beaming from ear to ear. Hebe's and Vestas' gowns drew audible gasps of admiration from their guests as they glided between the two columns of chairs. There was many a god who would have been happy to change places with Heracles or Hephaestus and many goddesses vowing to go on diets and do something different with their hair.

"Do you Hebe and you Vesta take Heracles and Hephaestus as your wedded husbands? Will you love them, honour them and obey them.."

"No!" The two goddesses chorused at once. Hebe wagged her finger at Janus. "We talked about this; we will not be obeying anyone. We are not lesser things than our husbands or any god for that matter. We will love, honour and respect them, but don't expect anything more than that."

Several of the gods who'd been wanting to swap places with Heracles or Hephaestus suddenly changed their minds. Several goddesses were heard to mutter "Right on," and there were a number of meaningful looks exchanged with their husbands.

"I do apologise. You're quite right, it was discussed. I just didn't cross out the phrase in my notes. Ahem, as I was saying, will you love, honour and respect them above all others for as long as they keep you happy and help out with the cleaning from time to time?"

"I do," said Vesta loudly.

"I do," declared Hebe.

"Thank you. Now, Heracles and Hephaestus, do you take Hebe and Vesta as your wedded wives? Will you love, honour and respect them, listen to their opinions and not judge them for moments of irrationality until the end of time?" Janus looked at his notes. "Hang on a minute, who added in that last bit? You goddesses can't expect your husbands to stay until the end of time if you'll only stay as long as they help out with the housework! That's hardly fair."

"Don't worry Janus, if helping out with the housework is what it takes to stay with our goddesses for eternity, we'll do it happily," Heracles spoke clearly but then turned to Hephaestus who muttered something under his breath. "But we won't do the ironing."

Hebe and Vesta had a short discussion. "Agreed, as long as you agree to deal with any big spiders that come into the villa."

Zeus, who was rapidly losing patience, yelled out from his front row seat, "Couldn't you have worked all this stuff out beforehand? Get on with it will you!"

Vesta turned on him instantly. "This is how a democracy works, Zeus. Get used to it!" Turning back to Janus she said, "I think you can now pronounce us husbands and wives."

Janus was looking utterly bewildered. "Do I? Right, yes, OK, I now pronounce you husbands and wives. Grooms you may kiss your brides." Vesta and Hebe both glared at him. "Or not, whatever you like; it doesn't matter who initiates the kissing...."

The guests all clapped politely, but many of them were chattering amongst themselves.

"Did you hear what she said?"

"I can't believe she spoke to Zeus like that!"

"What's a democracy?"

"Is the bar open yet?"

The happy couples were blissfully unaware of the mutterings from their guests as they made their way back down the aisle. Hades and Pan opened their jackets and twirled; they were bitterly disappointed that the garish linings didn't cause more of a stir.

"They have no fashion sense at all," moaned Hades. "Bloody peasants!"

The guests followed the newlyweds to the vast chamber that had been prepared for the reception. It had been tastefully decorated in metallic tones that ranged from gold to bronze, and a huge fireplace had been installed in which burned a suspiciously shaped flame. Vesta had insisted on the installation of the fireplace, "We spent so many happy hours together; I couldn't deny the phallic flame a place in my wedding." Hephaestus had so many questions; wisely, he kept them to himself.

The two brides and their grooms cut the enormous seven-tiered cake, a vast confection of chocolate and strawberries and then the party began in earnest. As was typical when the gods and goddesses got together, vast amounts of alcohol were consumed, and tongues began to loosen. Hebe and Vesta were inundated with questions from the other goddesses, many of them asking for advice on how to control their errant husbands.

Heracles and Hephaestus were also besieged by the gods who teased them mercilessly about being pussy-whipped and advised them to get their goddesses in line. The two gods took it in stride, insisting that they'd never been happier and that there was nothing quite so sexy as a strong female who knew what she wanted from her mate.

Heracles winked at the gods surrounding them and said in a low voice, "Trust me when I tell you this – let your goddesses take control in the bedroom and then come back and tell me if it's worth the odd bit of cleaning." Hephaestus nodded his emphatic agreement and the gods fell silent as they contemplated what they'd been told. They quickly dispersed after muttered "Congratulations" in search of their wives, most of whom were just taking their leave of Vesta and Hebe. The couples made their way to the dance floor where there was a brief struggle as they decided who should lead, and then they all relaxed and started to enjoy themselves. The dynamics of several relationships changed that evening, and oddly, there were no complaints from either side. The goddesses painted their faces and arranged their hair in becoming styles but insisted that the gods take out the rubbish. The gods helped out around the various villas, evicted spiders and looked forward to being led to the bedroom.

Life on Olympus and the gods and goddesses who lived there were changing. On the whole, everyone agreed that it was all for the better. Apart from Zeus. He still hated the humans and blamed them for the fact that he now had to work for his pleasure. He was also terrified of spiders.

## Chapter 34

Some years later, things had changed enormously for the gods and goddesses. Vesta, Hebe, Pan and Hades had become trendsetters. All but the most ancient had discarded their togas in favour of human styles of clothing; there had been several divorces and, most recently, a marriage between two goddesses – Astraea and Dike.

"I really think that you could try something just a little more colourful, Janus." Pan was showing Janus swatches of coloured silks in an attempt to liven up his wardrobe which consisted, primarily, of grey suits.

"I am not wearing an orange suit; it just wouldn't be proper." Janus tried to move away from the long mirror in front of him as Pan held up a length of amber coloured shantung silk against his chest. Unfortunately, Hades was standing to his other side; Janus was, effectively, trapped between the two gods.

"But with your colouring, Janus, this would look absolutely marvellous, and with the soft peach shirt and bronze tie, you would be such a hit with the goddesses."

Janus shooed him away, "Look, I've already said that I'll take the pink shirt and the maroon tie, but I'm sticking with my grey suits."

"How about a nice pocket square to complete the look?" Pan waved a scrap of maroon silk under his nose.

"No! Look I came down here because I wanted to talk to you both, not to go clothes shopping!" Janus slapped away their hands. He looked around the room, the walls of which were lined with suits, shirts, dresses, scarves and other fashion paraphernalia "Where are you getting all this stuff by the way?"

"The dead are making them all for us, when they're not helping out catering the parties that is. We had to torture them a bit until they learned how to sew, but we've got quite the little production line going now." Hades looked extremely pleased with himself.

"Hades, I wouldn't presume to tell you your job, but aren't you supposed to be persecuting them for eternity rather than turning them into waiters and seamstresses?"

Hades looked slightly guilty. "Yes, yes I know but this works out well for everyone; the dead keep busy, and we all have nice clothes and great parties; it's a win-win if you think about it."

Janus was not convinced, but Hades was Lord of the Underworld, so it was up to him how he dealt with the residents.

"Anyway, that's not what I came to see you about. Zeus and Saturn need to see you, and they've asked that you join them in Zeus' villa. They thought it would do you good to have a bit of fresh air."

Pan and Hades both looked suspicious. "What are they up to? Why can't they come down here?"

Janus held up his hands. "There's nothing funny going on; don't worry. They want to meet with Hebe and Vesta as well and it just seemed easier, that's all. Besides, Zeus has availed himself of your hospitality enough times, so it's about time that he returned the favour."

Pan looked at Hades. "He's right you know; that old letch has worked his way through an enormous amount of our booze over the last few years."

"That's true. It wouldn't do him any harm to open his wine cellar once in a while," Hades said. "OK, tell him he's on; when does he want to meet?"

"I thought you could come back with me now if it's not too much of an inconvenience," Janus said casually.

"All right, give me a few minutes to get changed and feed Cerberus, and we'll get going." Hades set off in the direction of their vast wardrobe.

"I'd get comfortable if I were you," advised Pan, "he's likely to be in there a while."

As it was, Janus had to wait for several hours. Hades decided that it might be nice to take a short holiday, so he had to arrange for someone to take care of Cerberus in his absence and then he and Pan both had to pack.

"We'll need something for the evening, obviously," said Pan looking at his huge array of suits, "and different daytime looks as well. How many shirts do you think I should take?"

Hades reply was muffled as he was in the very back of the wardrobe looking through his collection of shoes and sandals. "At least fourteen if we're going to be away for a week. Don't forget to pack your swimwear as well; Zeus has a great pool."

"Oh damn, I'd forgotten about that. In that case we'll need to take robes and sandals as well. Do you think these sandals will go with my lemon shorts?" Pan held up a pair of gold sandals that laced half-way up his calves.

Hades emerged from the wardrobe. "Not with the lemon shorts, no, but they'd look fantastic with the apricot pair."

In the end they re-joined Janus with eight suitcases between them and two holdalls (for hair and skincare products).

"Do you think this will be enough?" asked Hades anxiously.

Janus was getting impatient, "I bloody well hope so. Now, let's go. Hades say goodbye to Cerberus, and I'll call the lift."

They were delayed for several more minutes as Hades called out frantic last-minute instructions to one of the dead who was going to be looking after his dog. Then he insisted on going back for a last hug.

"Of course, he'll miss you," Pan comforted him. "Just remember, it will only be for a week; you'll see him again in no time."

A sniffling Hades was led to the lift, and they made their way to the surface where Sharon was waiting for them.

"Is he all right, poor lamb?" he asked of Pan as he guided Hades onto the boat.

"Yes, don't worry; he's just had to say goodbye to Cerberus, that's all. We're taking a little holiday."

Sharon looked at the huge pile of cases on the jetty. "How long are you going for? A week? Ten days?" He jumped down and began loading them.

"Just a week," Pan replied.

"You should have enough then I would have thought as long as there aren't too many parties. Did you remember to pack your sunscreen? You've been down here for a while."

Pan slapped his hand against his forehead. "Damn, I knew I'd forgotten something." He got up and made his way to the front of the boat, ready to jump off.

"Oh no you don't." Janus grabbed him by the collar and forced him into his seat. "You're a bloody god; you don't need sunscreen! You've gone millennia without once getting sunburned."

Pan looked militant. "The sun can be very aging you know."

Janus threw up his hands in exasperation. "You're sodding immortal!"

The three gods bickered all the way across the Styx with Sharon throwing in the occasional "Right on, sister!" for good measure.

Eventually they arrived at the door to Zeus' chamber. Janus knocked, and they all traipsed in. Zeus was sitting behind his desk, and Saturn was lounging in a chair in front of it; there were three more chairs one side of him and two to the other.

"Excellent! Come in you three; have a seat. We're just waiting for Hebe and Vesta to arrive. Fancy a glass of wine while we're waiting?"

Pan and Hades glanced at each other suspiciously; it was most unlike Zeus to be so hospitable.

"That would be great, thanks," Pan replied quickly before Zeus could change his mind.

"So how have you been? Enjoying life in the Underworld, Pan?" Saturn asked pleasantly. Pan opened his mouth to reply but Zeus jumped in.

"Don't know how you stand it down there; bloody depressing if you ask me. I admit you've brightened the place up a bit, but it still gives me the willies."

"You're just jealous brother!" Hades snapped "I am Lord of my world, what are you? Just a drunken old letch who relies on 'Panacea' to keep all your mistresses happy and relieve the incessant boredom."

Zeus choked on his wine, and Saturn had to slap him on the back. "That was a bit harsh, Hades. I am sure Zeus didn't really mean anything by it; you know what he's like."

"Yes, unfortunately, Saturn, I do know what he's like, and he's been critical of the Underworld ever since I took it over. He didn't want it, Poseidon didn't want it, so it was left to me, and he just can't stand the fact that Pan and I have made such a success of it."

"Maybe in the beginning, but he's mellowed a lot over the last few decades," Saturn was trying to placate a seriously upset Hades.

"I am bloody here you know!" Zeus had stopped coughing and took another slug of his wine. "I just said the place gives me the willies, that's all. If you must know, I get a bit claustrophobic, and it creeps me out having the dead wandering around all over the place."

"Oh," Hades deflated a little. "Well why didn't you say so? I always assumed that you didn't come to visit because you didn't want to see me."

Zeus reflected briefly before answering. "Don't take this the wrong way, but, in the past, I didn't really want to see you; you were a miserable sod."

"You bastard!" Pan was ready to leap to Hades' defence.

"Hang on a minute before you get all bent out of shape," Zeus held up his hand. "I said 'in the past'; since you all got back from Brighton, Hades has been like a different god, and now I enjoy his company. When he's not shouting at me that is." He sat back in his chair and turned his attention back to his glass of wine.

"Oh right, well, OK then." There was a knock at the door and Hebe and Vesta entered. "Hebe, Vesta, how lovely to see you," Hades jumped up from his chair to give the goddesses a hug, happy for the distraction. The others all followed suit, except Zeus who trotted down to his wine cellar to pick up another couple of bottles. Once everyone was comfortably seated and had a glass in their hands, he spoke.

"So, you're probably wondering why I called you all here." He didn't wait for a response. "The thing is, Saturn has been doing some stock taking, and it appears that our supplies are not replenishing as fast as they have been over the last few years."

"Are you sure it's not just because you're drinking more?" Pan asked.

"It's not just the wine supplies; it's everything. We have less food, yes, less wine and, more importantly, less gold."

"Why? What's been going on?"

"Since when?"

"Have we still got enough dogfood?"

The gods all spoke at once, firing questions at Zeus.

"If you'll let me bloody finish, I'll explain. Just be quiet all of you for five minutes. As I said, Saturn has been doing some stock taking, but he's also been doing some analysis, and it seems as though we are losing human followers again. A new generation is now influencing their beliefs and support for us and our products is wavering. It will continue as long as those that you helped and worked with are still alive, but after that, I think we risk being forgotten again. Panacea is still popular, but there are other drugs on the market that claim to have no side effects. Light of Aphrodite's sales are good, but it's less popular than before, and the young girls who slavishly bought Athena Cosmetics are now grandmothers." Zeus grabbed the bottle of red from the corner of his desk and topped up everyone's glasses while they digested what he'd just told them.

Finally, Janus spoke, "I assume that we're the first that you've told, when are you planning on telling everyone else?"

Zeus looked at Saturn who replied, "We're not planning on making an announcement. We've come up with a plan, and if it works, there should be no need."

Hades looked suspiciously at Saturn; he had an idea where this was going. "OK, so what's your plan?"

Saturn glanced at Zeus and gestured with a nod of his head.

"What?" Zeus' face was a picture of innocence.

"Tell them what the plan is," Saturn spoke through gritted teeth.

"Why can't you tell them?"

"We spoke about this; you said you'd tell them."

"Oh, for crying out loud! One of you, please, just tell us!" Hades was losing patience; he wanted to enjoy his holiday, not be stuck in Zeus' office all day.

Zeus crossed his arms and his supercilious smirk was designed to cause Saturn maximum irritation. Saturn glared at him. "Fine! I'll tell them." He turned to face the gods and goddesses.

"The thing is, we all thought that bringing back followers would be a permanent fix, but we didn't factor in that humans are not immortal."

"No shit, Sherlock!" Pan muttered under his breath.

"Anyway, we need to replicate what you five achieved when you were living in Brighton to ensure that we won't be at risk of popping out of existence any time soon. So, basically, we need you to go back." Saturn plastered a fake grin on his face that made him look slightly deranged.

Janus was the first to speak. "Well, I'm not going back, no way. My wife gave me hell when I got home last time; I'm not risking my marriage."

The others looked at him, all with the same shocked expression on their faces. Hebe was the first to speak.

"I didn't know that you had a wife, Janus, I've never seen you with her."

Janus looked slightly uncomfortable. "Her name is Camise. She's an excellent wife, but she's not really what you'd call a people person. She's always been a bit jealous to be honest and doesn't like it when she's not in a position to be able to keep an eye on me."

"She can't know you very well," Pan scoffed. "You never so much as looked lustfully at a human female all the time that we were there."

"Which is more than we can say for you!" Hades was bored and starting to get huffy.

"I know I didn't," Janus sighed "but she has fixated on the fact that I am, literally, two faced and has assumed that the same is true of my character." He looked deeply embarrassed. "Look, she might not be perfect but she's my wife, and I love her and want to do what I can to keep her happy, so there's no way I'm going back to Brighton."

## Chapter 35

Janus walked out of the meeting and refused to discuss the subject further. Hebe and Vesta said that they would discuss it with their husbands. Hades and Pan said they would think about it, but for now, as they were on holiday, they were going to party. Saturn and Zeus were left alone.

"Do you think they'll do it?" Saturn asked, opening yet another bottle of wine.

"Of course they will." Zeus held out his glass. "They enjoyed their time with the humans."

"Yes, I know, but I'm not sure it was good for them. Look what they were like when they got back."

"They wouldn't have to be there long, a couple of decades or so should do it. Besides, what choice do they have? I'm damned if I'm going back to having no wine and no cash." Zeus took a long sip of his wine. "Anyway, if they don't want to go back, I could always give it a shot. I'm sure the humans would love to have me amongst them for a few years; think what I could teach them."

Saturn sat bolt upright, spilling most of his wine. "NO! Absolutely not! Look what you did to humans when they first came into existence!"

Zeus had the grace to look slightly guilty. "I've mellowed since then but what was I supposed to do? A completely new species with four arms, four legs and two heads; it just wasn't natural."

"You could have given it a little while to see how their race panned out, but no! As usual, you completely over-reacted and cut them all in half. No wonder they're all so hung up on finding their 'soul mate.' It doesn't do them any good you know, always wandering around looking for their other half," Saturn wagged his finger sternly.

"Oh, don't give me that, they love it! Look how much music it's given rise to over the millennia; do you think James Blunt would have had the success he's had if it weren't for my interference?"

Zeus had become quite a fan of James Blunt ever since he'd heard "You're Beautiful" at Pan and Hades' wedding.

"Oh, you've got an answer for everything, haven't you! Look, you're not going among the humans and that's final. I wouldn't mind, but you don't even like them very much." Saturn rolled his eyes in exasperation.

"It's not that I dislike them, I think, as a species, they're quite interesting, but sometimes they do get up my nose with the way that they carry on. Look at how they used to sacrifice each other all the time and in *my* name. Bloody cheek!" Zeus had drunk far too much wine and was starting to get belligerent.

Saturn was equally inebriated and got to his feet, shaking his fist at Zeus. "And what did you do? Hmm? You persuaded Poseidon to flood the world and nearly killed the bloody lot of them!"

Their argument quickly progressed to a physical dispute which only ended when Zeus tripped over the edge of his toga and bashed his head on the corner of his desk. He was unconscious for several hours which gave Saturn time to put some coffee on.

Meanwhile, Pan and Hades had decided to go to the pool and invited Hebe, Vesta and their husbands to join them. Pan and Hades watched Heracles and Hephaestus do cannon balls into the water from the comfort of their silk covered sun loungers.

"Bravo!" Yelled Pan. "Do another one!" He and Hades clapped as Heracles launched himself into the sparkling blue water.

"Will you two concentrate?" Hebe said sharply. She rather regretted inviting Heracles who had large muscles and a particularly small bathing suit. She knew, deep down, that Pan and Hades only had eyes for each other, but she couldn't help but feel a little possessive. "We need to talk about this."

Hades dismissed her with a wave of his hand. "We will but not now, we're on holiday. Pan, my love, do you think you could order us a couple of cocktails? I fancy something pink with an umbrella in it."

Pan grinned and blew his husband a kiss before snapping his fingers at a passing wood nymph. "Of course my dear, anything for you. Do you guys want anything?" He asked.

"Hebe's right, we really should be talking about this," Vesta hesitated "but, since you're offering, I'll have a glass of champagne. What about you Hephaestus? Do you fancy anything?"

"Only you, my sweet." Hephaestus vaulted out of the swimming pool and wrapped his arms around Vesta who giggled most uncharacteristically. "Actually, I wouldn't mind a glass of wine, Pan."

Heracles could see that Hebe was losing her patience. "We'll both have some champagne too, then we can sit back, relax and talk about whatever is making my lovely lady so uptight." He kissed Hebe lightly on the lips. She was slightly miffed by the "uptight" remark but still leaned back against him as he sat behind her and circled his arms around her waist.

Once they all had their third round of drinks (the first two rounds really relaxed them, and they lost time chit-chatting and cracking jokes), Hebe explained the conversation that they'd had with Zeus and Saturn.

"So, basically, if we want to get the humans back on our side, we need to go back amongst them and educate another generation."

"When you say 'educate,' what do you mean exactly?" Heracles asked.

"Well, last time, we had to look at their deepest fears and their insecurities and try to find ways to address them so that they would stop worrying about everything. After that we had to create 'miracles' that their limited understanding could cope with and believe in."

Hephaestus was the most traditional of the assembled gods. "Does that mean that the humans now have shrines and alters to us? Do they worship as they did in the old days?"

Vesta answered him. "No, my love, it's not like the old days at all. We couldn't risk them returning to traditional worship; you remember what it used to be like? Sacrifices of goats, sheep and each other on occasion; it was all too messy. We just had to get them to believe that we could offer them something they weren't getting from other humans and we did it through business."

Hephaestus looked shocked. "Do you mean that you *worked?*"

"I told you about the business," Vesta was affronted.

"Yes, you did, but I rather assumed that you had minions doing everything for you. I didn't realise you actually had to work."

Vesta glanced at Hebe who was glaring at Hephaestus. She felt like glaring at him herself, but as they were newly married, she tried to keep her temper.

"Goddesses are perfectly capable of doing anything that a god can do. Janus, Hades and Pan all worked, so why shouldn't we?"

Hephaestus looked round at the assembled group who were all looking at him expectantly. "Right, yes, quite so, no reason at all. Anyway, how long would you be gone for?"

This time Vesta did glare at him, as did Hebe and he realised that he'd put his foot in it once again. Unfortunately, he had no idea how.

"What did I say?" he asked desperately.

"You said how long would 'I' be going for. Do you think that I would go without you? Would you want me to go without you?" Vesta snapped.

"No, of course not, but if you'll only be gone for a couple of days, I can get some work done at the forge," Hephaestus looked to Heracles for back-up.

"He's right. Of course we'd miss you, but there's plenty to be getting on with. I was thinking of putting in a pool at *our* villa; I could have it ready by the time you got back."

The two gods grinned hopefully. Pan took pity on the pair of them. "There's something that Hebe and Vesta neglected to explain. We wouldn't be gone for a few days; it would be more like a few decades."

"What!?" Heracles and Hephaestus leaped to their feet.

"So, *now* you want to come with us?" Hebe was still a little uptight about having been called uptight. She and Vesta looked up at their husbands as they paced around the pool, trying to come to grips with the new information.

"They can't force you to go, Zeus and Saturn, can they?" Heracles demanded. He was known as a great warrior and was quite prepared to take a swing at Zeus, should the occasion demand it.

"No-one's forcing my wife to do anything she doesn't want to!" Hephaestus said. "Come on, Heracles, let's go and have a word with Zeus; he won't be oppressing my wife!" He slapped Heracles on the shoulder, and they both turned towards the villa.

"May I suggest that, if you want to be taken seriously, you put on some clothes?" Hades drawled. "Calm down you two; no-one is forcing anyone to do anything. Saturn and Zeus asked us if we would go back and we said that we'd think about it. However, we also have to think about what we could be facing if we don't go back. At the moment, we have a life of luxury, but that won't last if the humans stop believing in us again; we can't just think about ourselves."

Heracles and Hephaestus returned to their seats, still looking slightly shell-shocked.

"What's it like down there?" Hephaestus asked as he picked up his drink.

"It's fun," Pan didn't hesitate. "Different from here obviously, and the humans are a bit strange until you get used to them, but it's definitely fun."

Hades took his hand. "The humans are much more open than us, more accepting of change, and they're very tolerant. They have their funny little ways, but they know how to enjoy themselves; I guess because their lives pass so quickly, they have to make the most of them."

"And they…well most of them believe in equality. They do have their hierarchies, but they're not rigid like they are here, or should I say, used to be here. We learned a lot when we were with the humans." Vesta smiled at her new husband encouragingly.

Hebe took her turn to speak. "It's exciting as well and there are so many opportunities if you're prepared to get out there and take them. The humans are incredibly innovative, and their world moves so much faster than ours." Hebe remembered the buzz of energy that she'd felt when she and Vesta had been running Goddesses. Although she'd been happier than ever since she'd met Heracles, she hadn't felt that same sense of purpose as she'd had when they'd had the business.

Heracles and Hephaestus looked surprised; their fellow gods and goddesses had spoken with so much passion. They both sat deep in thought for a few minutes, and then Heracles asked, "What's the food like now, and do they still have wine?"

Hebe laughed and hugged him, "Always thinking of your belly! Yes, they do have wine and so much more, but the food is not as good as it is here; however, they do some wonderful things with fish and potatoes."

They spent the next few hours drinking, splashing about in the swimming pool and relaxing in the late afternoon sunshine. They agreed that they would meet with Zeus and Saturn the following morning.

## Chapter 36

The six of them dressed carefully the next day, and after breakfast, they went en masse to Zeus' office. They hoped that they would find him sober and in an accommodating mood; they'd agreed that neither of those things was particularly likely but decided to take the chance anyway.

"Come in!" Zeus bellowed from behind his office door.

They trooped in and were surprised to see both Saturn and Janus comfortably installed on chaise lounges.

"It looks as though you were expecting us brother," said Hades.

"Well, seeing as you all spent all afternoon getting drunk at my pool, your discussion was bound to get back to me wasn't it?" Zeus gave a smug smile.

"Bugger!" Pan muttered under his breath.

Vesta decided to take charge. "Right, so you know our decision, and I assume, you know our terms? One, we want.." Zeus cut her off.

"Yes, I know your terms, and I agree to them."

Vesta was immediately suspicious. "All of them? Will you put that in writing?"

Zeus laughed and nodded at Janus who presented Vesta with a carefully laid out contract, written in golden ink on thick white parchment. Vesta read it carefully before presenting it to the others. None of them raised any questions, so they each took their turns to sign. Zeus and Saturn then signed their names and Janus sealed the document with gold-coloured wax.

"Right, that's it then; when are you off?" With business concluded, Zeus was eager to get about his day of drinking and debauchery.

"We've already packed, so we'll be leaving after lunch if you can arrange for us to be transported back to Brighton."

"Yes, yes, no problem. Off you go now." Zeus got up and ushered the gods and goddesses from his office. He'd decided to sprinkle some 'Panacea' on his cornflakes that morning and was now having some pressing urges that he couldn't ignore for much longer.

That evening, Hades, Pan, Vesta, Hebe, Heracles and Hephaestus were comfortably installed in their new home in Brighton. It had eight bedrooms, all with en-suite bathrooms, an indoor pool, a huge garden and an impressive staff.

"Well, this is certainly better than the 3-bed semi- that we had before," Pan said happily. "I can't believe that Zeus came through for us."

"I know," Hebe agreed "I really thought he'd put up a fight. We've got the funds to start new businesses, spending money and all this. I felt sure he'd want to negotiate at least some of it."

"He couldn't really," said Hades quietly. "You saw what he was like when he thought there'd be no more cash and, more importantly, wine. Zeus would do anything to maintain his lifestyle. He's a selfish bugger really."

Pan nodded, "Yep, I can't say *I'll* miss him. I will miss the Underworld though and our parties; they were fun. Mind you, I guess there's no reason why we can't do the same for the humans – give them 'dreams come true' parties or something like that. I'm sure there'd be a market for it. Maybe we could even open a nightclub and we could call it...get this...Pandemonium." Pan grinned delightedly.

"That's a wonderful idea." Hades took his husband's hand and smiled lovingly at him. "I want us to do something in fashion too; clothes that would flatter anyone, whatever shape or size they are. What do you think you guys will do?"

"I'm going to stick with what I know," said Hephaestus "I'll set up a forge and make indestructible weapons for the humans."

"I think maybe it would be better if you made indestructible saucepans or something my love; humans can't really be trusted with weapons." Hephaestus looked slightly crestfallen but then perked up when Heracles said that he'd worked in a forge and was sure that they could come up with a plan between them. A brief argument ensued as they tried to decide between "Hephaestus Ironware" or "Heracles Kitchenware" but peace was restored as they settled on "Olympus Steel." They both agreed it had a very masculine ring to it.

"What about you Vesta? Hebe?" Pan was curious.

The two goddesses smiled. "We'll be going back to our old business. Goddesses was never shut down and is still profitable so we're going to take it over. We'll say that we're long-lost relatives of the original owners or something like that. Hebe will work her magic, and we'll soon have our old fame and fortune back." Vesta sat back on the comfortable sofa looking immensely pleased.

"We've come up with some ideas for new product ranges as well," added Hebe "creams and lotions to suit every age group. That way our products should stand the test of time. There'll be 'Hebe Dream' for the younger generation, 'Vesta Vitality' for the more mature woman and, of course, we'll restart promotions for 'Light of Aphrodite,' promising a *magical* new formula."

"The names haven't been set in stone though, we could well change them." Vesta glared at Hebe who gave her a sly grin.

"That's it then," Pan said as he poured them each a glass of champagne. "We each have our plans. I have to admit I am rather glad that we're back in Brighton. I have missed this place. Cheers."

They all chorused "Cheers!" and clinked glasses.

"Hang on a minute," exclaimed Hades. "Who shut the bloody back door?"

"I did," replied Heracles. "Hebe was feeling a bit chilly. Why?"

Hades got up from his chair and marched across to the huge double doors that fronted the garden from the living room. "You've bloody shut Cerberus out, that's why! Poor little thing, he'll be worried out there all alone without his Daddy." He yelled out into the darkness, "Cerberus, come on boy." Several seconds later, he was knocked flat on his back as Cerberus, magically minus two heads, came flying through the door. Hades laughed as the huge dog sat on him and then licked his face.

"Even Cerberus likes Brighton!" Pan exclaimed as he rushed over to rescue his husband.

Zeus looked down on them from Olympus and raised a silent toast, happy in the knowledge that his plan would ensure the gods were never forgotten by humans, and that he would never run out of wine.

The End

Printed in Great Britain
by Amazon

49069880R00137